THE BEGONIA BRIBE

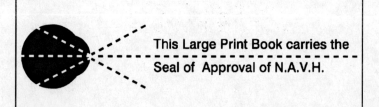

A GARDEN SOCIETY MYSTERY

THE BEGONIA BRIBE

ALYSE CARLSON

WHEELER PUBLISHING
A part of Gale, Cengage Learning

GALE
CENGAGE Learning·

Farmington Hills, Mich • San Francisco • New York • Waterville, Maine
Meriden, Conn • Mason, Ohio • Chicago

GALE
CENGAGE Learning·

Copyright © 2013 by Penguin Group (USA) Inc.
A Garden Society Mystery.
Wheeler Publishing, a part of Gale, Cengage Learning.

Wheeler Publishing Large Print Cozy Mystery.
The text of this Large Print edition is unabridged.
Other aspects of the book may vary from the original edition.
Set in 16 pt. Plantin.

LIBRARY OF CONGRESS CATALOGING-IN-PUBLICATION DATA

Carlson, Alyse, 1966–
    The begonia bribe / by Alyse Carlson. — Large print edition.
        pages ; cm. — (Wheeler Publishing large print cozy mystery) (A garden society mystery)
    ISBN 978-1-4104-7354-7 (softcover) — ISBN 1-4104-7354-6 (softcover)
    1. Beauty contests—Fiction. 2. Gardening—Societies, etc.—Fiction.
3. Murder—Investigation—Fiction. 4. Roanoke (Va.)—Fiction. 5. Large type books. I. Title.
PS3603.A75275B44 2014
813'.6—dc23   2014026642

Published in 2014 by arrangement with The Berkley Publishing Group, a member of Penguin Group (USA) LLC, a Penguin Random House Company

Printed in the United States of America
1 2 3 4 5 6 7 18 17 16 15 14

For Leanne Rabesa.
With hedgehogs and otters.
Thank you!

ACKNOWLEDGMENTS

This book was my first second, if you will. And as such, held some special challenges. Where to draw the line so readers starting here would still follow easily, but readers who began with *The Azalea Assault* won't get too much repetition. It took me several iterations, and much patience from my editor at the time, Emily Rapoport — so thank you. I'd also like to thank my ever-reliable critique partners, Leanne Rabesa and Stacy Gail; my agent, Ellen Pepus; my new editor, Michelle Vega; and the amazing art team at Berkley Prime Crime for my fabulous covers on their editions.

TO: *Roanoke Tribune*
FROM: The Little Miss Begonia Pageant
RE: State Little Miss Begonia Pageant
   Finals to be held in Roanoke

The Virginia State Committee Advancing "Miss Pageants" has chosen Roanoke for the state finals of the Little Miss Begonia Pageant this year. The pageant, a tradition since 1973, will be hosted by the Roanoke Garden Society and held at Elmwood Park. Facilities at the Roanoke Library and the Roanoke Arts Commission have been reserved for staging, rehearsals, and inclement weather backup. During the last week of July, thirty finalists between the ages of seven and ten, representing the ninety-five counties and forty independent cities in Virginia will compete. Local teen favorite, singer Kyle Lance, will broaden audience appeal and thrill participants. The winner of the Little Miss Begonia Pageant will participate in the Little Miss Cherry Blossom national competition in Denver, Colorado, in November.

Television coverage for the pageant will be provided by WONK television, and the competition will be judged by TV talk show host Telly Stevens, local columnist Barbara Mackay, and radio personality Clancy Huggins. The Mistress of Ceremonies this year will be none other than Roanoke's own Former Miss Virginia, Evangeline Patrick.

CONTACT: Camellia Harris

CHAPTER 1

Cam Harris slammed the phone down and spun. "Just shoot me now!"

"Bang." Annie, her best friend for the last twenty years, obliged her in spirit.

"How do I get sucked into these things?"

"Indiscriminate taste in friends?" Annie offered.

Cam launched herself at Annie, hugging her tight. "My taste is fine. I just happen to love some troublemakers."

Annie extricated herself from the bear hug. "Okay, I'll give you that. So what are these *other,* more troublemaking friends doing now?"

Cam snorted. Annie had been her best friend since seventh grade, but it was rich of Annie to call other people "troublemakers." Annie's relationship with rules tended to include a lot of sneers and mocking.

Cam didn't mention that, though. "You know that pageant the Roanoke Garden

Society is setting up for?"

"Yeah?" Annie's face looked pained.

"Well, Evangeline is on the pageant board and offered me a moonlighting gig while things with RGS are slow. In addition to coordinating and publicizing the RGS side, she asked me to do pageant publicity and coordination."

"Just tell her you can't," Annie offered.

"That's the thing. She sweetened the pot and I can't refuse."

"Seriously?" Cam watched the corners of Annie's nose rise and took a breath.

"You know I've been saving for that Mustang. She offered twenty-five hundred for this gig, which is above my regular salary, so I could finally afford payments. I could really use your help, though — that last week in July, I mean."

"Are you forgetting the last time I worked with these nuts they accused me of murder?"

"That was Jake, who you seem to have forgiven fine."

Jake was the police officer who'd investigated a pair of spring murders that the Garden Society had been entangled with. He was now Annie's boyfriend, so "forgiven" was an understatement.

"That wouldn't have happened if your

12

nuts hadn't framed me."

"Not nuts. Nut. And that's done with."

The meeting where RGS's involvement in the pageant had been decided had been held a month earlier on the covered back porch of La Fontaine, Neil and Evangeline Patrick's grand home. The gorgeous hibiscus that lined the sunny edge of the deck in big pots were tickling Cam's nose with their fragrance. From this angle she couldn't see the flower mural the Patricks' garden created, but the colors had changed from the white, red, and pink of spring to purples with a bit of gold and white. She thought from the balcony above them, it probably looked like some variety of iris, or perhaps a clematis. From Cam's position in a patio chair, she could see a border layer of lobelia in lighter and darker shades of purple. Cam was a little surprised because normally lobelia liked shade, but it must have been close enough to the taller plants that it was shaded for much of the day. Behind them stood Virginia Blue, larkspur, iris, and finally hollyhocks. She knew there was a lot she was missing from this angle, though, as the garden was designed with the balcony view in mind.

When Mr. Patrick called them all to order,

he sputtered a little but then seemed to find his resolve.

"You know why we've had a break. But the Roanoke Garden Society means something to all of us. I don't want to see it dissolve because of the bad behavior of a few people."

Mrs. Pemberly, a crabby older woman who had never participated but always wanted to give her opinion, started to speak, but Cam saw her husband pinch her.

The first item on the agenda was the election of an interim president, as the leadership that had been in place during the spring events had felt it best to step back while the scandal settled. Mr. Pemberly had to poke his wife several more times, but finally, one of the founding members gave her a look that silenced her and asked the key question.

"Did you have someone in mind?" Holden Hobbes was the oldest man present. Cam thought he had to be at least eighty, though he was healthy and spry.

"Actually, Holden," Evangeline Patrick said, "We hoped as a past president, y'all might be willing to act as president until proper elections can be held. We take a break in August, so you could take your normal holiday, and we could hold elections

14

in fall like we always do."

Holden Hobbes was a beloved local figure; in fact, he'd once held the state senate seat that Annie's father had eventually assumed. But Holden was a soft-touch politician — speaking quietly and seeking consensus and cooperation — a gentleman's gentleman.

"What's that? Six months?" Holden asked.

"Yes," Evangeline said.

"Well, I suppose I might live that long," he answered with an eye twinkle.

"Then you'll do it?"

"There needs to be a vote," Holden said.

"All in favor?" Evangeline said.

All the hands except Madeline Leclerc's and Cam's own went up. Madeline was her boss, the fund-raiser and manager for RGS. As hired staff, they didn't have voting privileges.

"My first act as president," Hobbes said, "is to ask Neil and his lovely wife to kindly carry on, as they have a much better idea what's going on than I do." Everyone laughed. "I trust they will bring me up to speed after the meeting."

"You know we will." Evangeline winked.

"Darling, the next up is you," Neil said to Evangeline.

"Well, then." Evangeline stood. She was a former Miss Virginia and was every bit the presence she'd been twenty years earlier, tall, curvy, and very pretty. "We've had a request for assistance."

Evangeline described a call from an old friend regarding the state finals for the Little Miss Begonia pageant. They would be held in Elmwood Park in Roanoke in July, and the committee had requested assistance in beautifying the space.

"Now, Elmwood Park *is* spectacular in spring, but in late July they could use a little help. I hoped maybe we could, either formally as a group or some of you as individuals, act as gardening experts to make the park look gorgeous. I think it would be a nice boost to our image."

"Well, we obviously need to get proper publicity," Mrs. Pemberly said. "Otherwise it's a lot of work for nothing."

Neil Patrick laughed uncomfortably. "Well, of course we will. Cammi is very good at making sure we get our due."

Cam smiled. He was a sweet little man about her father's age, but his trim white mustache and formal demeanor made him seem like he'd stepped out of another decade. She wished he wouldn't call her "Cammi," but at least he thought highly of her. When she looked back to her notes, Madeline had made an exclamation point, letting Cam know her supervisor agreed strongly with the annoying Mrs. Pemberly. It was true, though, that if they were going to the effort, they might as well let everyone know what amazing things their expertise could do with gardens, and Elmwood Park would be a wonderful canvas.

July was obviously a challenge because of the heat, but the park was watered at least daily, so they decided the biggest issue was the suspect soil quality of a location that gardened for the short term. They wanted to ensure their work had a lasting impact. Much of the park border was also shaded by large dogwood trees, so flowers that were shade friendly would need to be chosen.

As much discussion as had been needed for the plan, in the end, the group bought into formally helping for the goodwill it would create. Though Cam understood she was to give that goodwill publicity a giant boost.

In June, Cam helped Evangeline collect sponsors, as pageants cost money to put on. Their early conversations revolved around contacts made at *Green Living,* a Sunday morning public radio feature RGS contributed to regularly, both financially and in terms of content. The host, Clancy Huggins, had made friends with several Garden Society members. But in addition, RGS members had also met some of the other regular guests, including Nell Norton.

Nell owned a chain of nearly forty nurseries in Virginia, North Carolina, Kentucky, and Tennessee, but Roanoke boasted her original store and corporate headquarters.

When Cam called, Nell was rather short with her, but Cam had heard enough about her not to be discouraged. She was a sharp businesswoman, used to getting her way, but she wasn't a person to say no to an opportunity without weighing the facts. Cam summarized their goals, and Nell agreed to meet her and Evangeline for lunch the next day.

In person, Nell was an odd contrast of gardener and businesswoman. Her suit and hairdo were impeccable, the former in cornflower blue and the latter carefully highlighted in copper, gold, and bronze. Her fingernails, however, were short and, in spite of evidence of scrubbing, had soil under them, and she appeared to have forgotten more formal shoes. On her feet was a lilac pair of Crocs. Cam smiled. A true gardener was someone she and Evangeline could really talk to, no matter how many millions she had made being shrewd.

"Mrs. Norton, it's such an honor to meet you," Cam said. "This is Evangeline Patrick . . ."

"I know who Evangeline is." The voice wasn't impatient exactly, but neither was it warm. She scrutinized Evangeline by holding her head at a strange angle so she could look the much taller woman in the face through the reading portion of her bifocals. She shook Evangeline's hand but made no effort to hide her curiosity. "So you're the one who married Neil?"

"Well . . . yes . . . Do you know Neil?"

"Oh, not directly. I went to high school with him but was younger, so it was more . . . I knew *of* him. He was considered quite the catch . . ."

"Well, yes, he is . . . a catch, I mean."

"Back then none of us had the confidence. We thought we were too young . . . clearly we weren't young enough . . ."

Cam held her breath, worried Nell had provoked Evangeline. Evangeline was some thirty years younger than her husband, and here was Nell Norton suggesting three years had been too many. But Evangeline handled it with her usual grace.

She laughed. "When I was sixteen, my daddy grounded me for a month because

19

he found out I went on a date with a boy who was eighteen. Oh, how things change once we become adults!"

Cam was relieved that Nell laughed in response. "I like you! You've got spunk!" Then she turned her gaze on Cam. "Now who are you?"

"Camellia Harris. I'm the . . ."

"Vi and Nelson's daughter."

"Well, yes."

"I knew your mother; she was skilled with roses. Small town, isn't it? And I know your daddy a little bit. More than that, though, I've seen some of the beautiful garden structures he's built. Does he still do that?"

"Only for close friends. He's retired. But thank you."

"We have a trellis he built at our house," Evangeline said.

"I saw that in *Garden Delights* magazine earlier this month. It's lovely! I'd sure like to run into him again." Cam smiled, glad she knew Nell Norton was married, which eliminated her normal worries where her dad was concerned. He just seemed to draw a fan club way too easily.

The three ordered lunch and chatted about their gardens until their food arrived, and then Evangeline smoothly segued into the pageant, the flower theme, and the need

20

for a local sponsor.

"Well, I suppose I support it in premise. What media coverage would we get?"

Cam took over with the preliminary support they'd received from WONK, a local television affiliate with a producer who knew Evangeline.

"Does this support have to all be cash, or can some of it be in-kind?"

Cam and Evangeline looked at each other. Evangeline nodded.

"Actually, the event is to be held at Elmwood Park, which has some beautiful plants but at the end of July could use a bit of help. We would love it if a significant portion was seasonal plants. Summer is so much prettier with some nice annuals. Plus, we'd really like to include some lasting plants," Cam said, "as a legacy to the park."

"And I can trust your group to get it planted right?"

"Of course you can," Evangeline said. "We'd really like the background to display the floral glory Virginia is capable of, even in late July." Cam hoped she wasn't meant to be part of the planting team. It was a huge park, and July could be miserable to work in, but they did know a lot of experts.

"Any chance if I do all this, I might run into that daddy of yours?" Nell asked.

21

"Well . . . I think so," Cam said.

"I'd like that. He always could make me laugh. So now your group . . . I suspect they have some specific ideas of what they'd like to display then?"

"You know we do," Evangeline said. "But we also understand you are donating, so we can compromise if necessary. Here is our wish list."

Evangeline pulled out a list from her purse and unfolded it onto the table. It included a handful of low bushes, hydrangea, and azalea. There were a variety of lilies, too, as they were a dramatic centerpiece flower that liked shade. And then the list was rounded off with annuals that were more colorful.

"Well, the bushes and lilies are on the expensive side, though they will make nice focal points. Gladiolus is too unpredictable as to how long the blooms will last. Impatiens probably need watering more often than the park does it, at least when newly planted. And I've had trouble keeping enough dahlias in stock for my stores, so those might be a problem. Petunias and geraniums are great for color splashes. Maybe salvia at the sunny edges?"

"That's so generous," Cam said. She liked to see that the woman talked herself through these things very much like Cam did when she was trying to make initial gardening decisions.

Nell smiled.

They hammered out the other details in dollars and cents and then toasted the upcoming pageant with sweet tea. Cam figured they needed a half-dozen more sponsors, but none as big as this, so she was sure between her and Evangeline they'd have their list by the weekend.

A few days later, Cam received a call from Evangeline. "Cam? I have two pieces of good news and one bad."

Cam sighed. She didn't have the patience for kid gloves. "Sandwich them."

"Well, first, we've convinced Kyle Lance to help us out. He's agreed to be here all week, opening the show and then performing several times in the last two nights."

"Kyle Lance, isn't he . . ."

"Very famous, yes!"

Cam had meant to finish with "twelve," but whatever his age, if he was actually very popular, she could work with that. "Okay, bad news?"

"We don't have a choice about Telly Stevens as a pageant judge."

"Because?" Telly Stevens was a morning talk-show host at WONK with a reputation for womanizing.

"Because if he isn't, WONK won't air the pageant."

Cam grimaced, frustrated. "And we lose three-quarters of our sponsors if we lose WONK because they are set on air time. But why do they want him? He's a sleaze." Admittedly, a sleaze known well in Roanoke, but still a sleaze.

"He's married to their executive producer."

"Your *friend* the executive producer?" Cam asked. That sounded familiar, now that she heard it. It was probably the only reason he was still on the air, but it annoyed her that Evangeline hadn't anticipated this. There was nothing to do about it now, though. "Got it. We'll work with him. He fits our theme, anyway. What was the good news?"

"We have all our judges!"

Cam squashed back the comment that that was obvious.

The next several weeks flew by in a daze of planning and coordinating. As the eve of pageant week arrived, Cam was preparing for the large supper party for media, pageant staff, and judges, so she was double-checking her list from home when her phone rang.

"Cam, how's everything going?" Evangeline asked.

"So far, so good."

"I was just thinking about that comment from Nell. Can your dad come to tonight's dinner?"

Cam sighed. If she were more honest with herself, she would have seen this coming. "I can check whether he's available."

When she hung up, she called him.

"Daddy?"

"Hiya, sunshine. How's shakes?"

"Pretty good, but you've been given a special VIP invite for our supper tonight."

"It's not one of them fancy things, is it?"

"You know it is. It's for the judges, main sponsors, media, and executive staff."

"Who'd want a gaffer like me at a fancy supper party?"

"The request came from Nell Norton. She says . . ."

"She was a friend of your mother's. I remember."

"I think she's just feeling sentimental — she's married . . ." Cam wasn't sure what made her blurt it, except it seemed her dad was a hot commodity among women over fifty.

"Well, of course. I remember Byron, too."

Cam thought that was Nell's husband's name.

"So you'll come?"

"It would be antisocial not to, it seems."

"Thank you, Daddy. I'll have Annie pick you up about quarter to seven."

"You do that," he said before he hung up.

Cam shut her phone and stared at it.

She refilled her coffee cup and then went upstairs to see Annie. Her best friend was already planning on attending the supper party in order to take pictures, so Cam didn't think it would be a problem.

"You want a hot date tonight?"

"I might. Who's asking?"

"My dad."

"Is he taking me to Disney World?" Annie jumped up and down as she said it.

"Just the same old party you were already going to."

"Well, I suppose it ups my value to show up with a hot guy on my arm."

"Excellent!" Cam knew her dad was one of Annie's favorite people, so unlike with the other favors she asked — and there were a lot of them — she didn't feel too guilty. "I told him you'd pick him up at quarter to seven."

"Nice! An excuse not to be there too early."

Cam shrugged. "I owe you one, in any case."

Annie grabbed her chin and looked upward. "You owe me nine million and forty-three."

"Probably." She gave Annie a hug. "You really are the best, *best* friend ever."

CHAPTER 2

Twelve guests had grown to thirty faster
than Cam could say "pretentious pageant,"
and she found herself in the awkwardly
familiar spot of greeting guests in the
Patricks' foyer. Both times she'd done this
before, people had died, no matter how
much she didn't want to think about that.
Instead of guests wafting in with the smell
of honeysuckle and jasmine as they had
then, they now carried the sweet aroma of
the gardenia that framed the Patricks' front
walk.

Evangeline and Neil Patrick were shuf-
fling about in the day room upstairs where
the reception would be, and Cam expected
Lydia Fennewick, the pageant chair and a
friend of Evangeline's, to arrive from the
guest house any minute.

The first other guests to arrive were Trish
Tait and Jenny Andrews, volunteers who
would be helping with the pageant. Cam

was glad. They'd make excellent minglers as the more prestigious guests arrived. Both were socially skilled, attractive, and committed to the pageant's success. Cam sent them up the stairs to wait for the other guests.

Clancy Huggins, one of the judges and host of *Green Living,* arrived next with a pretty woman Cam didn't know.

"Mr. Huggins! Welcome! I'm Camellia Harris, the event coordinator."

"Miss Harris, lovely to meet you in person. And this is my dear friend, Jessica Benchly."

Cam had half expected to hear the name Jessica Rabbit, with the unrealistic proportions and beauty of the woman, though Jessica Benchly was dark haired with large dark eyes. She casually hung on Clancy's arm. Dear friend could have been literal or a euphemism — there was no way to know.

"Wonderful to meet you, Ms. Benchly. We're having cocktails up in the drawing room." Cam gestured toward the stairs, then had to turn back to the door as guests began to arrive in earnest: Nell Norton and her husband, Byron; Telly Stevens and his wife, Judith Towers-Stevens — the executive producer who'd insisted her husband judge, Annette DiFlor of Anna Banana's Tween

Fashions; Holden Hobbes and several more.

Cam had a headache. She'd been a part of a lot of formal festivities, but this one seemed to have a higher ratio of important people and fewer allies to help her when things went wrong. She wished her boyfriend, Rob, hadn't had a dinner scheduled with his editor at the *Roanoke Tribune,* as it would have been nice if he could have been here for her. She felt like squealing when her dad and Annie finally arrived, though she knew Annie was only looking at this as a job. Her camera was draped over her neck to document the party.

After another half hour of greeting, Cam finally felt she was OK to join the guests upstairs.

Instead of air conditioning the grand, garden-view drawing room, the Patricks had thrown open the wall of windows and glass doors and had a half-dozen ceiling fans circulating the summer air. The delicious floral scent from the garden drifted in. Cam was glad the temperature was lower than they expected the rest of the week, which made this possible. It was warm but worth it. And the room provided the ideal angle to view the elaborate garden.

As she stood in one of the French doorways that led to the balcony, Clancy Huggins and Jessica Benchly climbed the balcony stairs from strolling the garden. Cam had been right that the mosaic effect of the garden below was that of an iris. There was a vast array of purple blazing star, iris, and gladiolus, shot through with yellow foxglove and white calla lilies. Nearest the fountain at the center was a delightful cluster of sunflowers, perfect for the stamen at the center of the flower. The bit of conversation she heard from Clancy and Jessica was about the specific strains of oleander and the variety of lilies Clancy admired, while Jessica favored the hibiscus.

As they passed her, Cam heard an ominous feminine growl from inside. "What is *she* doing here?" Cam looked for the source. Judith Towers-Stevens glared at Clancy and Jessica, then stormed away from her husband and caught Nell Norton's hand. She changed faces like a chameleon as she began to ask recommendations for keeping a floral garden through August, which could be challenging in the Virginia heat.

Cam felt guilty for her relief that Judith Towers-Stevens could take care of herself, as a look to another French door and the hungry look of Telly Stevens explained why she was so angry. Her husband definitely lusted after his fellow judge's date. She wished she could smack him upside the head, but it wasn't like they didn't know about his personality. And it was Judith's fault Telly was involved — she'd insisted.

Cam tried to evaluate if there were other problems, though a romantic triangle among judges was problem enough.

She looked at her watch for comfort but didn't find it. She wandered over to Annie with her new concern. "It's not like Petunia to be late." Petunia and Nick, Cam's sister and brother-in-law, ran a small restaurant called Spoons, and Cam liked to hire them whenever RGS had catering needs, so they were expected at any minute.

Annie looked at her own watch and raised an eyebrow.

"Okay, technically, they aren't late, though they're pushing it. And Petunia is usually a little early."

She walked out onto the stairway landing and realized the Spoons van was sitting on the street waiting for one of the guests to park so Nick could pull past and get close to the house. When the car had finally cleared, he pulled up near the front door. Cam ran down to greet them.

"Everything all right?" she asked.

"Why wouldn't it be?" Petunia sneered.

Cam started to help, but Annie pushed past. "Let me do it first. She won't refuse me," she whispered.

It was true. Petunia liked Annie a lot, in spite of Annie being Cam's best friend and the daughter of a former state senator, a position Petunia's reverse-snob tendencies would normally shun. It was largely because they both were a bit snarky, though Annie's snark held significantly more humor than Petunia's, in Cam's opinion. But Annie also shared Petunia's reverse classism.

Cam waited until Annie had grabbed a box without being yelled at before she joined. Petunia still glared but didn't stop Cam from taking a tray.

"Dining room!" Cam called. She hoped they'd find it. The parties Spoons had catered at the Patricks' before had been outside or upstairs. When Cam arrived at the room, she was relieved to see Petunia opening wine bottles and Nick heading back outside for the last bowls of fettuccine.

The table looked lovely. Cam had rarely seen a table that could comfortably seat thirty — most dining rooms couldn't hold one — but this one had extra room. It was set elegantly with the Patricks' fine china and crystal glassware.

"Are you two staying?"

Petunia shook her head decisively. "You'll get the pans, won't you, Cam?" Petunia blinked innocently. Cam found her sarcasm annoying.

"We'll be back in about ninety minutes," Nick said, taking his wife by the elbow. "We need to get the dessert, which is ice cream." Cam knew it was for the best if they left anyway.

"Sheesh. Petunia's crabbier than usual, isn't she?" Annie said.

"No kidding," Cam agreed. For Annie to say it, it had to be pretty obvious.

Cam started to follow Petunia to see if there was a real problem, but was intercepted by a very late Jimmy Meares — probably the parker who had been in Nick's way. Jimmy was Kyle Lance's manager. Kyle was the tween pop star who had agreed to help with the pageant, and Cam thought it was cheeky of Jimmy to show up without Kyle, but she led him upstairs. She waited about ten minutes before she called the guests down to supper as Annie took pictures to document the gathering.

In the dining room, Cam suggested seating as people came in. She hoped to avoid the judge issues, so she sat Clancy Huggins and Telly Stevens at opposite ends on the same side of the table. She tried to alternate sponsors, pageant staff, and media, hoping it would encourage camaraderie, and took the last empty chair between Barbara Mackay, the third judge, and Jimmy Meares for herself.

"He did *not* just spike his tea." Evangeline's voice was quiet, but she looked scandalized. Cam thought only she, Neil, and Barbara had heard, but all of them turned to see Telly Stevens pouring from a silver flask into his goblet of sweet tea.

Evangeline made a point of pouring wine. It wasn't as if they were asking people to teetotal. There'd been cocktails upstairs, and Cam wondered why Mr. Stevens hadn't just brought a drink down if he preferred bourbon over wine.

Each quadrant of the table had a large bowl of pasta and one of salad, along with garlic bread, fancy olives, and fresh Parmesan. Cam helped her neighbors get served before serving herself.

When everyone had full plates, she surveyed the table. For the most part, people looked content. Cam thought it was possible Telly had his hand on Trish Tait's leg, but Trish didn't seem to object, and Judith Towers-Stevens was engaged in conversation with Holden Hobbes, who Cam knew could be terribly charming.

She had to stop herself from rolling her eyes when her scanning reached her dad, down a few chairs on the same side of the table as she sat. Older women always latched onto him, and there he sat, with Lydia Fennewick on one side and Nell Norton on the other. Both looked completely enthralled by some story he was telling. Thankfully Nell was happily married, so this was just entertainment on her part.

Jimmy Meares mistook Cam's leaning to look at her father as leaning toward him, and he leaned toward her in return so their shoulders touched.

Cam pulled back. She would not have been interested, even if she was available.

"There now. No need to be so jumpy. What's your role in this little shindig?" he asked.

Cam frowned at him. "I *planned* this little shindig. I'm the event coordinator."

"Oh! So you and I are sort of the same," he said, pressing closer again.

His hair was slicked back and long enough to curl at the base of his neck. She supposed it was sort of a Hollywood casual formal thing. His eyes seemed a little too pleased with something.

"And why would you think that?" Cam

asked, hoping she didn't sound as annoyed as she felt.

"I'm the man behind the story — the planner — the one who makes it all happen."

"Well, you have a talented artist to work with. I'm sure that helps."

Annie snapped their picture, and Cam gave her the super-secret glare. Jimmy hadn't even noticed; what's more, he seemed not to have heard her.

"And it seems you're the force behind this deal. We ought to get together and compare notes."

"As tempting as that is, I'm afraid I have too much to do." Cam stood and rushed out of the room, hoping she could think of some task to perform so she could return with a realistic story after Jimmy had cooled off.

She double-checked the dessert table. While they were eating, the staff was meant to clean up the sunroom so when Petunia and Nick returned with the trays of ice cream delights there would be room. The desserts were beautiful little squares, much like petit fours, but they had ice cream in them, so they were perfect for a warm day.

The room looked great. She'd known it would; she called Nick to make sure they'd be back by eight. When he answered, she heard an annoyed Petunia in the background, so she whispered to Nick, "Just tell her I only made the call as an excuse to get out of talking to an obnoxious rich person."

Nick laughed. If anything would work on Petunia, that ought to.

She caught Giselle, the Patricks' housekeeper, on the way back to the dining room and suggested she could open some of the bottles of red wine to let them breathe.

"*Oui,* mademoiselle," Giselle said and rushed off.

Giselle was no more French than Cam was, but the staff at La Fontaine seemed to play at it to make their jobs more interesting. Cam supposed there was no harm if it worked.

"Everything all right?" Evangeline asked as Cam came back in.

"Of course it is, love. Cammi's on top of everything." Mr. Patrick patted his wife's leg and smiled.

"I was just double-checking on dessert," Cam said. "With ice cream, timing matters. Eight o'clock, they said."

She sat down again, pulling her chair just a little closer to Barbara Mackay. She would explain later. Barbara worked for the same newspaper as her boyfriend, Rob, so Cam knew her slightly and she thought Barbara would understand.

Evangeline looked at her watch. "That's in about ten minutes. Looks like we timed this just right. Do you think the servants are ready for us to get a glass of wine?"

"I know they are." Cam smiled.

Evangeline stood and clinked her glass. "Everyone, there's no rush, but when y'all are ready, if you could make your way back to the sunroom . . ."

A few people began to stand and move. Others, in pairs, lingered a bit.

"Why don't you and Neil go ahead," Cam suggested to Evangeline. "I can stay for the stragglers."

Evangeline winked, then took her husband's arm to lead the procession.

Jimmy Meares looked ready to stay put with Cam, but Cam ducked over for an urgent word with Annie, hoping it didn't look too obvious.

"Is he gone yet?" Cam whispered.

"Wait for it," Annie said. "Lingering look . . . and . . . he's gone."

"Thank goodness," Cam said.

"He's a little slimy."

"Understatement," Cam said.

She turned back around to see her dad standing, Lydia Fennewick clinging to his

39

arm, laughing.

"It's not his fault he's a babe magnet," Annie whispered behind her.

Jessica and Clancy rose, too, finally heading out, and Cam spotted the danger. This was what Telly had been waiting for.

Cam pounced. "Mr. Stevens! I hoped I might have a word."

He looked irritable. "Now?"

"Just briefly. I wanted to double-check what you needed for interviews." Telly's manager had agreed that he would interview all contestants for the pageant promotion.

"Let's walk and talk at the same time, shall we?" he said, taking a shot from his flask.

Cam nodded but made a point of moving slowly.

It wasn't slowly enough, however, to miss seeing Judith Towers-Stevens pull on Jessica's unoccupied arm, spin her around, and give her a slap.

"You're a home-wrecker, you tramp!"

"Judith!" Clancy and Telly swore at the same time.

"You see that? She's got both of them wrapped around her little finger!" Judith accused, looking around the crowded corridor.

Cam watched Jessica. She didn't argue or

defend herself, but she did turn a sickly green and rush out the front door.

Clancy started to follow her, but Telly grabbed his arm. His words were quiet, but his voice was made for broadcast media; the tenor trembled within hearing range.

"Why did you bring her here? Tonight, of all nights?"

Cam wondered what was so special about this particular night, but the men just stood and glared. Telly had forgotten Cam entirely.

Thankfully, Nick came through the front door with a tray, giving Cam something to do. She rushed over.

"Hey, sis — glad to see you. There are three of these and Petunia's sort of . . . indisposed . . . You mind grabbing one?"

"Of course."

Cam rushed out to the van and retrieved one, glad for a concrete task at the moment. She could hear retching behind a bush. Was it Petunia? Or Jessica? She worried either way but grabbed a tray. She had barely reached the stairs when Nick rushed back past her for the last one.

The little squares of ice cream were beautiful. Chocolate on some, white chocolate on others — each with a small flower in pink, yellow, or lavender.

When Nick set the last tray down, she

grabbed his arm. "Is Petunia okay?"

"Yeah, just . . . well, she'll explain later."

He splayed his hands and Cam knew he meant Petunia was throwing up. It *had* been her Cam had heard.

"Out there?"

He nodded. "Behind a bush. Something set her off."

"Poor thing!"

"I'll get the dinner dishes now, but can you . . ." He indicated the three trays. "We still have another few deliveries."

"Of course!" It was funny to hear the word "dinner" for "supper," and with Nick's New Jersey accent, it was really closer to "dinna." "You come say good-bye after you're loaded, okay? Let me know that Tunia's all right?"

He clicked his tongue and gave a half grin — a sort of wordless affirmative in Nick's world. He seemed to do whatever he could to avoid language.

As Cam watched Nick leave the sunroom, Jessica came back in. She looked better — a lot better. Cam was impressed with how dignified she could look after the scene downstairs; she was the picture of elegance. She looked around the room and then made her way over to Clancy.

In slow motion, it seemed, Telly went

toward her and his wife grabbed his arm, throwing red wine in his face.

"I will not have you chase after that floozy in my presence!"

Judith stormed out and Telly stood there, looking like an idiot.

Nobody rushed to help, as they all seemed to think he'd asked for it, until Giselle handed him a towel and then carefully began to dab at a wine-splattered tapestry.

Cam went to her. "Do you have any seltzer? It might work better."

Giselle looked up. "It will? Yes! The mini-fridge." Giselle rushed over to the bookcase and pulled a book out, which revealed itself to be a false front. She took a bottle of seltzer water and Cam did the same, then closed it again.

By the time Cam turned around after cleaning the stains, Telly, Judith, Clancy, and Jessica were all gone. Evangeline and Neil chatted amicably with sponsors and members of the media, and Cam's dad seemed to have a harem, if not for Byron Norton also hovering. Nell, Lydia, Annette, and Barbara Mackay all appeared rapt at his story.

Jimmy Meares loitered near Annie, and Cam took mercy, deciding her best friend needed rescuing. She went over and leaned in, whispering loudly.

"You meeting Jake later?" Cam asked.

"Maybe. He went to his mom's for dinner, which often requires Annie therapy afterward. What about Rob?"

"Hopefully."

Jimmy wasn't as thick as he'd acted; he understood the conversation meant the two women in his age range weren't available. He said his good-byes and left.

CHAPTER 3

Cam had an appointment the following morning to supply Telly Stevens with portfolios of the contestants for the interviews that would occur in the coming days. She looked around WONK, with its chrome-and-glass lobby. A small, perky receptionist led her into a studio that was familiar and not at the same time: Telly Stevens's talk show set for *Roanoke Living.* The stage looked eerily empty without lights, host, and guest, but the chairs and background, a grand shot of Roanoke she'd seen on television a hundred times, were well-known.

"Mr. Stevens?" the receptionist called. Her voice was slightly nasal when she shouted.

Telly Stevens came out a side door wearing a shirt, tie, and vest, but had apparently discarded the jacket for the time being. His hair was combed straight back to reveal a widow's peak, but the salt that tempered his pepper kept it from looking too menacing. She realized she'd avoided looking at him very closely the night before, probably because he'd made such a spectacle, so it felt like her first close-up look at him.

"Well, hello there," he oozed.

Cam repeated her mantra: *professional. Professional. Professional.* She knew his reputation and was not interested, but neither did she want to jeopardize the pageant by offending him. She thought if she were distant, she could avoid any misinterpretation.

"Mr. Stevens, nice to see you again. I wanted to go over the parameters for the Little Miss Begonia interviews."

"Well, sure, darlin'. Come on in." He was shameless — not a word or look of apology for the scene he'd caused the night before.

Cam followed him into his office and sat across from the main seat. A bookshelf sat to the side, the top lined with a handful of high-end liquor bottles. A similarly sized gift box sat on his desk. She suspected that was a well-known way to butter the man up.

To her alarm, instead of going around to his side of the desk, he settled in the guest chair next to her. She plowed ahead, presenting what his team had agreed to in terms of the interviews with the girls and how the clips would be used in the pageant and for publicity.

He scooted close to her and rested the back of his arm on her leg to hold the packet, even as she tried to push it to him.

"And this was all scheduled with my secretary?" he asked.

"Yes. Of course."

"Then I suppose we're set."

"I just wanted to talk about tone and see if you had any questions. I know you've done pageants, but these girls are only seven to ten years old."

His mouth twitched like he'd bitten into something bitter.

"They'll be very star-struck and excited to be in the studio," she said. "The first few will come in this afternoon — local girls — after you're done filming *Roanoke Living.*"

"Well, if my secretary scheduled them . . ." He hadn't removed his arm from her leg. He then turned his arm over and patted her knee.

Professional. Professional. "We confirmed six a day through Friday."

He squeezed her knee and smiled. She had to work not to swat it away.

"Well, I'm glad you let me know. I barely keep up with my calendar most days, but

I'd like to prepare a little for this."

Cam breathed a sigh of relief when he leaned back and let go of her knee. She handed over the packet she'd prepared for him.

"This should help. It's all about the pageant. Do you have any questions, Mr. Stevens?"

"Can I get your phone number?"

Cam was horrified, then realized he might have a professional need.

"Of course you can. And you can call me for any trouble with these interviews or questions the packet brings up. Will you be at the welcoming supper for the girls tonight?"

"Wouldn't miss it." His teeth gleamed, but his eyes didn't crinkle. He'd gotten her hint about the phone number. She felt dirty when she escaped, and it was barely nine in the morning.

Cam arrived at the Patrick Henry just ten minutes later. The old hotel was a comfortable walk from the studio, but the morning meeting with Telly Stevens had drained her. She found her way to an empty pageant office and turned on her laptop to organize her day. Once her planner was double-checked, she went into Evangeline's office to see how things were going, but as soon as she got there, the bell chimed, signaling they had company in their suite.

Cam turned and her heart stopped. Three months earlier, Dylan, the man now loitering in the doorway, had guarded her as she was briefly — and, it turned out, benignly — held hostage. There was electricity between them, regardless of how badly Cam wanted it to go away. Her face grew hot. She wasn't quite a redhead, but her complexion thought she was. She blushed easily.

She looked around for a distraction and saw that Benny Larsson, son of Henry Larsson, the premiere local gardener, had come in to Dylan's left. Benny usually worked for his father, who in turn worked for half of the Roanoke Garden Society.

"Benny! Hi! What are you doing here?" Cam hoped her enthusiasm hid her embarrassment about Dylan.

"Mrs. Patrick hired me and a few friends to help with aerating the soil, then planting some stuff for this pageant thing."

"They're your staff, Cam." Evangeline smiled as if this were a grand treat for Cam.

"Staff. I see." Cam blushed again, so she turned back to Evangeline to keep Benny and Dylan from seeing. "Thank you."

"Well, of course, honey. There's lots to do.

Why don't you have them get started?"

"Right." Cam turned back to them. "Just you two?"

"Until eleven, then we have two more," Benny said. "We also brought a bunch of tools."

"That's good. It's a lot of area to cover and I don't think the soil has been treated for years. They normally just use bedding plants, changing them out a few times a year, so they can tolerate poorer soil. The Memorial Day batch has run its course, though."

On the elevator, without looking at her, Dylan said, "I'm glad I'm getting to work with you, Miss Harris."

Her stomach protested and her spine felt weak. "Me, too. We appreciate it." Her answer felt canned.

Cam looked at Benny. He was chuckling quietly, seemingly pleased with Cam's discomfort.

She led them out of the Patrick Henry and headed toward the clamshell at the park. The area behind it would be most visible, and would therefore get the most flowers.

She pointed out the priority area and let them know the soil supplements and first batch of flowers would be arriving soon, so they could just get started prepping the

50

ground. As she left, she scolded herself for feeling like it was a narrow escape.

Cam had plenty to do before she began checking in pageant contestants at three. The event staff all had to be situated in their various places at the Roanoke Arts Commission and the Roanoke Library. All the goodies for contestants had to be in place in the amphitheater, and she had to confirm that a shuttle would run hourly to the Hotel Roanoke and the Travelodge, the two closest hotels that had had rooms blocked for the event.

As she made her way back to the Patrick Henry, trying not to think about Dylan, Cam called Petunia to make sure she didn't need help with the fajita buffet that would serve as the supper in the park.

Cam's cell phone buzzed as she tried to put it back in her pocket. She hadn't even made it back up to her office yet.

"Got a truckload of flowers down here. Where you want 'em?" Cam didn't recognize the voice, but she'd been expecting the flower delivery.

"Oh! Wonderful! Can you see the men turning over soil?"

"Yeah?"

"Just drive across the grass and park near

them. The flowers will be planted under the dogwoods, and the shade will be better for them until they're planted."

"That's city property," the man said.

"And the city is thrilled to have an outside group donate and plant flowers for them."

"Okay! No offense, I just like to make sure. People who get kicked out don't pay their bills." It sounded like he was removed several steps from Nell Norton or he'd know these were a donation, but Cam decided to be nice.

"Understandable. I'll meet you in ten minutes with your receipt. Just unload under the trees, if you would."

"Will do."

Cam hoped they also had the fertilizer and compost she'd requested. She wanted a lasting benefit to her favorite city, so she'd been pleased with the arrangement they'd made with Nell. Benny would know which plants needed greater acidity and which preferred alkaline soil, so she trusted optimum growing conditions would be set.

She reached the second floor and peeked into Evangeline's office. "Flowers are here. Could I get that non-profit voucher? Nell will want her tax deduction."

Evangeline nodded, pulled out a receipt book, and wrote one up for Cam. Cam took it and hurried back toward the elevators, feeling like her entire day would probably be spent running around like a chicken with its head cut off.

She met the truck on the grass near the row of trees that lined Williamson Road, forming the eastern border for the park. Two men were diligently unloading, and she noted they'd included several bags of compost and manure.

Benny heaved his shovel into the soil so it stood upright, and walked over to Cam. "What's up?"

"This is first priority, now. I hope you've made good progress because these bushes and flowers need to be planted by the time the sprinklers come on at six."

"Holy crap!" Benny said.

Cam eyed him. "I'm sure Evangeline told you."

"Yeah, and there are four of us. But that's a lot!"

Benny's friends had all joined him and Cam looked at Benny, waiting for introductions. They didn't come, so she began. "I'm Cam Harris."

Benny jumped. "Right! Miss Harris, this is Scooter and Jed."

"Nice to meet you both," Cam said. "The

bushes and lilies take priority as focal points. The annuals should work around them as complements. Benny is expert enough to guide you. I just wanted to make sure you knew they were the priority."

Dylan was behind the others, as he was taller, and made a point of grinning in a way that made Cam feel naked. That's when a hand from behind touched her waist and she jumped.

"Sorry! Intense flower discussion?" Rob asked.

She kissed him quickly so no one mistook who he was, then said, "Just a second." She rushed over and handed the man from the nursery the receipt slip and then came back to Rob and quickly made introductions. Everyone else dispersed, but Cam felt at least one set of eyes on her.

"What are you doing here? I don't have time for lunch."

"Then I'll bring you some, but I have news," he said.

"Good news? Bad news?"

"Yes."

Cam raised an eyebrow.

"I get to cover the murder trial next week," Rob said. It was Cam who had solved the murders that had plagued the RGS the previous spring and Rob had reported on them, so it wasn't surprising he got to cover the trial. But Cam could tell there was more.

"And?"

"And as payment, I have to cover the Little Miss Begonia Pageant."

Cam laughed. "Oh, you poor macho stud! How will you save your reputation?"

"I thought maybe I'd request a brawl."

Cam laughed again. "Actually, I think these things can get pretty nasty, though I'd appreciate it if you covered it as warm and fuzzy."

"I'll cover what happens."

"I know. News is news." Rob wasn't actually a high risk for tabloid-style journalism, so she felt fairly safe unless something went drastically wrong. Unfortunately, if the pageant-judge love triangle didn't sort itself out, they might have a little of the wrong kind of excitement. She just hoped this event would be significantly less eventful than the last one. A nice, smooth competition with a deserving winner might not be exciting, but at the end of July it was newsworthy. And it was certainly what the pageant committee hoped for, as well as RGS, which was even more important to Cam.

"So what's the agenda?" Rob asked.

"Setting up until three, then I start check-ing girls in and getting them to their hotels. At six, there is a buffet supper in the circular courtyard by the library. Afterward is a meet-and-greet ice cream social. Back to the hotel by eight, and tomorrow we start rehearsals."

Rob's eyes glazed over.

"Hopefully that won't put you to sleep," Cam said. She considered telling him about the potential judge scandal but decided against it. She wanted the girls to be the focus.

"Can I talk to the contestants?"

"If their guardians don't object and you promise to be nice."

"Would I be mean to ten-year-old girls?"

"No, I'm teasing."

"And what's your next step?"

"I need to bring over all the check-in packets. We'll do it at the band shell."

"I'll help you."

Cam was glad for the help. She could have recruited one or two of the men planting flowers, but they were better off uninter-rupted and Cam didn't want to encounter Dylan at the moment. She liked this solu-tion for help until the cadre of volunteers began to arrive around two.

■ ■ ■ ■

The heat threatened as Cam and Rob crossed the lawn to the band shell weighted down with the boxes of materials for participants. It was noon, and Cam thought it might have already hit the predicted high of ninety.

She carried a box and Rob maneuvered a hand truck that held four similar boxes. He looked too warm, but didn't complain. She led him up the ramp onto the shell.

"Crap!"

"What?" he asked.

"Look!"

Rob looked around. The inside of the shell had been vandalized with a lot of spray-painted writing, though the only recurrent word was "Exploit."

Cam set the box down and jogged back down the ramp, Rob on her heels.

"Benny!" she shouted as she approached the trees.

"Yeah?" she heard from the far end of the row.

"Did any of you see anyone go in the band shell today? It was fine this morning, but somebody has had a heyday with spray paint since then."

"I didn't see anyone," Benny said.

"Couple people went by," Scooter said. "You guys even."

"Who was here since the last time I was here?" Cam prodded. She was annoyed to have to be so explicit. Anyone should know what she meant.

"Kids on skateboards?" Jed said.

"When?"

"A half hour ago. I think there were three."

Cam frowned. "How old?"

"Middle school, probably?"

"Probably not them," Rob said. "Whoever this was seems to take issue with the contest — this looks like an adult."

"I agree," Cam said.

"Little old lady?" Scooter asked.

"Maybe." Though Cam didn't think that sounded very likely.

"I saw one. Big handbag. Looked like she was going to sit on the steps for lunch."

"Did you get a good look at her?"

"Big hat. Those" — Scooter made a slashing motion at his calves — "pants . . ."

"Cropped?"

"Yeah. Cropped pants. A little hunched. That's why I thought she was older. I didn't see her well enough to say otherwise. Mighta been wearing a light blue top — like denim?"

"That helps. We'll watch for her, anyway. Thank you."

Cam felt ready to cry. They didn't have time to have someone come paint over the graffiti before the show, and she swore to that effect. "Why does everything have to go wrong?"

"You should cover it up," Rob said, rubbing her neck to relieve the tension.

"What?"

"Get . . . like drapery or something. It would make the inside look elegant, and then nobody would have to paint."

Cam closed her eyes to try and envision it and realized it would be actually nicer that way.

"We need somebody to frame it," she said.

"Good thing you know a carpenter with some free time," Rob said.

Cam frowned again. Her father was indeed a retired carpenter, but this would drag him just that much further into everything. She adored him, but somehow he always ended up center stage. This time, literally.

CHAPTER 4

Cam managed to reach park staff and arrange a cover for the band shell so nobody would see the offending graffiti.

Fortunately, the first event tent was up by two o'clock, and Rob helped Cam move all the check-in materials, along with making a sign so people would know where to go. He was a little more enthusiastic than she would have liked about a story on sabotage, but she appreciated the help. At two-thirty, before any contestants began appearing, the two volunteers from the dinner the night before arrived and were willing to check girls in. They'd been part of the plan, but since Cam hadn't worked with them before, she hadn't known if she could count on their promptness. Their arrival freed her to inspect and supervise.

Annie appeared with her camera, smelling of buttercream. Annie owned a bakery called the Sweet Surprise, which specialized

in cupcakes, though she sold other desserts as well. Cam knew Annie had asked the young girl who sometimes worked with her to fill in some extra hours this week to free Annie to act as photographer for the pageant.

"I'm glad to see you. Did you look behind there?" Cam pointed to the band shell.

Annie snuck off, then returned with wide eyes. "I guess somebody doesn't like beauty pageants."

"It's not a beauty pageant," Cam corrected.

"Yeah, well . . . That fanatic doesn't seem to know that. Erm . . . and it wasn't me."

Cam laughed. She knew it hadn't been her best friend, but it wasn't that different from how Annie felt about the whole thing.

"Should we check and make sure all the stations are set?" Cam asked.

"I'm going to stay here and see if I can interview anyone," Rob said.

Annie looked at Cam, confused.

"It's true. He was assigned the pageant beat," Cam said.

Annie snorted. "Oh, Rob, you get to practice all your *pretty* words!"

Rob glared and Cam pulled Annie toward the library for their first inspection. The library had a community room and had

agreed to allow the pageant committee to set up lockers for each girl in there.

She posted another volunteer with a list so as people came through, she could assign each girl one of the rented lockers. Cam thanked the volunteer, and then she and Annie headed northeast toward the Arts Commission building.

"I thought we'd direct from here, since both the parking garage and shuttle stop channel people past here. You want to get some arrival shots?"

"Nothing would make me happier." Cam noted Annie's sarcasm, but if she was honest, she enjoyed the humor. Usually.

"Oh, look. There's one now," Annie said, snapping a picture.

Cam went down to greet the mom and daughter and directed them around the building toward the park. This continued in an increasing stream for the next hour.

"Do *not* tell me *that* is participating!" Annie hissed behind Cam.

Cam looked up to see a familiar woman helping a little girl from the car seat of a minivan. Another girl, taller and fairer than the first, came around from the other side.

The woman, Mindy, had gone to high school with Cam and Annie and had been a

notorious snob. In spite of that, Mindy had once vouched for Cam against one of her rich friends when the friend had cheated off Cam on a test. The teacher had given Cam a zero until Mindy came forward, admitting what she'd seen — losing social status for a while. Cam and Mindy had been friends after that, though they'd lost touch since then. "You be nice," Cam told Annie.

"Do I have to?"

"Yes." Cam thought maybe Annie had mentally blocked the story. Even if she hadn't, Annie and Mindy had their own history that, in Annie's mind, would no doubt trump the single good deed.

"Cam!" The elegant woman spotted her and came forward to the entrance of the Arts Commission. "Do you have a daughter participating, too?"

"Hi, Mindy. No, I'm the event coordinator. Registration is in a tent just around the corner."

Mindy turned her eyes to Annie. Her nose went up like she smelled something unpleasant. "Oh. Hello, Annie."

"Hi, Mindy. So nice to see you."

Cam almost snorted out loud. Annie sounded so unlike herself that it took everything Cam had to keep a straight face.

"Lauren, Lizzie, these are friends of mine

from high school. Mrs . . ."

Cam shook her head. "Just call me Cam, and this is Annie. Nice to meet you, Lauren and Lizzie."

Lauren gave them a very polite greeting, but Lizzie was examining the camera that dangled from Annie's neck.

"What are you taking pictures of?"

"The Little Miss Begonia Pageant," Annie said.

"Cool! I like to take pictures."

"Come on, girls. I'm sure Cam and Annie are very busy." Mindy hustled to lead the girls around the corner.

"Cam, you should walk Mindy over, check on things," Annie said. "I can keep directing people." Cam thought about it and decided Annie was right, so she ran to catch up.

"Is *she* really working with the pageant?" Mindy asked as Cam caught up. She sounded alarmed.

"Annie's a brilliant photographer, so yes, she's helping." It was hard to hit the right tone — a little scolding without being offensive — but Mindy seemed distracted and apparently felt neither.

"Is it all . . . *out* here? In the *open* like this?"

"Well, we hope so! It's a lovely venue for a

pageant." Cam spotted the work crew. They'd made good progress.

"But . . ."

"Is one of your children heat sensitive?"

"No. I just feel sort of . . . exposed."

Mindy was one of the few people Cam knew who was fairer complexioned than she was. "There are some boutiques not far from here if you need a broad-brimmed hat."

Mindy jerked her head and stared at Cam like she'd forgotten she was there. "Oh! Yes. I'll have to go look."

Cam thought Mindy hadn't meant sun-exposed, but Mindy was a former pageant girl herself, so surely she would expect the other exposure. A girl didn't sign up for pageants to hide.

They finally reached the tent and Cam led Mindy to the sign-in table.

"Lauren and Lizzie Blankenship." Mindy smiled, every bit as sincere as Cam remembered, which was to say not at all. But instead of looking snobbish, as Cam expected, Mindy looked nervous.

The younger daughter pulled on Mindy's shirt. "Can I go back and take pictures with that other girl?"

Cam squatted, though she saw a warning glance from Mindy. "Her name is Annie, but you know what? She's working, so now isn't the best time. She'll be here all week, okay?"

"Come on, Lizzie. Cam is working, too," Mindy said.

Cam wondered what was up with Mindy. She would have expected a lot more nose-rubbing from the one-time debutante about her successful marriage and status, which was clearly wealthy, but Mindy seemed to be posturing, hiding something, almost timid.

Cam double-checked that Trish and Jenny, the volunteers, had been giving directions and the time for the supper buffet. She greeted a few more entrants, then left the tent, only to find Rob interviewing Lizzie, Mindy standing nearby.

"Well, you've made a friend," Cam said.

"Cam, this is . . ."

"I've met Lizzie. Actually, Mindy and I went to high school together," Cam said.

"You two know each other?" Mindy asked, eying Rob with interest.

Cam started to say something about small towns, but Rob scooped her around the waist and tried to kiss her, catching her cheek.

"Yes. Rob and I are seeing each other," Cam admitted, realizing she'd blushed more

66

today than she had in months.

"Well, good heavens! Marry the boy! He's terribly charming!" Mindy said.

Cam thought she might die. She got a fair bit of flak for not being married at thirty-two from the matrons in her life, most of them Roanoke Garden Society members, but she didn't want Rob to feel pressured. She didn't want to get married until it was right for both of them.

That's when Benny appeared. "Erm, Miss Harris. I think we found something that needs your attention."

She apologized to Mindy and followed Benny. Rob stayed behind, figuring it was a floral detail, an assumption Cam shared. Benny led her away from the tents; she saw a cluster of people in the shrubs behind the Arts Commission and felt her stomach somersault. Her heart leaped into her throat and stayed. She sprinted as well as she could without being able to breathe.

"What happened?"

"It's that T.V. guy who's judging," Benny said.

"T.V. guy" took a minute to register. "Telly Stevens?"

Benny nodded.

"What did he do?" She pictured another scene.

"I haven't gotten close. Scooter found him. He was planting salvia at the far end and spotted a foot in the bushes."

Telly Stevens was in the bushes? Cam stood on her tiptoes and could see Scooter standing guard in front of a prone body. Her heart thumped, but surely this was just a case of overheating or something. Somebody who Cam thought might be Michelle, the choreographer, leaned over him, trying to administer CPR. She was only doing the heart part. Cam rushed forward to help, though her own training was very rusty, but when she got to her knees, Michelle shouted, "No!"

Cam looked at her, fighting anxiety. This was a lot worse than she'd feared.

"Look at his mouth — that foam — I don't know what that is, but it might be poison. I don't think it's a good idea to get close to it."

The paramedics arrived then, and Cam and Michelle were glad to step away and let the professionals take over.

"Ma'am, how long did you try CPR?" one of them asked Michelle.

"Somewhere between five and ten minutes, but I couldn't do the breathing," Michelle said. "Look in his mouth."

The second EMT looked and pulled a

needle from a box and shot it into Telly Stevens, but nothing happened. The other man shrugged.

"It was a long shot. That foam could have indicated an allergic reaction." He turned back to Michelle. "That was smart not to get too close. I don't know what that is, but it might be dangerous."

"Is he dead?" Cam asked, and then spotted Stevens's flask off to the side. She thought about picking it up, but then thought better of it.

At that minute, Jake arrived with a female deputy. Cam swerved and pointed out the flask to Jake. She told him she'd seen Stevens with it the night before. She felt, though, that her best efforts should be spent keeping people involved in the pageant away from this until the scene cleared.

As soon as the area had emptied, Cam went up to their offices to explain what had happened to Evangeline.

"We've got a problem," she said quietly, hoping there was no one to hear.

"Close the door," Evangeline said.

Cam did and then told her about what had happened.

"Shoot! We are back to looking for judges!"

That hadn't been the response Cam had anticipated, but it was true. Nobody had really liked Telly, so it was also possible the pageant would go more smoothly with a different judge, if they were able to manage the press of the matter.

They decided for the time being, at least, they would assume the tragedy was unrelated to the pageant. It was an unfortunate event, but until they knew differently, it was easiest to assume it was just an unfortunate medical incident.

Nick and Petunia were setting up under a tent canopy when Cam and Evangeline reached the park lawns on the far side of the library a few hours later. The van was pulled onto the grass so they didn't have to move things far, but there was a lot of food, Cam knew, as she was the one who'd ordered it.

Cam had forgotten the Petunia-Evangeline dynamic momentarily, since the two hadn't encountered each other the night before. Evangeline and Nick had a rather colorful history together, and no matter how it was argued, Petunia refused to believe it was only platonic. Cam jumped into their lineup to help unload and Evangeline grabbed a salad bowl, until Petunia pulled it back saying, "I'm sure that's not necessary."

Cam hoped Evangeline didn't hear the rudeness under the words. She wished Petunia could just believe Evangeline and Nick were only old friends and let the past go. Whatever the case, Evangeline took the cue to go into the tent next door and make sure all the participants had arrived. Evangeline returned just as Nick and Petunia were shutting the van to re-park it on the street during the supper.

Annie returned then, cleaned up and in a sundress. Cam envied her the shower, but then Cam had started work three hours later than Annie and hadn't spent any time with an industrial oven. She was just glad her best friend had been willing to pitch in over and above her own business.

"I came with your dad," Annie said. "He insisted on dropping me off and then parking."

"He does that, but I'm glad you came together. That way you can keep track of him."

"You think I'm going to keep someone out of trouble?" Annie asked with a raised eyebrow. "Didn't seem to work last night."

Cam debated telling Annie about the dead judge but decided it needed to wait until later. "No, but I don't think you've completely lost anyone since college," she said.

Annie nodded, conceding the point.

Not two minutes later, Cam saw two older men crossing the grass together, chatting amicably. Evangeline rushed to one of them and kissed her husband. He was thirty years older and two inches shorter, but they really seemed to adore one another.

"Daddy! Thank you for coming." Cam kissed her dad's cheek.

"Well, another free supper . . ." he said.

Cam tilted her head, but he was unabashed.

"So why don't you show me this project before they let us eat? Is it where all that yellow tape is?"

"No. I will explain that later. Come with me." Cam led her dad to the band shell, where they slipped behind the curtain.

"Oh boy. Somebody doesn't like pageants much."

"It's true. And we can't have it painted. There's no time. Can you think of anything?"

"I've got some lattice. We could weave . . . what's this . . . Miss Honeysuckle?"

"Begonia!" Cam scolded.

He waved a hand in front of his face. It was the same difference to him. "Weave some flowers and leaves into the lattice, then it's just a couple hours' work to put it up. Wait 'til the day of the pageant and you don't risk anyone ruining that, too."

"That's perfect! And I bet Nelly's Nurseries would help us out. It increases their visibility. I wish we could cover this in the meantime so the girls could practice up here. But I think you're right. It's better to avoid further vandalism."

They headed back to the tents.

"Is Rob coming?" her father asked.

"He was here already. He was assigned the story."

Her dad chuckled. "I bet he likes that."

"He requested a brawl."

"He may get one! Your mother tried to enter you into one of these once, but I'd seen what could happen. No, sirree, not my girls!"

"That doesn't sound like her at all. How'd she get involved?"

"Oh, she and Lydia were friends. They went to high school together."

"That's right. Nell Norton, too, apparently. So that was what all of you had to talk about last night?"

"Well, sure. We had lots to talk about." Her father seemed to attract far too many women who thought he was the perfect eligible older man. She didn't say anything;

73

she wanted him happy. She just wished he'd meet someone nice and settle down again.

When they arrived back at the supper tent, Cam could see about a dozen participants coming across the lawn, mostly in mother-daughter pairs, though one young lady was with her dad and one held the hands of both parents. Cam didn't like to make assumptions, but she guessed the girl with both parents was at least somewhat local. Families who began pageants so early in life just couldn't all take off work for a whole week every time there was a final. She was sure all the dads would be there by Thursday night when the competition really got under way, but not for the opening supper.

She kept an eye on things as everybody arrived. Rob had returned and brought her a plate of chicken and salad. More than once, he'd seen her forget to eat when she got busy, and the consequences weren't pretty. She wondered if she should mention Telly Stevens but decided it had to wait until after the supper. Then she'd tell Rob and Annie together.

"I wonder where Mindy is," Cam said as Rob handed her the food and she thankfully took a few bites.

"Mindy from this afternoon?"

"Yeah."

"Maybe two kids at once is a lot to handle at a pageant. Lizzie didn't really want to be here."

"She's the little one?"

"Yeah, but I got the feeling the older one was only doing it for her mom, too, even if she gave the expected answers."

"She's playing a role for her mom?"

"Yeah."

"That's awful."

"Maybe, but I bet she's not the only girl who feels that way. I talked to three whom I got that impression from, and I only met about half the girls."

"Are you writing that?"

"Not until it's over, and not mainstream — I'll change names of everything, but yeah, I can't not write it. I won't mention the pageant name or location. I'll just say a Southern state. The *Tribune* is too conservative to cast doubt on an old institution like pageants. I can find a magazine, though, that wants the article."

Cam sighed. "I guess I don't disagree. Thank you for not outing *here*, though."

"I bet it's the case everywhere. Some mom was a former beauty queen, or mom *wasn't* a former beauty queen and is bitter and has a pretty daughter . . . wants to live through

75

her child . . ."

Cam hated that she thought he was probably right, but she suspected he was.

When Cam thought everyone had arrived who was going to, she began her announcements.

"Can I get your attention?" She waited for the faces to turn. "My name is Cam Harris, and I am coordinator for this event. That means if you have any trouble or questions, you can come to me. We have offices on the second floor in the Patrick Henry Hotel, which isn't actually a hotel, as I think you've all heard." She pointed at the beautiful old building across from the northeast corner of the park. "I hope to talk to everyone regularly enough that you don't have to go there. But if you need something and can't find me, they will know where I am. I have an agenda and some standalone media packets up here." She indicated the box next to her. "The bigger deal, though — all this coverage will go to your local newspapers, but if you are from a city whose local paper has closed or gone online, or if you are lucky enough to be from a place with a new paper, I'd appreciate your help in identifying those." Cam held up a clipboard. "This has a sign-up sheet to add to our email list. An actual URL or email address is nice, but if you don't have it, the page or paper name and city will do. I'm pretty good at finding these press sites." She smiled and the audience chortled.

"Now, the goal tonight is to get comfortable and get to know a few people, so when I bring you an agenda, I am also bringing you a Bingo board. Instead of letters and numbers, it has things like" — Cam looked at the page to read a few examples — "plays polo or tap dances. I want you — the girls here, not their parents — to ask other girls questions and if they do anything on your Bingo board. If they do, they can sign their name. There will be a prize for the first Bingo and also for the girl who signs the most different boards. Only one signature per board, please. And don't start until everyone has one."

Cam handed a stack of handouts to Evangeline and together they distributed the packets. It didn't take long, as all the girls had come close when Cam started explaining.

She had to laugh. As soon as she said "Go," a half-dozen girls descended on Lizzie Blankenship, undoubtedly for the box that read "is under four feet tall."

She was still laughing when Mindy gave a

choked sound. Cam made her way over to her friend.

"Is this true?" Mindy asked.

Cam, thinking Mindy was upset her daughter had been swarmed, looked with confusion at the woman. The goal of that particular box in the Bingo game was to give positive attention to the smallest girl. "Is what true?"

"Telly Stevens . . . a judge for this event? I just thought . . . he was a judge last year . . ."

"Was he? I didn't realize . . ." She wasn't willing to explain it was no longer true, as she just couldn't afford to open that can of worms at the moment. She wasn't sure why being a judge two years in a row would be an issue.

"Why?" Mindy asked.

Cam looked around. Nobody else was close enough to hear. "Honestly, the television station required it or they wouldn't air us. Is there a problem?"

"No." But if ever a "no" had meant "yes" more, Cam hadn't heard it. She felt guilty for feeling relieved that Mindy didn't want to share.

She patted Mindy's arm. "I don't think he will bother you."

When the girls had been seen off for the

night, Cam groaned. The sponsors and judges were having a high-end cocktail party in the Patrick Henry offices at the same time, and Cam knew they would wonder where Telly Stevens was. She had to make an appearance. To top it off, Annie *had*, in fact, lost Cam's dad. He was nowhere to be found.

She thought Neil Patrick had probably dragged her dad up to the party, so Cam found Annie and Rob and they made their way there.

The party was surprisingly pleasant, possibly helped by Telly's absence. Lydia Fennewick seemed to be orchestrating people into small groups. Her dad was indeed at the center of one of these, all women but himself.

Cam made the rounds and said hello to all, making sure each knew what her schedule for the week would be. When Evangeline arrived to oversee everything, Cam made her excuses about needing to send press releases and escaped with Rob, leaving Annie to extricate her dad.

It was time to confess to Rob what had happened.

CHAPTER 5

Cam's phone buzzed. It was the party supply company that was meant to make a delivery of thousands of tissue flowers early the next day. Their van was broken.

"I don't have anything to transport them. Are you sure you don't have another way?" she asked.

The negative response verified this project would probably give her an ulcer by sending a pain through her abdomen.

"Well, I'll have to brainstorm. We definitely need them by tomorrow, but I need to see what I can find to transport them." She snapped her phone shut.

"That sounded bad," Rob said.

"Forty thousand tissue dogwood flowers and their van is broken. They can't deliver!"

"I hate to ask the obvious here, but why do you need dogwood flowers? And if you do, why couldn't they just hold the pageant when the dogwoods are in bloom?"

Cam rolled her eyes. She'd asked Evangeline Patrick the same thing, but she wouldn't admit that to Rob. "The local pageants are held in spring, almost all when the dogwoods are in bloom. The teen class is Miss Dogwood — the state flower — and the theme unites all the pageants. But the state pageant is a week long and the local winners all need time to prepare, so they hold it in the summer."

"I see," he said. He looked skeptical.

"Where are we going to get a van?" Cam asked.

"You ask Petunia?"

"Yeah, that'll go over well." Cam knew her sister had already had her quota of Evangeline Patrick for the day. It didn't help that the word "pageant" also riled Petunia. Petunia hated any system that dubbed any person superior to others. "I'll call Nick," Cam said, fearing a bad pattern had been set. "You go back inside and get Annie."

Cam pressed "N" and Nick's number popped up.

"Yeh?" Nick answered. It was typical. He wasn't one for niceties or . . . words, really. But he had a heart of gold and treated her sister like a gem — something not easy, in Cam's opinion. Petunia was definitely prickly. Cam thought Nick probably deserved sainthood.

"Nick? Can you talk?" She hoped Petunia wasn't right there.

"Yeah?" Nick said.

Cam waited, but that was all he said.

"Is there a good time in the next fourteen hours for me to borrow the catering van for . . . maybe three hours?"

"One to four A.M.?"

"Preferably not, but I'm desperate enough." She hoped he was joking.

"Last catering job is done at ten. You help me clean it up, it's yours until nine in the morning."

"Deal! Thanks, Nick!" Cam hung up just as Rob reappeared with Annie.

"You're a chicken," Annie said.

"What?" Cam turned to look at Annie.

"You knew Petunia wouldn't help because it's for Evangeline," Annie said.

"Which doesn't make me a chicken. It makes me smart. So are you in?"

"Transport off-season tissue dogwood flowers? Do I have to?" Annie looked to Rob, who was chuckling.

"Yes," Cam said.

"Can I complain on my blog?"

"I'd rather you didn't." Cam wasn't sure whether Annie had a blog or not, she'd never mentioned it before if she did, but there was no reason to tempt it. "At least not until this whole pageant is done," she amended. The artist in Annie might rebel if Cam came across too strong.

"Usual gang?" Rob asked.

"Something happened this afternoon. A body was found on the side of the Arts Commission."

Rob stared at her for a moment. "Body?"

"Not just a body. One of our judges. Telly Stevens. Jake was here looking to see if there was foul play."

"I'm going to get scooped," Rob accused. "You could have told me."

"They don't know if it's foul play or not," Cam said.

"I'm only helping if Jake will meet us after and get me up to date," Rob said.

"He'd probably be happy for the break," Annie said, taking out her phone.

The three of them beat the van to Spoons. They joked in an alley behind the restaurant as they waited. Annie made outrageous dares, but neither Cam nor Rob took her up on them. Finally, the Spoons van pulled in.

Petunia jumped out as soon as it stopped. "What's this?"

"Hi, Tunia. Nick said if we helped clean it, we could borrow the van for the night," Cam said.

Petunia, all arms and legs, rounded on her husband, who probably had ninety pounds on her. She hit him until he picked her up and whispered sweet things nobody else could hear. Finally, he set her down again.

"Just tell her, Pet. She's your sister."

"Tell me what?" Cam asked.

Petunia scowled at Cam, turned back, and scowled at Nick, then scowled at Cam one more time. It was crabby, even for Petunia. Finally though, she squinted and spoke.

"I'm pregnant."

Cam shrieked, joy flooding out all her other emotions. Tears flowed as she rushed over and hugged her sister, then she stood back, only to have Annie rush in for a hug.

Cam looked at her sister carefully. "Why aren't you happier?"

"You try nausea every waking minute. See how happy you are. Then . . . last night . . . I hope that's just a one-time thing!"

The pieces fell into place for Cam about the retching the night before. "Oh. Sorry about that. But Tunia, I'm thrilled for you! A baby!" Cam said.

"They came to help so you could go rest, Pet. Why don't you head home, have a bath, and get some sleep," Nick said.

Cam knew she hadn't agreed to cleaning everything, just the van, but she also recognized Nick getting the irritable Petunia out of the way for the moment would save time. Besides, with the four of them, cleanup would go quickly. And, she was going to be an aunt!

Just over an hour later, they were headed for Blue Mountain Events to pick up the tissue flowers. The salesperson, probably the owner, had agreed to meet Cam there because of their broken van, but he still seemed grouchy about the hour.

Their shipment was a dozen huge boxes, but each was no heavier than a box of shoes.

"So what's in here?" Rob asked again. He was lifting two boxes at once into the air and acting like it proved great strength.

"Weren't you listening? Paper dogwood flowers," Annie grumbled.

"Seriously?" he said. "I hoped she was kidding."

Before Cam could stop Annie, she had pulled out a box cutter and sliced one open to prove it. She tucked a flower behind each of her ears and then did the same for Rob.

"Toilet paper flowers?" Rob said, examining the flower Annie had put behind his left ear.

"It's tissue. It's the most like real flowers for the television cameras," Cam said.

"It better have come cheap," Annie scolded.

They weren't, but Cam wasn't going to fuel Annie's fires. It was none of her business.

"Just load the boxes, would you?"

Rob headed out with the two he'd been lifting. Cam followed, and soon Annie was the only one not helping, which pushed her into motion, too. She liked to ask questions, but she didn't like to look lazy.

Three trips moved all the boxes to the van.

"We're going where?" Annie shouted when she heard Cam's directions.

"Neil Patrick rented offices at the Patrick Henry, but is letting Evangeline use them for pageant administration before he moves in."

"But it's haunted," Annie complained.

"Oh, will you stop? You're the one who used to scare *me*, remember?"

It was true. Annie had always gotten a kick out of raising a response from people by any means necessary.

"Yeah, but that was all fake stuff. This isn't."

"Well, it's the closest place to where we need the flowers to be for the setup crew, so that's where we're taking them."

"And then beer?" Annie asked. "Jake said he could meet us by midnight."

Cam raised an eyebrow. Annie obviously wasn't *that* concerned about the haunting nonsense if in the next sentence she could change topics to beer.

"I wish he could make it sooner," Rob said. "*Tribune* has a staff meeting in the morning."

They began lugging the boxes to the Patrick Henry from their spot in the loading zone.

"I can stay here so we don't get towed," Annie offered.

"We don't need you to. This is what a loading zone is *for:* loading!" Cam said.

Annie stuck her tongue out and then launched into ever-sillier faces until she was again the last to grab a box.

The upscale restaurant on the ground floor of the Patrick Henry building appeared closed for the night, but they heard piano music from the bar and a nicely dressed couple came out as they entered the former hotel.

"Should we be using a freight elevator?" Rob asked.

"Probably, but I don't know where it is. I only have a key to the office, and this is the only way I know to get there," Cam said.

As they stood, a businessman joined them waiting for the elevator, so Cam and Annie got in with their one box apiece, leaving the businessman room to stand without being jostled. Rob and his two boxes waited for the next elevator.

"Second floor!" Cam called out as the doors closed.

"Second floor? You aren't robbing the bank?" the man joked.

"Making a deposit," Annie said, holding out her box.

Cam clarified. "Neil Patrick leased space on the second floor, which he's kindly lent to the Little Miss Begonia Pageant through the end of July."

To her surprise he raised an interested eyebrow. "Are you working with Evangeline?" The elevator had stopped and Annie got out, but the man was holding the door and partially blocking Cam's way.

"Yes. Are you a friend of hers?"

He laughed. "Oh, I'd hardly put it that way. Still, I'd like to run into her." He finally backed against the wall, allowing Cam room to maneuver out of the elevator. The doors shut behind her.

"See? Haunted," Annie said, picking up her box again.

Cam laughed. "Yeah, I'd go along with that." She found the heavy glass door, currently unmarked, and unlocked the deadbolt at the bottom. She turned on a light, which spilled out into the dim hallway just as the other elevator door opened. Cam and Annie watched as Rob wrestled his boxes out of the elevator.

As they brought in the boxes, twice Rob shouted "Boo!" behind Annie, delighted to finally have an advantage on his girlfriend's best friend. Annie had teased him a lot over the years. They finished and made two more trips, storing the boxes in a side room. Cam left Evangeline a note, and then they were free to get their beer before calling it a night.

Jake actually beat them to Martin's. For the four of them, Martin's Downtown Bar had become a sort of tradition.

Rob sat across from Jake and leaned back. "So tell us about Telly Stevens," he said.

"Definitely died of poison," Jake said. "The initial lab results have identified it as plant matter."

"Oh, crap," Cam said. "Murder?"

"Suicide is possible, though the M.E. said it was a horrible death. A guy who knew anything about whatever plant it was wouldn't have picked it."

"And Telly did," Cam said. That had been her concern: knowledge. Plus, anything plant-related pointed to the Roanoke Garden Society as the experts. She worried someone she worked for might be suspected. Again. "What about time of death?"

"Difficult to say with as warm as it was. Body temperature doesn't change much when the air outside is so warm. No rigor mortis yet, though, so less than two hours before he was found."

"And the men planting didn't see anything?" Cam asked.

Jake just looked at her.

"I just thought . . . they were there all day except their lunch break. You could find out when they took that, and it should help identify when he got to that spot."

"That's not bad, Cam," he said.

"Do you have any suspects?" she asked.

"No fingerprints on that flask except his own. We canvased his coworkers and some of his social connections. Everybody has a theory — they all seemed to know someone who didn't like him, but all claimed they personally did. It's a pretty large field of suspects. I think I should leave it at that, though."

He clearly didn't want any more questions. That was okay. Cam didn't want to get involved, either. Rob was eating up the details, though, and she was sure she would hear about it if there was any reason she should be worried, aside from general damage control.

When Cam got home, she sent out a press release about the unfortunate demise of Telly Stevens.

"The cause of death is still being investigated." If it was murder, the word would eventually be out, but there was no reason to hurry it. The only real guilt she felt was not telling Rob about her hunch that Telly's death had not been accidental. He'd be irritated if he thought she'd hidden it, so she was willing herself to believe it really was accidental. Before they heard otherwise, she hoped the pageant would be over. If he learned it was murder now, he'd report it and the effect on the pageant might be devastating, a possibility she wanted to avoid.

Cam arrived at the Patrick Henry the next morning, found her way to her empty office, and turned on her laptop to organize her day. The first full day of pageant activity was likely to be chaotic, even if they hadn't had the dead judge to worry about.

"I've been thinking about replacement judges," Evangeline said.

Cam started and looked up to see Evangeline in her doorway. "I didn't know you were here!" She took a minute to catch her breath and then looked back to Evangeline. "We interviewed five, based on the RGS screening. Should we go to the next on the list?" Cam said.

"Yes and no. If Toni Howe is available, that would be great. She was actually our third choice for a judge until we were blackmailed by WONK. She would have been second on my list. Whatever the case, Vicky Wynan was last on everybody's list, so if Toni isn't available, we need to look further."

"What's wrong with Vicky?" Cam asked.

"She has no manners! She offended every person she talked to. Believe me. She almost needed to *try* to rank behind Telly Stevens."

"Okay . . . We'll skip Vicky. I will check with Toni, though, and see if she's available." Cam looked at Evangeline, who nodded. "Then I guess I will let Benny and company know about these boxes of dogwoods."

"They should love that," Evangeline said.

Cam had to laugh at Evangeline's sarcasm; she didn't stoop to it very often.

"By the way," Cam said, remembering their elevator ride the night before, "a man who must live in the building was asking about you."

"Really?"

Cam described him, but Evangeline couldn't seem to match it with anybody who might be looking for her, and Cam needed to get back to work.

She went out to fetch the work crew. Only Benny and Dylan had arrived so far, but she wanted to get them started on the dogwoods.

She retrieved them and had each man grab two boxes from the office where they'd been stashed the night before. She grabbed one, heading for the elevator with as little talk as possible.

"You'll need to put these on all the dogwoods that will show behind the stage when the camera is running."

"Put what on the dogwoods?" Benny asked, eying the boxes suspiciously.

"The dogwood flowers. It has to look like they're in bloom."

"Why?" Dylan sounded incredulous.

"Because the dogwood flower unites all of the Virginia State pageants, and it needs to look authentic."

"Dogwoods blooming in July is *not* authentic. But I guess *we're* getting paid and *you're* the boss," Benny said. Dylan just winked.

They deposited the boxes to the side of the amphitheater and then Cam made both men follow her to a central audience spot so she could point out the most obvious trees to attend to.

"You can see the whole tree from this angle," Benny complained.

"And?"

"We have to get these up really high."

"I'm sure there's a ladder or something." She wasn't, but Cam had never let the truth interfere with telling people what she thought they needed to hear. Plus, if there wasn't a ladder around, she'd find one, so it was only a small lie.

"Catch me if I fall?" Dylan asked, looking at the treetops.

Cam rolled her eyes, more to avoid looking at him than anything else. She wasn't sure how she could deal with this for the next several days. If she were a free agent, some sort of liaison might be poorly advised, but feasible. The problem was, she was happily attached to Rob.

No. That wasn't right. Rob wasn't the

problem. Dylan was the problem. But the fact that she had to keep reminding herself of that was *also* a problem.

She called Evangeline to clarify about the ladder, then told the boys it was coming soon and to start on the branches they could reach. She couldn't afford to get sucked into this distraction, so she headed back to her office to finish organizing her day.

Once her planner was double-checked, she went into Evangeline's office to see how things were going for her.

In the lower level of the Roanoke Arts Commission was a large room that the pageant had been lent in exchange for including the commission's name on the program and promotional materials. Michelle would use it to teach the girls three choreographed numbers for the pageant. Cam wondered if she was sufficiently recovered from the trauma of finding Telly the day before.

Two of the routines the girls would perform were fairly simple: just walking in a certain pattern, but the third was intended to evaluate fitness and coordination, and so would take some effort. Three girls from one of the local high school dance teams had signed up to help Michelle, so they could work in smaller groups to learn faster. Two of them were present already when Cam got to the room. She decided to avoid mentioning what had happened the day before, as she didn't want to alarm the girls.

"Hi, girls. Michelle not here yet?"

"I saw her, but she said she forgot her microphone in her car, so she ran back to get it."

"Yeah, I imagine getting the attention of thirty young girls takes some volume," Cam said.

"No kidding!" one of them said. Cam thought she was called Chelsea. "I just helped coach a cheerleading camp for middle-schoolers. My word!"

They all laughed.

"Should we test the music? It's all set up, isn't it?" Cam hoped if they were busy, she could more easily have a quiet word with Michelle.

The other girl shrugged. Her name tag read Ashley. "I think it's all on her iPod." She went over to look, found the iPod, hooked everything together, and looked at the song options. She frowned. "Chel, does this look right?"

Chelsea joined her, looking at the options. "I've never heard of these songs, but maybe she just called them something funny." She pushed play.

Cello overtures of a loud, depressing Wagner tune blared.

"No!" Ashley yelped, hitting stop. She tried another, which was more energetic but just as dark. "It's all this Wagner guy!" she said it like an American, though Cam knew better.

Vogner.

"Maybe you're just in the wrong folder. A lot of people love Wagner." Cam pronounced it carefully so the girls might learn, though she was thinking "for mourning" as the most appropriate timing for the tunes.

The girls had pushed play on one last song when Michelle came in, cringing. "Zoiks! Who's the morbid one?"

Cam and the girls turned.

"It's not you?" Cam asked.

"Oh, Cam. I'm aware it's ignorant, but I've made a point of avoiding any classical music that isn't featured in a game arena or pop song since I was allowed to quit piano at fourteen. No. Not mine. Mine's the . . ." She stared and pulled the iPod off of the player. "Mine looks just like this, but this is *not* my music. And my music is gone!"

"Are you sure you left yours here? Black is a common color," Cam said.

"Positive. I left everything I worried I'd forget." She glanced to the side to check on the props, but then nodded.

"So someone came in here, but not to steal . . . they just wanted to wreak havoc?" Cam asked.

"Looks like it," Michelle answered, running a hand through her hair. She looked frazzled, but given the last twenty-four hours, that was understandable. Cam doubted the iPod switch was related to the probable murder, but it certainly compounded the already unpleasant morning.

Cam reached into her bag and pulled out her laptop. She touched Michelle's shoulder and met her eyes to show support, then put the laptop next to the music equipment. "If you connect to your account, you can get it, right?"

"Not all of it, but most of it — definitely the songs we're using in the pageant."

Cam logged on to her laptop and let Michelle download her songs again. She left her computer there and rushed out. She wanted to double-check with Celeste that nothing had happened at the library.

Thankfully it hadn't. Nell Norton was in one room setting up for her side project, and Celeste seemed fine taking in props and supervising the changing room.

When Cam got back to the Arts Commission, girls were starting to arrive, so she spent the next twenty minutes greeting them. The teens helped, starting some jumping jacks with the girls and then moving on to stretching. By the time Michelle was needed, she had her music back in order and seemed to have calmed down, but Cam was beginning to wonder if their vandal had better connections than they had assumed. Getting inside a locked building meant the person had to have legitimate access. She hoped he wasn't also the murderer.

When she left the Arts Commission, Cam spotted her dad's car through the trees and realized he was working already. She found him under the grand curtain.

"Hi, Daddy."

"Hiya, sunshine!" He was measuring the space so he could build his lattice. "Boy, somebody sure doesn't think much of beauty pageants."

"Not to mention they don't understand this *isn't* a beauty pageant."

"It's not?" Her dad looked confused.

"No, Daddy. This is little girls — seven to ten. It's far more rounded than that. Talent, intelligence, grace . . ." Cam wasn't sure she believed what she was saying, but it was what she'd been told. It was almost lunch-time, so she asked her dad to join her.

"Are you sure you aren't trying to make me fat?" he asked.

There were sack lunches for the girls and a vendor selling a handful of options for all the loitering parents. Cam spotted no less than three mothers she wanted to throw pickle slices at because they were making their daughters continue to practice instead of letting them sit down to eat. It was a fast time frame to learn routines, but the poor girls needed their fuel.

"Cam! There you are!" Cam turned to see Mindy.

"Oh! Hello."

"I just . . . I didn't mean . . . well, I'm sorry if I was strange yesterday."

The fact that Mindy was apologizing was even stranger. In four years of high school together, she didn't think it had ever hap-pened.

"Oh, don't worry. I know these pageants can be stressful," Cam said. She was sure Mindy didn't know the half of it.

Mindy bit her lip.

"Was there another reason? Something you want to talk about?"

"Of course not. Though . . . Lizzie has been asking about Annie."

"She should be here around three. She owns a cupcake shop, so she works during the day."

"Annie has her own business?" Cam was offended at how shocked Mindy sounded but tried to temper her response.

"Yes. A successful one."

"Oh!" Mindy looked confused for a minute. She tried to smile, but failed, then said, "I'm glad it's successful." Cam thought the statement lacked conviction.

"Tell me about yourself, Mindy," Cam said, trying to change the subject. "Are you a stay-at-home mom?"

"I'm afraid it's not very interesting," Mindy said.

"Well, that depends. What does your husband do?" Cam asked.

"Barry's in real estate." Mindy's smile looked strained. "He was just made a regional manager, but Cam, I just wanted to ask about . . ." She looked either way and gave an apologetic gesture, then rushed off. Cam was confused, but didn't have time to dwell on it.

Cam had to get on with her day. Her first stop was a classroom in the library with all the contestants. Nell Norton was nothing if not a genius. She had requested time with the girls, since most of the week would be taken with physical rehearsals, but they would all need breaks from that. Nell wanted to present them with a project and had asked that the pageant schedule give each of them a two-hour block at some point each afternoon for "research" and presentation development.

Cam was curious about what she had in mind, so she joined at the back of the room.

Nell showed a short, warm, fuzzy video narrated by a team of endangered animals and then talked briefly about what kids could do in their homes and gardens to lower their carbon footprint. She gave handouts on composting and how much better it was for the earth if everybody grew some of their own fruits and vegetables.

"Now, I happen to know that the very best ideas come from kids. You don't have a lifetime of people saying something isn't possible, so you are more creative and more hopeful. On Friday night, to open the competition, each of you will have three minutes to give an idea, and the best idea will earn a separate scholarship of one thousand dollars that has nothing to do with winning the overall pageant.

"Three minutes isn't much time, so all you need to prepare is a statement on why you think it's needed, and then a description of what you would do. Because I know a lot of you may not know very much about the topics, I'm handing out a list of words that I think might give you good ideas to search, and there is a website with videos that will tell you what we know now so that you don't suggest something that's already being done. I've also got several of my friends from the Roanoke Garden Society who have volunteered to answer questions."

Cam was surprised to hear that and looked behind her to see Neil Patrick, Holden Hobbes, and Mrs. Pemberly.

Evangeline was there, too, but Cam thought her interest was mere curiosity, like Cam's had been about what Nell planned for the green project. Cam edged closer for confirmation.

"Oh, of course I was curious. But honestly," Evangeline whispered, "I had to get away from the phone. Did you know I've been getting crank calls all day?"

"You have? I wonder if it's our vandal."

"That could be. It's just heavy breathing, but I needed a break."

"Understandable," Cam said, and looked back to the room.

Several girls and all the moms had perked up at the prize offer. The whole pageant was only worth $2,500 to the winner and $1,000 to the first runner-up. The winner didn't even earn a semester's tuition at most colleges. Cam doubted this group was shooting for community colleges when they finished high school.

"I better get back to it," Cam said. She waved as she left the library.

On her way out, Jake approached her. He looked exhausted, and Cam wondered if he'd really gotten a break.

"What's up?" she asked.

"Well, I just had a witness from the Arts Commission tell me he saw a woman arguing with Telly yesterday morning — he identified Telly from his television show, so he was sure it was him. I wondered if I could get a list from you of who was around related to the pageant yesterday morning."

"The pageant?"

"It's just to complete the list. I am getting them from the Arts Commission, library, and Patrick Henry, too. You just have the only other set of people . . ."

Cam felt better when he put it that way. "The pageant didn't even check in until three, so it would only be staff. Come on up to my office and I can print you a list."

"I can't now. I have too much to do, but if you could have it ready in an hour, I would appreciate it."

After Jake left, Cam went to her office feeling frazzled. She found the lists to double-check so Jake would get a complete list and compiled it. She printed it up and put it in her handbag. She looked at her watch and realized Annie might already be on the grounds and breathed a sigh of relief.

She found Annie with a small group of girls who were having a water break. Annie was showing Lizzie how to aim her camera. Cam suspected it was a little painful to let a seven-year-old handle the $1,500 piece of equipment — the brand-new replacement for the camera that had recently met its ugly demise.

Annie seemed to be taking it in stride, though, and Lizzie looked like she was in heaven.

"Hey there," Cam said.

Lizzie pushed the camera back at Annie and rushed over to Cam, bubbling with excitement.

"Annie let me take two pictures!"

"That was nice of her. Did you tell her thank you?"

"Thank you, Annie!"

Lizzie hugged Annie just as the group was called back to walk through one of the routines.

"You're a saint," Cam said.

"I prefer goddess, if you don't mind."

Cam smirked. "Fine, oh, anointed one."

"Anointing! Now there's an idea. I think Jake needs to anoint me with chocolate."

"Well, I'm sure there's nobody more deserving."

"Oh, stop it or I'll start crying, then you'll start crying, then we'll be a big snotty mess."

"Fine. I have work to do anyway."

Annie punched her arm, and Cam went to check with Dylan. He was stashing the flowers they hadn't managed to get planted in the back of a pickup parked on Williamson.

"You all set?"

"For now. I need to rest up because tomorrow I have both planting and lighting. We should finish the planting part, though, so that's my only really long day."

"Lighting? Really? Well, we appreciate it."

"No problem."

Cam waved and turned to find Rob right behind her.

"Who's that again?" Rob's narrowed eyes followed Dylan.

"Friend of Benny's." Cam thought she might die under Rob's questioning look.

Rob stared. "I know *who* he is. What I

meant was why does he seem to know you?"

"I met him with . . . you know . . . last time . . ."

Jake arrived then, at exactly the wrong time, and stuck his hand out for Cam's list.

"Listen, Jake," Cam said, "I've been thinking about the lack of fingerprints. Telly gets gifts of liquor at his office. I saw one when I was there. Maybe that is how the poison arrived?"

Jake narrowed his eyes and then nodded. "I'll look into that, too."

Cam breathed easier, but Rob gave her a piercing look that let her know she just admitted to knowing this was murder.

"I think since the pageant crew is on its own tonight — rehearsal's over — I'm heading out with Jake now on this search for the mystery woman," he said.

He was avoiding her. Cam was disappointed but not surprised. She would have to think of a way to make it up to him.

In an effort to make things right, Cam decided a partially home-cooked meal for Rob was in order. She walked north to Awful Arthur's for an order of fresh crab legs to go. She had wild rice at home and salad vegetables in her garden. She thought she could make a nice meal.

She called Rob as she walked home to convince him to come for dinner once he was done with Jake.

"We are onto something. Can we make it seven?" he asked.

"We can."

She put a bottle of white wine in the refrigerator to chill and picked lettuce, tomatoes, and a cucumber from her garden and washed them. Then she decided to use the waiting time to answer some emails and draft the first part of her press release on the talent portion. The talent competition wouldn't be over until Thursday night, but she knew what each of the girls was doing, so there was no reason not to get started on the text.

Two hours later, Rob arrived with his own bottle of wine.

"I'm sorry I was short earlier," he said.

"You weren't. And I guess it's a little flattering for you to get jealous," Cam said.

"I wasn't jealous," he said.

"Mmm-hmm," she said, knowing it would make him nuts. She took the wine to the kitchen, uncorked it then poured them each a glass, and starting the sauce pan while she was at it. Most of dinner was ready, but she needed to melt lemon butter for the crab.

"So what did you find out?" she called.

Rob was putting on music in her front room.

"Well, the studio keeps a log of gifts. The secretary said it was to send thank-you cards. Unfortunately, there are several anonymous ones each month. On the plus side, he goes through them sort of fast — the liquor gifts, I mean. So whoever sent this, sent it in the last week. But since they were intent on murder, it was probably sent anonymously. Anyway, all the bottles were taken in for prints and testing of the contents."

"I guess that's something."

"It's a better start than they had. The whole world seemed to hate the guy."

"Though nobody would admit it," Cam said.

"Yeah. There's that," Rob said.

CHAPTER 6

Cam arose at 7:30 the next morning and showered, but before she'd even put her contacts in, Evangeline called in a state of panic.

"Cam! You've got to get here as fast as you can! It's awful!"

Cam thought it must be related to Telly's death. She worried the press had leaked something. "I can be ready in fifteen minutes, but walking will take another fifteen."

"No! I'll be there! See you in a few." Evangeline hung up before Cam could respond. Cam was going to tell Evangeline she sounded too upset to drive, but before she knew it, Evangeline was waiting at her door. The short but erratic ride downtown proved Cam's impulse was right; she was a little queasy by the time they parked.

Evangeline swerved and talked, looking more at Cam than the road. "The dogwoods! Someone took a hose to them!

They're destroyed!"

"A hose destroyed the trees?" That sounded implausible.

"Not the trees. All the flowers those boys put up."

Cam breathed easier. It was bad, but not something they couldn't recover from. "Benny and Dylan only spent about two hours on those yesterday. There are lots of flowers left — all but two boxes, I think."

"And the flowers!" Evangeline looked up. Cam had learned this was an effort she made to keep herself from crying. "A lot of those are lying flat, too."

"That's horrible!" This was significantly worse. "The flowers were worth hundreds of dollars!"

"I don't look forward to requesting more from Nell. And all the work! What kind of monsters would do that to those gorgeous flowers?"

Cam liked that Evangeline cared as much or more about the work and beauty as the money, but they still had a problem. "So what should we do?"

"I hate to bring in the police. Their presence would call such attention to the problems we've been having. I was hoping you might investigate. You did such a great job with . . . well . . . you know."

With the last fiasco. Cam knew. That had involved two murders. At least she didn't have *that* investigation on her plate this time. Surely a little vandalism wouldn't be hard to investigate, but Cam had a full agenda with the things she'd been hired to do. And the murder that *had* happened might be a press fiasco, even if she wasn't meant to be solving it. She wasn't sure she had the time or the energy for a vandalism investigation.

"I'll brainstorm and see if I can figure out a way to flush them out," she said.

"Oh, good. I knew you wouldn't disappoint me."

Cam wasn't sure she'd agreed to that much, but she'd do her best. When they arrived, she saw the dogwood flowers had indeed been ruined by what Cam thought must have been a high-powered hose; that and at least half the flowers that had been planted had been trampled.

"How do we proceed?" Evangeline asked as they crossed the grass.

"I think we should see what Benny and company can save, first, so we know what we need to do to replace them. Nell isn't here today, so we can wait until this afternoon to call her. I also think we should maybe post a guard through the end of the pageant."

"This is Roanoke! We shouldn't need one," Evangeline complained.

"No, but apparently *somebody* is very anti-pageant. Until we know who, paranoia can save us a lot of grief."

"I know. I sure hate looking for the worst in people, though."

Cam, with her career invested in damage control, always had to look for potential problems, but she admired that Evangeline saw the best. It was a good quality.

"So what do we have up first?" Cam asked.

"Talent. Groups one and two will work with tech, and Celeste, the other volunteer I told you about, is meeting with groups three and four to go over props and organization. That way, we can put them in an order that will be best for the staging people and audience. It's all in the library. The girls are supposed to be there by ten."

"When do Benny and company get here?"

"Shortly. I'll leave you to meet them, if you don't mind."

Cam could hardly argue. It *was* what she'd been hired for. She nodded and then headed toward the destroyed flowers to assess the damage from a nearer vantage.

On approaching, her throat caught. So

much senseless destruction of such gorgeous flowers made her sad. Many of the lilies were toppled, though on closer inspection, most of their stalks had not been broken.

"Holy mu . . ." Cam turned and Benny stopped himself. "What happened here?"

"A vandal. Probably the same anti-pageant vandal who graffitied the band shell, and we also had some music sabotaged yesterday. Any ideas how you'd catch the person if it were up to you?"

Benny looked confused, then said, "Well . . . might or might not help, but the library has video surveillance. So does the parking garage."

"That's two more options than I had a minute ago, so it's worth a try," Cam said. "Say, I wonder if the Arts Commission has anything."

"What do you want us to do?"

"Save what you can. Clean up what can't. Assess the damage. Look for clues while you're at it. Do you know anyone who might be willing to . . . act as a guard?"

"We can find someone."

"Thank you! Listen, I need to check on several other things. Do you mind?"

"Under control. The others should be here soon."

"Thanks, Benny!"

He saluted as she rushed off.

After talking to Benny, Cam went to the Arts Commission to see what she could find about building security. It took some effort, but she finally found the building manager, who gave her the number for the security office.

"Arts Commission," the man answered. It sounded like she'd woken him up.

"This is Cam Harris, part of the Little Miss Begonia pageant staff. We've had a couple acts of vandalism. Are you on location?"

"Where at?"

"The Arts Commission leased a room in the basement to us and sometime night before last, somebody broke in and sabotaged the music. I hoped there might be video footage of who came and went."

"You know we have a bigger problem than a little vandalism?"

She knew he was referring to Telly Stevens's body.

"I realize that's much bigger, but what if the two are related?"

"You know what time?"

"No."

"Can't help you."

"Listen, I know you can. You're saying you *won't.* I honestly doubt this is related to that man's unfortunate death, but I suspect the same vandal destroyed hundreds of dollars' worth of flowers overnight. Would you like *that* bill?" Cam knew she didn't have legal ground to stand on with the threat, but she hoped he didn't know.

"Sheesh. No, lady. It's just hours and hours to watch. If *you* want to, you can."

"What room are you in?"

He told her and Cam rode the elevator. As expected, she found a man in his early twenties not quite ready to think about anything serious.

She lectured him on the importance of the task, then grilled him on how the system worked, verifying that they could indeed watch in fast motion, with a digital read marking where things were so they could easily find the same spot again if they had questions.

"Great. There will be a rotation of people through here to watch that whole night. They should write down every single entrance and departure from this building. Later, we'll all go through together to see if there's a match for what Benny's crew saw a couple days ago when the spray painting happened."

The young man didn't look happy. He sputtered as if he wanted to protest a few times, but he also clearly didn't feel he could disagree.

Cam left again and found Benny to tell him her plan. She thought they could cover the night's footage if they each took a turn watching for an hour. It was a nice break from the heat. Benny wasn't happy at first. They had a lot of work to do. But when she reminded him they might be looking for the same vandal who had destroyed the flowers, he changed his mind. That made him angry enough to put in some effort, so he set up the rotation with his crew.

After lunch, the girls were assembled in four groups on the grass in front of the stage, staggered in their lines so they all had enough room to move without kicking each other during the dance routines. Parents watched from the periphery. Michelle called for attention and asked the high school girls to help call roll. They each quietly found a group and began calling names to make sure everyone was there. Cam didn't pay much attention until Chelsea's tone changed.

"Lizzie?" she said, her voice rising above the others. She looked across all the girls and then called again. "Lizzie Blankenship?"

Mindy rushed to Lauren, and Cam was sure she was asking if she knew where her little sister was. Lauren shook her head.

"Lizzie!" Mindy shouted. She sounded scared. Cam thought about the nerves Mindy had displayed over the last few days; she might crack.

Cam rushed over to the three men who were helping with the gardening and asked if they'd seen anything. None had, so she enlisted them to help look.

Cam then ensured the volunteers present would keep the girls calm and keep them working before hitting speed dial to get Evangeline.

"Stop calling!" Evangeline shrieked.

"Evangeline, it's Cam!"

"Oh, dear. I'm sorry." Cam thought she might be crying. "That prank caller just keeps at it. He just called my cell this time, since I haven't been answering the other. I thought he'd called back."

"Vange, we have a bigger emergency."

"Oh, dear! What?"

"Lizzie Blankenship has disappeared."

Evangeline sputtered a little, so Cam expanded.

"Lizzie Blankenship, the littlest girl? You

remember?"

"Well, yes, of course! What can I do?"

"Search your building. Ask security for help. Make sure to check everywhere."

"Of course!"

Cam hung up and saw Annie walking across the lawn with a frown.

"What happened?" Annie asked.

"Your little buddy, Lizzie, disappeared."

"For real? What can I do?"

"I think you should take Mindy and check the library."

"Take Mindy?" she whispered. "Are you sure?"

"It's a big building and one Lizzie might like. Split up if you need to."

Cam then went to the Arts Commission building and straight to the security office.

"We lost a little girl! She disappeared after lunch, so within the last hour or hour and a half. Can you see if a little girl came in? She's tiny, really — only seven."

"Sure." Cam was glad the man sounded far more helpful than he had earlier. Either he'd made friends with the crew, or he felt like a little girl was a higher priority than a little vandalism, which it was. Jed, one of the gardeners, waved at her from a monitor to the side, but he kept watching video.

Cam leaned over to write down her cell

phone number for the man, whose name was Todd, but then spotted the live monitor.

"Him." She pointed. "Who is he?"

"Must work in the building. I see him almost every day."

Cam frowned. It was the creep from the elevator in the Patrick Henry. "Do you have his name?"

"No. We have a building directory you could look at."

"That's not necessary, but could you email me that clip?"

"Sure thing, Miz Harris."

"Thank you. And call me immediately if you see the little girl."

"Will do."

Cam went back out to see if anyone had found Lizzie. A crowd had started to build. It was amazing, in the most disturbing of ways, how stress acted as a people magnet.

"Lizzie?" She shouted as she reached the crowd.

Cam looked around desperately for security people, feeling it had reached the time where they needed to call the police. Fortunately, she spotted Annie and Mindy coming from the library, Lizzie plastered to Annie's front with her head on her shoulder. Mindy tried to take Lizzie a few times, but

Lizzie stubbornly clung.

Cam ran over to them. "You found her!"

"Reading. She was cuddled in a corner in the children's section — went there after her interview with Rob because he asked about her talent, and the idea came from a book." Lizzie had a *Little Mermaid* book clutched in her hand.

Mindy looked like a wreck. Cam tried to steer them away from the commotion. Rob joined them. He'd heard about Lizzie and wanted to make sure she was okay.

"I'm glad you're safe, Lizzie," Cam said. "Please don't go anywhere without telling your mom or your group leader, though, okay?"

Lizzie nodded, her head drooping.

"Nobody's mad at you. We were just really worried."

"Okay," Lizzie said.

Cam looked closely at Lizzie. "Annie and Rob will stay here and talk to you for a little bit, okay? I have to make a phone call."

Cam realized time was running out to tell Nell about the flower fiasco before she saw it for herself. It also behooved them to let her know while she could still get something going to solve the problem. She steeled herself for the call.

■ ■ ■ ■

Vandalism and murder were not the best press complements to a children's pageant, but as long as she was in the domain of bad news, this was as good a time as any to alert Nell to the vandalism she would see the next day.

Cam punched Nell's number into the phone, fighting the catch that her breath kept trying to make. She hated difficult conversations. In writing, she was fine — she could think and edit and make sure the details were presented in the right order. In person, she both had to stay on message and navigate someone else's agenda. She preferred more control.

"It's Nell!" The woman was such a forceful presence, even over the phone.

"Nell? It's Cam. I'm afraid we have some bad news."

"Well, spit it out."

"We had some vandals last night — they destroyed a lot of the newly planted flowers. The lilies, with those sturdy stalks took the worst of it — they break instead of just leaning."

"And I'm just hearing now?"

"I wanted our gardening guys to sort what

could be saved first so that we had a bottom line for you. I have to admit I thought it was worse when I first saw, but it's still pretty bad. They had planted almost everything — we estimate about 30 percent was lost — horrible people."

The phone was silent for a while.

"Those tubers will come back."

"That's true. It's just . . ."

"This year. Yes, I get it. Pretty pageant . . . I just think it might be best to replace with annuals. It's cheaper for me by a long shot — there are several blooming right now. And since the tubers will come back . . . I think perhaps even begonias. I had an overshipment of red wax begonias, and I have several other varieties I could choose from."

"It's a perfect solution. It definitely fits the pageant theme. Thank you so much!"

"Be sure to file a police report. I can recover some of this with insurance if we do. I don't suppose you've caught the vandal?"

Police report. Nell had a point. Cam supposed it was inevitable at this point.

"No suspect yet, but somebody also spray-painted the stage. My dad is building a trellis to cover that, and we'll want to buy some flowers to weave in there, too."

"Buy, nonsense. On a stage you want silk

flowers — no water source. Real flowers would need to be replaced daily — more often in the heat they say we'll get. I've amassed a collection over the years. I'll bring them along."

"Oh, you're a lifesaver! Thank you!"

"Any chance of increasing the font size for Nelly's Nurseries?"

"No, but there's a strong possibility that Nelly's Nurseries will make the news for their generosity after these vandalism events."

"Well, then, it's a good deal."

Cam bit the inside of her cheek. She hated to do this, but Nell would be upset if she heard it elsewhere.

"There was one other thing, probably unrelated . . ." She went on to describe what had happened with Telly.

"Oh, my. When you say 'one more thing,' you don't skimp, do you?"

When Cam hung up, she had to just breathe for a few minutes before returning to her friends and Lizzie, but she finally managed. It was time to get back to pageant preparation.

"Maybe you should let Lizzie's mom get her back to rehearsal and I'll tell you about my day," Cam said to Annie. Rob, it seemed, had found another story angle to investigate and had taken off.

Lizzie started shrieking at the suggestion of leaving Annie; everybody turned to stare.

Annie squatted and set Lizzie in front of her so their noses were almost touching.

"Remember how I said you could help me later?"

Lizzie nodded.

"Well, if I want to be free for that, I have some things I need to get done now." Annie shook Lizzie's hand and Mindy and Lizzie left.

"Poor kid. Her mom doesn't get her at all."

"You aren't biased?" Cam asked.

"About Mindy? Probably. She's a status snob. But those were Lizzie's words. She said, and I quote, 'My mom doesn't get me.' And then she told me what she really wanted to be was a photographer. Well . . . maybe she called it a picture-taker, but I knew what she meant. I get her."

Cam wasn't sure how much free time there would be to indulge this, but it seemed to be keeping Annie a little more mellow than normal and was probably relaxing Lizzie, who clearly didn't want to be there.

Cam looked up and saw Evangeline marching toward them. Cam quickly explained that the resolution with Lizzie had

125

been fine and that Nell Norton had proven herself enormously generous about the flowers, provided they report to the police so she could make an insurance claim.

Evangeline put her hands over her face, expressing perfectly how Cam felt. It was always something — in this case several somethings — and the pageant was starting that night.

"Let's go back to the office and sort this out."

"What about . . ."

"Our volunteers seem to have it under control, but why don't you check and meet me up there in a little bit?"

Annie headed with her camera toward the crowd.

Cam felt resigned. "Guess we should get back to normal, whatever that is," she said, though as she looked up, she knew she'd spoken too soon. Benny was walking toward her with purpose. "I'll meet you up there soon."

"Three suspects. We'd like you to look at them," he said when he reached Cam.

Cam followed Benny back toward the Arts Commission building.

"We saw Michelle leaving, so we watched the tape from there. Overnight there weren't that many . . ."

"That's good. It helps. Anybody coming in at night or early in the morning has some story. Maybe the security guard could help with who works in the building?"

Benny's eyes lit up again. "Right! Good idea!" Cam frowned. She wondered how much of Benny's response was automatic from years of *acting* stupider than he was and how much was actually missing stuff because he'd played dumb so long.

They reached the room. Cam had to first reassure Todd they'd found the lost child. She'd forgotten to call him when Lizzie was found. Benny then showed Cam clips that indeed looked suspicious — mostly because none of the people had used access cards to get into the building in spite of the hour. All had come in as someone else left. It didn't mean they didn't have access cards, but they certainly hadn't proved they did on tape.

The first was a man with slacks and a button-up shirt. Cam thought it hadn't been long since he'd removed his tie and jacket. The crisp white shirt screamed sales, though he looked a little disheveled. He appeared suspicious mostly because he kept looking around, as if he were being followed.

The next person was a woman who didn't look at all suspicious, except she matched the worker's description from the day before. She had khaki capris, a denim sleeveless blouse, and a broad hat. Sunglasses obscured her face and her hair was either short or tucked under the hat.

"Only identifiable thing about her is size," Dylan said.

Cam started, looking behind her. She hadn't realized he'd followed them in.

"Boo!" he teased.

Cam frowned and turned back. "What do you mean?"

"Back it up, Benny. There. See how the dead-bolt plate is almost at her shoulder? She's a tiny thing — only around five foot, I'd guess."

"I see what you mean," Cam said. "So where's our third person?"

"*People.* Couple."

The tape caught a couple necking on the stairs and when the door opened to let a businessman out, the boy, clad in skater attire, caught it and held it for the girl, who had hair Cam could only describe as tortoiseshell — it had blotches of black and orange.

"Ever hear the phrase 'get a room'?" Cam asked. "Those two are just looking for some privacy . . . probably not what this building wants, but I doubt they have anything to do with us."

"I agree, but no saying they didn't decide to pull some vandalism once they were here."

"Wagner?" Cam said.

"What?" Benny said.

"Whoever did this erased the pageant music and put a bunch of depressing classical stuff on Michelle's iPod. It was planned."

"I thought all classical stuff was depressing," Benny said.

"No, but even if you think so, Wagner takes it to a new level."

She heard Dylan chuckling behind her and turned to glare.

"Hey, I'm just agreeing with you. Classical in my book is Zeppelin or Black Sabbath, but my sister took a lot of piano, so I've heard more than a person should have to."

"Well, I'll defend most of it, but I would reserve Wagner for suicide," Cam said.

"Or wabbit hunting," Dylan joked.

Cam was surprised he knew the *Bugs Bunny* opera was Wagner. She laughed, but knew she had to get back to meet Evangeline or Evangeline would worry.

"I think that little woman is our vandal," she said. "But for now, I need to go. Todd, can you save all of these?"

Todd nodded.

Cam headed back up to the office to join Evangeline.

She rode the elevator to the second floor and locked the office door behind her. They needed a break.

Evangeline crooked her finger and walked to a side table in the large office. She pulled out a bottle of red wine and two glasses and began to uncork the bottle.

Cam thought it might be early to drink, especially with the pageant starting that night. But she also thought reminding Evangeline of that might make matters worse, so she just sat in the comfortable chair across the grand desk from where Evangeline would sit.

"Am I cursed?" Evangeline finally asked.

It was the last question Cam had expected. "What? No! You're gorgeous, talented, happily married, and wealthy. How could that be cursed?"

"Maybe I have too much and . . . God is trying to right things."

Cam leaned across the desk. "Evangeline, think of all the people with a lot more than you. The rich and famous, the politicians . . . Do you really think you have so much God would single you out?"

Evangeline sniffed. "Sometimes, but I know it's not rational. I mean . . . you know

I haven't always been good, but for a very long time I've at least tried not to be bad. And I try to show my gratitude."

It was true. Evangeline definitely had a colorful history, and some of it was not very flattering, but it was also true that she actively made a point of being kind and generous. Any past transgressions had been repaid long ago.

The phone rang and Evangeline's peaches-and-cream complexion turned to skim milk. Cam jumped to grab the phone.

"Little Miss Begonia headquarters. Cam speaking."

The dial tone came on and Cam hung up triumphantly. She reached for her wine and took a sip.

"Don't answer it," she ordered Evangeline. "Hey, wait a minute." Cam pointed at the computer. "Can I log on?"

Evangeline turned the monitor and pushed the keyboard to Cam. Cam clicked through to her email and found what she was looking for: the video clip from Todd Cummings. Cam turned the monitor back to Evangeline as she watched.

"Do you know this guy? There!" She pointed.

Cam paused the video and Evangeline stared for a long time and then frowned.

"Yes, unfortunately. Why is he on a video you have?"

"That was the man I told you about, the one who asked about you in the elevator. And he also has been working in the Arts Commission building. How do you know him?"

"I went to high school with him way back when." That was a little rich, Cam thought. Evangeline was only five or six years older than she was. "We went to a dance together, I think, but it never went anywhere. Then, when I first moved back to Roanoke — I suppose this was four years ago — my class was having its fifteen-year reunion. He and I ran into each other, had a few laughs, and then had a few dates. That's when I learned he was married. It was the last straw for me and men my own age. I appreciate Neil's maturity and integrity so much."

Cam could understand that, but she didn't want to lose direction. "Okay. So what's this creep's name?"

"Barry Blankenship."

Cam nearly choked on the wine she had in her mouth. "Like the father of Lizzie and Lauren Blankenship?"

Evangeline's face fell. "Really?"

"I don't know, but it might explain his hovering. I'll talk to Mindy and see if she can confirm who he is."

"Cam. He's a known liar, whatever else he is. He told me he was single and available, but he wasn't. And you just said he wanted to see me?"

"Yes?"

"I doubt his wife knows what he's up to."

Cam hated that idea, but didn't disagree based on what she knew. "I'll just see what Mindy has to say, okay?"

Evangeline sighed and took a large drink, then massaged her temples for a moment before swallowing.

"After this pageant, no more deviations from a normal routine for us, okay?" Evangeline said.

"Even though it would put me out of a job, I think I agree!" Cam swallowed the last of her wine.

Cam considered the luck they'd been having and felt quite fortunate that Toni Howe had been available. She hosted a live morning television show, but as a cost-saving measure, her station was running reruns through the summer.

Cam found Rob on her way out. He'd talked to girls about their excitement level, their respective talent pieces, and what it would mean to each of them if they won until they all left to gather their things for the evening performance. It was terribly cute to see handsome, athletic Rob talking to all these little princesses. They seemed very pleased with the attention. He'd done his last interview, though, an hour earlier and had been on his phone since then. The only people left on the grounds were setting up for the audience that would attend the pageant that night.

"Jake says hello," he said as he shut his phone.

"Any news on the poison?" she asked.

"Oleander," he said.

"Oh, yeah. That would do it," Cam said. Unfortunately, it reinforced that whoever had committed the crime was knowledgeable about gardening, or at least plant-based poisons.

She looked out at the men setting up chairs in front of the amphitheater and eyed the patched-up gardens and faux dogwood flowers. The begonias that would arrive the next day would do a better job hiding the damage to the lilies. They were also colorful and cheerful, something the sad, sagging lily heads were not. Most were currently bound to stakes to hold them upright, but they hadn't forgotten their abuse. Cam wished they'd been able to get the begonias in that day, even if she knew the television cameras would be too far away to notice.

CHAPTER 7

"I sure wish with a dead judge they would let us postpone!" Evangeline was matching invoices to equipment in the staging area. Cam thought her comment was really just stage-night nerves talking.

They both knew it was standard for television not to change scheduling because of advertiser expectations. Still, Evangeline seemed to want to talk about it.

"Have you appealed to Judith Towers-Stevens?" Cam figured with a dead husband, she might feasibly try to find a loophole.

"She's the one who told me."

"She's working? It's only been a few days! And isn't she a primary suspect? That won't be good for publicity."

Evangeline shrugged and nodded. "She won't bow out and the station is supporting her."

"Well, Toni is on board. I guess we can do

it if we have to," Cam said.

"Why do people die on our watch, Cam?"

"I wish I knew."

Cam looked up and saw Judith Towers-Stevens walking straight toward them. She wondered if the woman's ears had been burning.

"You should talk to her," Cam said, thinking a society woman like Evangeline had a better shot at getting somewhere than she did.

"I'm sorry, Cam. I just can't." Evangeline ducked away, leaving Cam to face Judith Towers-Stevens alone.

Cam looked at her carefully. The woman was strangely dry-eyed as she got the camera crew into position for the evening.

Cam plastered on her most sympathetic smile. "Ms. Towers-Stevens, I'm so sorry about your husband."

Judith swiped a hand irritably.

"Are you sure you wouldn't rather have an assistant or somebody else take over?"

"Oh, they never get it right. And I've been working with Jimmy Meares, who will only work with me." Cam thought that was self-importance on Judith's part. Jimmy had seemed perfectly willing to work with Cam.

"Maybe I can convince him . . . don't you have a vice president of production or something you could call? Surely Jimmy would understand." Especially if she was young and pretty, Cam thought, though she didn't think sharing that thought was wise. She saw a flash of hope in Judith Towers-Stevens's eyes. "Tell me who I should talk up. I'll go work on him," Cam said.

"Hilary Sweeny has been my right hand for six years. She's very good."

"I'll work on Jimmy." Cam spotted an opportunity in the form of her work crew putting the finishing touches on the mended garden. She called, "Dylan!"

He wandered over more slowly than Cam would have liked and then just stood in front of Judith Towers-Stevens and her expectantly.

"Dylan, Ms. Towers-Stevens is the television producer. It was her husband whom Scooter found the other day. Would you be able to see that she gets home?"

Dylan looked at Judith quizzically, as if sizing her up. "Sure. If it's not far, I mean. I need to be back in an hour for lighting."

Judith's expression wasn't readable but she didn't argue, so Cam took that to mean she was close enough. Dylan must have understood the same thing.

"Car's just on the street over there."

Cam wondered if she'd regret this. She

didn't know Dylan very well, but she felt the sooner Judith Towers-Stevens was out of there, the better. It would help her argument with Jimmy Meares if Judith could be seen as too deeply grieving but that an excellent substitute was on the way.

Cam watched as Dylan escorted Judith toward the street. She looked a little like she had something under her nose, which probably reflected her opinion of men with dirt under their nails, though Dylan's hair might have been a little long for her professional pedigree and he had grass stains on the knees of his jeans, too. As she watched, she saw something else of interest.

Ducking behind the stage was a smallish woman built like the figure caught sabotaging things, so Cam sprinted in that direction.

Rob spotted her and gave chase, too. Rob was a baseball player, and extremely fast, so it didn't take him long to figure out who Cam was chasing and pass her in pursuit.

Tackling the woman onto the grass probably wasn't the best idea he could have had, but it was effective, and Cam met them where they lay sprawled.

"Violated!" the woman shouted. "I've been violated!"

"Stopped, more like," Cam said. "You planned more sabotage for the pageant, didn't you?"

The woman closed her mouth and wouldn't say any more, but Rob called Jake, whom Cam had seen go into the Arts Commission building a few minutes earlier. He was probably canvassing for potential murder witnesses, but he arrived within five minutes. The woman remained seated on the grass, glaring, and responded to the officer as expected.

"This young man assaulted me!"

"I tackled her to stop her from running. She'd . . ." Rob looked to Cam desperately. He didn't know what the woman had done.

"She is suspected of all the vandalism that's happened here," said Cam. "There are witnesses who put her at the stage, and the security tape puts her in the Arts Commission building the night our music was sabotaged."

Jake looked uncomfortable. "You just *think* it was her?"

"She was there two of the three times."

"Cam, that's circumstantial. I can't arrest somebody for that."

"Search her bag!" Cam shouted.

"And I can't do *that* without a warrant."

The woman looked very smug as she rose.

"Am I free to leave, Officer?"

"You are."

Cam thought they were lucky Jake didn't offer to press charges against her and Rob. The woman seemed just the type to do it for spite.

Jake eyed them both as he headed back to the Arts Commission. Cam recognized his "You know better" look. But she wasn't sure how to catch a criminal without chasing her down when you saw her. She decided to imagine they'd just avoided a huge fiasco by scaring this woman off.

The sound of someone screaming brought her back to the present, and the trio rushed back to the front of the band shell. It was delighted screaming. Cam rolled her eyes. In spite of the obnoxious show of his agent a few nights earlier and the agent's recent mention in conversation, she'd forgotten that Kyle Lance would be arriving before the show to meet the girls. Teen, or in this case tween, idols brought more emotion than any other kind of star.

She rushed back to the amphitheater. The curtain finally had been taken down to reveal her dad's spectacular skill with the lattice. She suspected Lydia Fennewick might have made herself available to help, as she was hovering now, eying Nelson Harris with a dreamy smile.

Cam went around the giggling girls.

"Daddy, it's gorgeous!" She hugged him.

"You sound surprised."

"I'm never surprised when you make something beautiful, but you had so little time! So I'm still impressed."

"What was all that excitement with you chasing that lady?"

"We think she's the vandal, but we don't have any evidence."

"That little thing?"

"She's been seen at two of the three crime scenes."

"Well, I bet a lot of people have."

"Oh, don't go defending everybody."

"Not everybody, just . . ." He paused and Cam could tell he didn't want to say it out loud, so she leaned in. "Just women of a certain age," he said sheepishly.

"You're a sucker for a pretty face."

"I suppose I am at that. Do you need anything else, sunshine?"

"I'd love it if you'd come back for the pageant. It starts at seven."

"I'll be here." He kissed her cheek and headed back toward his car, giving Lydia a friendly wave and smile as he left.

The crowd had mellowed considerably.

Kyle Lance had shaken each girl's hand and promised an autographed picture for each of them before the pageant was over. Cam could see his back as he returned to his limousine, accompanied by smarmy Jimmy Meares. She liked to think the boy was nice, but somebody advising him had very poor taste. She remembered, though, she had business with Jimmy, so she shouted and ran after him.

For all the fuss Ms. Towers-Stevens had made about having Hilary step in, Jimmy didn't seem to care at all. She was glad to check that off her list.

The supper buffet was off to one side. Hired helpers had set out chairs. Pageant veterans had spoken of the nightmares of pageant participants held up by slow restaurants. It was just easier to have it all done on location. Even if it was a little behind schedule, everyone had the same disadvantage, though Cam trusted Petunia and her luau bonanza to be right on time.

As they had the night before, Nick and Petunia pulled right onto the lawn behind the tent. The girls were starting to return from their hotels, so Cam went over to help Petunia unload.

Not five minutes later, Venus DiAngelo,

one of the pageant contestants, ran out of the library shrieking, her mom not far behind. Cam practically dropped the fruit bowl she was carrying and ran to head off the upset girl.

"Venus, what happened?"

"Somebody dumped all my makeup!"

"What? Come with me. We'll look into this." Cam turned the girl back around and headed toward the library, catching the mother on the way and explaining that she was there to help investigate.

"It's very expensive, you know," the woman said. "The very best stage makeup. Venus dances a ballet. She is dressed as a dragonfly."

"Sounds lovely!" Cam said. It actually did sound sort of cool, were it not dripping in pretension because this mother was absurd. But vandalism was vandalism, and it couldn't be tolerated.

When the woman showed Cam, Cam gasped. The makeup hadn't just been dumped, it had been taken into the main portion of the library and dumped onto a bookshelf. Cam shouted and stormed back out to where the girls were gathered and called everyone to her.

"Somebody here not only sabotaged a teammate, but vandalized library books.

Until the culprit comes forward, or somebody turns them in, *nobody* will be permitted *any* makeup. Violators will be disqualified."

Unlike on school grounds, pageant contestants held no disregard for snitches if it got the rest of them what they wanted. Within ten minutes, Delphinia Lovette-Hicks had turned in Skye Derringer. Skye swore Delphinia had dared her, and Cam left the outcome between the parents, but insisted on seventy-two dollars from each to cover the makeup replacement cost and took credit card numbers to address the book replacement. There had to be a no-tolerance policy or these nuts would bring chaos upon them.

The talent competition always caused high tension, or so Lydia Fennewick had told Cam. Cam had never seen a Young Miss pageant before. As she hovered behind the scenes, she felt a little dirty for being involved. Mothers rubbed Vaseline on their daughters' teeth to make sure they sparkled, and poked them into perfect posture, barking reminders every ten seconds.

When Alexandria pushed Andromeda over, though, Cam stepped in again.

"Do y'all want to explain what this is about?"

Neither girl would look at her.

Cam knew she had to be tough or she'd be dealing with this all week. "Let me rephrase. I saw Alexandria push Andromeda over. If you won't explain yourselves, I will just tell the judges and you'll both be penalized."

Andromeda's mom tried to protest, but Cam stared at her. "I have this authority. I suggest you don't interfere."

"Andromeda called me names," Alexandria said.

"No. I said hers was a white trash song," Andromeda argued.

Cam spun to stare at her. "Did you *not* hear the no-criticism rule?"

"I was trying to help. She needs a better song."

"You are not helping when a song has already been practiced. Keep it to yourself or go home."

Andromeda looked down as Alexandria smiled.

"You." Cam turned. "Pushing is physical. I could send you home this minute. Do you want that?"

Alexandria sobered and sputtered.

"You apologize, and if it happens again,

you're disqualified."

Alexandria nodded and muttered a quiet apology. Cam thought about harassing her for a better one, but it wasn't worth it. It was time to get this under way, and she had bigger things to worry about.

Sofie went on first with an impressive piano performance, followed by Delphinia's ballet and Alexandria's rendition of a song Cam had never heard before that indeed might fall under the category "trashy," but the performance of it was cute, rather than mortifying. Unfortunately, near the end, Mindy found her, needing urgent help.

"Come quickly!"

Cam rushed after her toward the library, where they found Lauren in tears. The blue formal gown she was going to wear for her song had been shredded with scissors, the white undercoats peeking through in grotesque, jagged lines.

"When did this happen?"

"We only brought it from the hotel just before supper."

"Celeste." Cam turned to the volunteer who was working the changing room. "Who's been in here?"

"Only the contestants and their mothers, and I've been here the whole time."

"Somebody is sabotaging Lauren!" Mindy

cried. "She's a favorite!"

Cam wasn't sure that was true, but she didn't say that to Mindy. This was much more serious than the makeup, in any case. Dresses could cost close to a thousand dollars, and Cam doubted Mindy was a bargain shopper, never mind the inherent threat implied by using a sharp implement for the job.

"You're sure it was fine before it got here?"

"How could it *not* be fine? I packed it myself in Lynchburg. It was fine then. Who would touch it in the hotel?"

"You're right. That's silly. For the time being, I'll get Lauren moved to Thursday for the talent piece. Hopefully you can replace it or borrow something by then?"

"This was specially made!"

"Mindy, I'm so sorry. And we will investigate, but it is her song that is the talent, right?"

Mindy looked furious for a minute but finally gave in.

"Mindy Blankenship?"

They both turned to find Jake in the doorway.

"Yes?"

"I have a few questions for you."

"The police are here already? I only just found it twenty minutes ago."

"Found what?"

"Lauren's shredded dress."

"Oh. No. I'm here because a witness saw you arguing loudly with Telly Stevens yesterday morning."

"Oh!" Mindy's pale face lost another few shades. Cam thought if she turned a light off, Mindy might glow.

"Do you need me to leave?" Cam asked. She didn't want to, but felt it was probably most appropriate.

"If you wouldn't mind," Jake said, which was his polite way of telling her to scram. But at the same time, Mindy shrieked, "No!" She grabbed Cam's wrist. Her eyes looked scared and a little desperate.

"Can I stay, Jake? It sounds like Mindy would prefer . . ."

Jake rolled his eyes. Cam read his meaning. She got entangled in these messes far too easily, but Mindy wanted a friend near. And if Cam was honest, she was dying to know what was going on. It seemed so unlikely, but Cam knew the argument was suspected of being related to the murder.

"Can you tell me what you and Mr. Stevens argued about, Mrs. Blankenship?"

"He was a horrible man," she said.

"So you confront all horrible men? Just out of habit? Or had he done some specific horrible thing to you?"

Mindy sniffed and looked up, then turned to look at Cam. She seemed to find courage.

"Telly Stevens was also a judge last year . . . Lauren was a local finalist then, too. I . . . he . . . It was important she win . . . we needed the scholarship. I saw him at the bar one night, about two drinks too late, and said something to that effect. He suggested I might earn my daughter an advantage . . ."

Cam felt her eyes bulge and couldn't seem to call her lids back down. She did, however, manage to keep from shrieking or gasping.

"Let's put it this way," Mindy said through a clenched jaw, "I followed through and he didn't."

Cam had to cover her mouth.

Jake's eyes narrowed. "I see. And so yesterday?"

"I just told him he was a bastard and that I couldn't believe he'd show his face near this year's pageant."

"And the man wound up dead."

"Officer, if this is how this man behaves, then probably half the moms here have a motive. I didn't kill him. I thought he had a heart attack until now."

"And what do you know about gardening?"

"What? Not very much, why?"

"Just answer the question."

"I did a special study with Cam's mom when I was in high school, but that was mostly so I could get a science credit without taking physics."

Cam frowned. She hadn't known that. It was always a little bit of a shock to realize her parents had led lives she didn't know about. Especially her mom, who had passed on more than three years earlier.

Jake didn't know anything about Cam's discomfort and continued his questioning. "And so you would know which plants are edible and which are poison?"

"Was he poisoned? By a plant?"

"I'm just trying to assess what you know."

"I know a few flowers make for a lovely salad — nasturtiums and violets. And I was warned about a few when I had small children. That is something you see in parenting magazines. So I know foxglove and I watch for nightshade. I haven't worried about it, though, other than to watch my girls."

"I'll need you to give an accounting of your whereabouts that morning and the day before . . . and who was with you."

"I was driving to Roanoke that morning — with my girls! We had errands to run and the hotel to check into. The day before, we were in Lynchburg. What could I have done from Lynchburg?"

Cam felt bad for Mindy. She hated the idea of the girls being questioned, but knew it would have to happen — they were their mom's only alibi.

When Jake left, Cam hugged Mindy and promised Jake was a good guy who was just trying to get to the bottom of this.

"What you must think of me!" Mindy said. "Cheating on my husband for a stupid . . ."

"I'm not judging," Cam said.

"I would. At least until recently. But the truth is my marriage was over before that. Barry left me eighteen months ago and spent the first nine months or so trying to get out of paying any child support at all. So when the pageant happened, I was feeling desperate about that scholarship money. Now Barry's changed his mind and is trying to act like a superdad. I think he wants to take the girls from me."

She broke into tears and Cam hugged her again as a pair of girls hustled in, grabbed props, and hustled back out. By the end of the talent night, Cam felt a little lost about the pageant process, but very glad for the next day. There would be no public show, so the girls could work on their coordinated routines.

CHAPTER 8

Cam slept in a little the next day and then had a surprisingly smooth morning until she got an urgent call from Dylan about an hour after lunch.

"Cam, I need to leave my post. I'm just guarding. Can you call Benny? And maybe cover watching while I'm gone?"

"Of course. I'll be right down."

She called Benny as she rode down the elevator, covering her ear to the piano music from the bar as she walked through the lobby. Benny agreed to be there in a half hour, so Cam resigned herself to standing on the lawn in her pumps until he got there. The heat had returned, so she took off her jacket as she came outside. Jake was talking to Dylan.

"Is there a problem, Jake?" she asked as she approached.

"I don't think you need to worry, Cam." He wouldn't meet her eye, which reversed the meaning of his words. "We just have some questions for Mr. Stevens."

Stevens. She had never heard that as Dylan's last name.

"Dylan, you're not . . ."

"Stevens? No. My last name is Markham."

"Then why . . ."

"He never married my mother." He left it at that. "I'll call you or Benny when I can get back to my schedule." He walked away with Jake and didn't look back.

Cam wondered how small a town Roanoke really was that a pseudo thug could be son of one of its most famous members. It made her wonder who Dylan's mother was, though given Dylan's looks, she was probably very pretty — just the type Telly Stevens had seemed to take advantage of.

As Cam waited for Benny, her cell phone rang. It was Mindy, nearly in tears.

"Cam, Barry called! He wants to take the girls for the afternoon, but I'm really worried if he takes them, I won't get them back! Please! Do you know somewhere to hide us? I can't take our car. I'm worried he'll tap into our GPS tracker. It's how he found out where we're staying."

"There's no . . . court order, is there? To let him, I mean?" Cam was worried about breaking the law. This domain could be so touchy.

"No! He never wanted to talk custody until recently. We're not even divorced, but I'm scared." Her voice quivered and Cam gave in.

"You're only about eight blocks from Sweet Surprise — Annie's store. Go there as soon as rehearsals are over and I'll meet you there as soon as I can." She relayed the address and gave directions, then hung up, thinking the day couldn't get any more complicated.

"And this was supposed to be my easy day," she grumbled.

"Talking to yourself might make people think you're unstable, Miz Harris."

"Benny! Thank goodness!" She almost spilled the beans about Dylan being the son of the dead man, but decided that if Dylan wanted people to know, he would tell them. "Are you okay with a longer shift?"

"Scooter's coming soon. I got it covered. Then I'll be back for six to midnight. Don't you worry."

Benny's reassurances didn't help. She needed to call Annie and get to the cupcake shop before someone, namely Annie, blew a gasket about the unexpected guests.

She rushed back to the office to tell

Evangeline she'd be available on her cell, only to find Barry Blankenship, culprit of the hour, hovering outside the elevator.

"Oh! Hello!"

"I wondered . . . my daughters are in the pageant . . ."

"You're the man who asked about Evangeline the other night," Cam said. She didn't want to let on how much she actually knew about him.

"I am." He didn't look thrilled to be remembered that way.

"Are you also the one who's been calling Evangeline?"

"What? Well, maybe a few times."

Cam almost called him by name, but caught herself. "If your name is on the forms, I can share information with you. Otherwise, it violates the legal agreement we have with the contestants. Who are your daughters?"

"Are there a lot of sisters?"

"Sir, for all I know, your daughters are by different mamas and have nothing to do with the other besides you. You said plural, so I said plural. If it's just one, it's easier."

"I think you know who I am."

"And I think you know the law is on my side."

Evangeline walked out then and stared

down Barry.

"I blocked your number, so now you turn up here?" she said.

"I want to see my daughters."

"I explained that, legally, his name has to be on the documents," Cam said.

Her phone buzzed. She looked at both Evangeline and Barry, as if daring them to stop her from answering.

"Cam Harris," she answered, her neck prickling from the uncomfortable conversation.

"What the hell did you send them here for?" Annie snarled.

"I don't know. My afternoon is swamped, but I'll see what I can do," Cam said, hoping Annie would take the hint.

"You owe me!"

"Oh, thank goodness. As soon as I can, then." She hung up.

"Barry, I'll get a restraining order if I have to," Evangeline said.

"Did you want to give me a card or something?" Cam said, hoping to defuse the standoff. "I can check the lists. Your daughters' names would help, too."

Barry glared and got on the elevator without sharing a card or any names.

Evangeline looked at Cam curiously. "So you know the story with his daughters?"

"I think so. He left the mom . . . completely for about nine months, but now seems to want custody of his daughters again. My guess is a lawyer told him how much a rich son-of-a-gun has to pay in child support if he's not the custodial parent."

"That sounds about right. And your phone call?"

"Personal obligation this afternoon." Cam didn't want to put Evangeline in an awkward position legally or ethically. "I'll have my phone and computer. You okay here?"

"You've put out the fires this week. I suppose it's my turn."

Cam made her way to Sweet Surprise, only to ask Annie another favor. She needed Annie's car to take Mindy and the girls to her house so they'd be more comfortable for the afternoon and evening. They could do the research there for the Green Project, which both were scheduled for.

When she arrived at Sweet Surprise, she whispered to Annie that the deadbeat dad was trying to change his mind about custody and they were stuck. She looked up at Lauren frosting cupcakes and Lizzie adding sprinkles, her mermaid book off to the side like a security blanket. Cam figured the only real tension was with Mindy, who was surely

159

eating crow after accepting Annie's help. Annie could act as irritable as she wanted. She'd won the battle of "who has a better life." Still, a little bribery could never hurt. Cam offered to buy Annie a six-pack of the finest microbrew and a bottle of Mexican vanilla, and then they might call it even.

"You girls ready to go relax for a bit?" Cam asked.

"No!" Lizzie yelled. "It's fun here!"

"I have it on good authority that Annie has to clean up next. Do you want to scrub the floor?"

"No, thank you." She frowned very seriously.

"I'll tell you what. For supper, we'll order some pizzas and Annie can come over. Does that sound okay?"

"Yes!" both girls shouted together.

Cam went over and hugged Annie, shoving a twenty in her pocket. "Buy whatever beer you need to make this bearable. Pizza is on us."

"Can the boys come?" Annie asked.

"Yeah, that's probably best."

"Tell Rob to bring the beer for you and him. I can't be seen buying that stuff. I have a reputation to uphold."

It was a jab, to be sure, but one Cam was familiar with. Annie liked locally brewed, strong beer. "If you can see through it, why bother?" was her motto. Cam and Rob tended to go with lower-calorie options. Cam could take the teasing. What she couldn't seem to take was the alcohol content in the strong stuff. She was a lightweight.

Davy Jones, the neighborhood stray, greeted them outside and it took some effort to convince the girls he didn't really need to be invited in. Cam watched Mindy's face as they entered the lower level of the split house Cam shared with Annie. She could see Mindy examining the little house, probably fighting her snobbery, but the girls jumped onto her futon in the front room and Cam turned on the Disney Channel.

She looked back at Mindy, who was biting her finger and looking distraught.

"What is it?"

"I'm just mad at myself — buying into all that 'stuff matters' and marrying for security without learning to create my own." She sniffed heavily and sat at Cam's kitchen table, out of view of her daughters.

Cam wasn't sure how to respond. "Do you want some tea? Wine?"

"Tea's good."

Mindy was crying openly now. Cam de-

161

cided just to listen if Mindy needed to talk. She filled the teapot and put it on the burner, then occupied herself putting tea-bags in a bowl, then sugar and cream. When she had the pieces assembled, she put them all onto a tray.

Mindy continued to whimper about choices wasted and never having had to support herself before.

"I mean, what can I do? The last job I had, I was twenty-three and living with my parents."

"I'm sure you have plenty of skills. What was your degree in?"

Mindy sniffed. "French. And I haven't spoken it since Barry and I honeymooned in Quebec."

"The girls seem well-adjusted. You've been a good mother. That's important."

"Lauren blames me for their dad leaving, and I don't even understand Lizzie. She's like some foreign thing."

Cam frowned. At least Mindy and Lizzie were on the same page about their relation-ship. That was something.

Cam excused herself for a little while to make the calls she needed to double-check everything, then she called Rob and ex-plained the situation. Mindy thumbed through a gardening magazine, but Cam was sure she didn't really see anything. Cam took the girls to and from an afternoon rehearsal, feeling Mindy needed the downtime. When they returned, the girls took turns at the computer for an hour, then Lauren got back to television and Lizzie curled up on a chair with her book. Mindy was still in a funk and couldn't even help Lauren sort through a tiered compost bin she was trying to design. Cam wished she could help, but as pageant staff, she felt it would be cheating. Instead, she gave Lauren some websites to check.

The girls giggled in the other room and Cam went out to talk to them. "What kind of pizza do you girls eat?"

Mindy spoke behind her. "Just cheese — that's normal, right?"

Cam suspected pepperoni was more common, but since she planned on veggie for her and Rob — a choice she knew Annie could live with if they got a side of jalapeños — she just shrugged and ordered one of each. Jake, the lone meat-eater, would have to cope somehow.

Annie and Rob arrived together, coming through the back door. Since Cam had borrowed Annie's car, she'd asked Rob to swing by and pick up Annie on his way over. Each of them carried in a six-pack of beer and stuck them in Cam's fridge.

"We won't insist you partake," Annie said to Mindy.

Cam made a face at Annie, hoping Mindy wouldn't hear it for the rudeness it was.

"When's Jake getting here?" Cam asked.

"His shift ended at four, but he's got the paperwork piece after that, and . . ."

"Yeah . . . I know murder investigations make for a busy day."

Mindy's expression changed, then changed again. She finally found some resolve and went into the front room to see her daughters. When Lizzie heard Annie's name, though, she shrieked and ran back to the kitchen, hugging her.

"Hey, squirt. What are you watching?"

Lizzie shrugged and took Annie's hand, leading her back to the television.

"You hear anything?" Rob asked.

Cam shook her head, though that wasn't strictly true. "You?"

He made a disgruntled face. He hadn't, either.

"Guess at the moment this mystery rests with Jake," Cam said.

"Unfortunately, I think he feels burned by the last time," Rob said. "He hasn't shared nearly as much."

Cam and Rob had both gotten a lot of information from Jake the last time there'd been a murder. And both had done a fair bit of investigating on their own, which Jake didn't like. "I think we should pool what we know, even if it isn't much, so he will trade with us."

Cam smiled and hugged him. It was nice that Rob could be a little devious in the same way she was. Neither of them would ever withhold anything from the police that would keep a crime from being solved. But they both had some skill maneuvering facts so they could obtain as much extra information as was available.

They liked Jake, but as a cop, Jake's job was to keep quiet as much as possible. Cam, under the heading of damage control, needed better information than that. Rob, a newspaper reporter, needed as much as he could possibly get.

Jake arrived about fifteen minutes after the pizza.

They all met in the front room. Cam noticed Jake looking strangely at Mindy and she remembered the questioning he'd given her. At the moment, though, it seemed like Mindy's fear for her kids was more important to Mindy than any residual awkwardness from the questioning, so she didn't seem to mind Jake was there. After they ate, Cam surveyed the leftovers and her companions and said, "Look at the time! You two girls need to be up early. One more slice of pizza and then Rob will give you a ride back to your hotel."

They started to complain, but when Lizzie yawned, they gave in.

"Thank you so much for having us here. I couldn't have faced Barry tonight — not after that questioning," Mindy whispered just out of earshot of her children.

"I'm sure there were several of those arguments," Cam tried to reassure her. "Telly seemed to make a lot of people mad."

"Maybe. But I'm sure I was the only one stupid enough to be seen. Even if there were lots of arguments, since mine was the only one witnessed, they wouldn't believe every other mother here had probably had the exact same argument with him. He was a horrible man."

Mindy saw Rob pull out a notebook and gasped. "You're not reporting on this, are you?"

"It's a good story."

"You can't write that! I didn't kill him!"

"They thought you did it?" Rob looked at Cam. She could have died. They hadn't gotten around to Mindy being questioned yet. Dylan, either, for that matter. She'd been saving her news for later, or so she had told herself.

Jake approached and Cam looked to him. "There was a whiskey bottle in Telly Stevens's office that was half oleander, according to the medical examiner. It was either murder or suicide, and nothing I've heard today leads me to believe the man had enough depth of feeling for suicide. So thank you for being so observant, Cam. We will have to go through the log of gifts, but chances are this bottle was sent anonymously."

Lauren looked over at them in alarm. Cam tried to give a warning look, but Jake was done and seemed not to be paying attention. He had turned back to his pizza choices.

When the girls had finished, Rob drove them and their mom back to the Travelodge and Cam pounced on Jake.

"Please keep murder speculation to a minimum this week."

"Cam, poison is usually murder. Besides, Rob's been shadowing me on this anyway, so I know you will hear everything he does."

"So, who are you looking at? At least nobody from my friend list, I hope."

"I can't talk to you about this."

Cam looked at Annie, who shrugged. Cam suggested tequila, hoping to extend conversation and maybe loosen Jake's tongue, but Annie suggested they go. She held out her hand and Jake took it, following Annie out the back door. It was some time before Cam heard the single set of footsteps on the stairs, which meant either Annie or Jake had decided to call it an early night.

It was probably for the best. In fact, Annie had probably saved Cam from alienating Jake permanently. Besides, they all had a big day the next day.

As she was finishing up dishes, she heard an unfamiliar pounding on her front door. People had fairly individualized knocks, but her most regular guests typically just let themselves in after a warning knock or two. This was someone who didn't visit her regularly.

Cam dried her hands and made her way to the front door. A small window in the top of the door revealed a sandy head of hair. She stood on tiptoes far enough to recognize Benny's eye and opened the door.

Benny burst in, followed more slowly by Dylan.

"Hi. Um . . . is there a problem?" Cam

asked. "Is the vandal back?"

"No, this isn't about the pageant . . . well, not exactly. It's . . . well, Dylan here . . ."

Dylan wasn't wearing his naughty smirk, and Cam thought he looked worried.

"It's like this, Miz Harris," Benny said, his words coming in spurts. "Remember how you solved the murder a couple months ago?"

"That wasn't exactly . . ."

"Yes, it was! I know the killer tried to frame your friend, so you solved it."

"Well, I guess . . ."

"The police are asking a lot of questions like Dylan did it. We wondered . . . well, I suggested . . . I thought maybe you could find out who did it, so Dylan doesn't have to go to jail."

"Benny, I'm not a detective. I wouldn't know where to start."

"But you're so smart! I know you could do it."

Benny played this very well — complimenting smart people and playing a bit dim himself was something he'd perfected, but Cam knew it was mostly an act.

She almost told him off because his game irked her a little — at least the idea that he was still trying to play it with her. Then she saw Dylan. He was licking his lips like a

169

man lost in the desert. His demeanor was very different from the cocky man he usually was.

"Sit." She gestured toward the couch. "Can I get you something to drink? Water? Beer?"

"Beer's good," Benny said.

"Dylan?" Cam asked.

He nodded. He still hadn't said anything.

She took them their beers and then opened a Diet Pepsi for herself and sat.

"What makes you think they'll blame you?" Cam asked.

Dylan looked up, took a drink, and then straightened a little. Cam thought he didn't really want to be there.

"I guess there's the money. A will. It's . . . I didn't even know there was a will, but that producer woman let me have it when she realized who I was."

"Let you have it, how?"

"I walked her inside her house — to make sure she was okay, like you said. I never put it all together. But inside there were old pictures — a local television award, stuff like that. And it was the show my mom had been on. Before she had me, she was a weather girl on a morning show and then she got fired when she got pregnant. I knew it was the show, so I said it to the woman

— that Towers-whatever . . . and she got really mad. She threw things and told me to get out.

"Then the police came — when I called you. I went down to the station to answer questions, and they started asking me about how I knew I was in the will. I didn't know anything until that first police officer said the dead guy was my father."

"You didn't know?"

"No. I called my mom after I got home, and I guess he bought her a little crappy house to shut her up — made her swear never to tell. It's a lousy house, but . . . you know . . . when a house is paid for, she could make ends meet, even without her weather job. Neither of us ever thought there'd be anything else. And my stepdad was there awhile — then another guy she never married. Heck, I didn't even know she knew who my father was. She never mentioned him. I thought she just worked and saved."

"Well, you can't be blamed if you didn't even know," Cam said.

"But they don't believe me. I've run a half-dozen cons and scams — get-rich-quick schemes — at any given time. I'm an easy target, and I think that Towers woman wants it to look like me because then I don't get any money."

"Do you know how much?" Cam asked.

"Would it matter?" Benny asked.

"I framed that wrong." Cam thought for a minute about what she meant. "If the wife still gets the bulk of it and you just get a little, it might not be worth it for her to try to frame you — too risky, so she's really just throwing the accusation and it can't hurt. But if you will get what she perceives to be a lot — then she may do whatever she can to make it look like you, regardless of who it was."

"Though if it's *her,* she might want him to look guilty no matter what," Benny said.

Cam snapped her head around to stare at Benny. "You think *she* did it?"

"Isn't it always the wife when a rich guy bites it?"

Cam thought about Telly leering at Jessica Benchly and thought it wasn't at all unlikely. She also thought, if things between Jessica and Clancy Huggins were at all serious, that *he* might have taken offense at Telly Stevens's behavior.

"I can come up with at least a few suspects. I'll ask some questions and hopefully we can throw enough doubt on you to make it stick." She doubted it would come to that, but it seemed easy enough, even so.

"Thanks, Miz Harris," Benny said, standing.

Dylan and Cam stood at the same time and found themselves in too little space. Cam could smell peat, the residue of aftershave, and a little sweat as she found herself staring at Dylan's shoulder. He was well over six feet tall, though she hadn't realized just how tall, since she hadn't stood this close to him before. Usually when she was this close to a man, she looked at eyes or nose. Rob was a nose man. Right now she was looking at a chin. She backed up a step.

He took her hand and kissed it — a proper kiss, like an old-fashioned gentleman — not the earth-shifting wrist-lick she'd gotten the last time he made the gesture. She was glad for that. She didn't think she could help Dylan if all she could think about was a quiver at the base of her spine.

CHAPTER 9

Cam slept lightly. Her brain tossed around themes about the love triangles, quadrangles . . . was "quintangle" a word? There was no solid answer except Jessica Benchly looked like the centerpiece. Cam wondered if she could think of an excuse to talk to the woman, since she wasn't officially a part of the pageant.

When Cam arrived at the Patrick Henry, she tried to keep her pace measured as she entered the pageant's suite and then the large private office occupied by Evangeline.

"I have a question."

Evangeline looked up. Her eyes were red-rimmed and Cam thought she wasn't the only one who'd slept poorly.

"Yes. When I blocked Barry on my cell, the crank calls stopped."

"Oh! Well, that's good." Cam felt a little guilty for having let Evangeline's problem fall off her priority list, but she plowed on.

"I was actually going to ask whether you knew Jessica Benchly before Monday."

"Well . . . 'know' has degrees. I'd met her. She was another former Miss Virginia, actually. She went further than I did — I think she was a national finalist. Probably she didn't have as much of an attitude. I think she was four years ahead of me."

Cam would never have said it. Evangeline looked great for the thirty-eight Cam thought she was, but she really never would have guessed that Jessica Benchly was another four years older. The woman looked perpetually twenty-five. Age, though, was not relevant to Cam's set of questions.

"Is she dating Clancy Huggins? Or is that . . ."

"Oh, honey, I have no idea. I've seen them places together before — for years, actually — and they're affectionate, but they've never called themselves a couple. Neither one is married."

"And what about Telly Stevens's feelings for her?"

"Just between us?"

"Of course."

"Telly had a reputation for . . . sampling the merchandise . . . he sort of thought if a beautiful woman was on his show, she should . . . you know . . . show her appreciation . . ."

"Ick."

"I know. Second-rate stars, though, were happy for the opportunity, and honestly, I've heard he was . . . now this is strictly rumor . . . skilled. He probably started the rumor himself. Anyway, the rumor is Jessica refused and then Telly, baffled, like the egomaniac he was, proceeded to follow her around because he didn't believe she was serious about not wanting him. Cam, this is totally gossip — please only take it that way . . ."

Cam nodded. "Now, don't shoot me. I have a guess on this, but I want your guess. If she turned down Telly, who was handsome, why say yes to Clancy?"

"I don't know that she did. They may just be close friends. But the fact that I believe Clancy Huggins would take a friend on dates speaks volumes. Even if Telly is better looking, Clancy is so much more interesting, and . . . where it matters — for relationships, he's loyal."

Cam nodded again. Her thoughts hadn't been so specific but were certainly along the same lines.

"Is Jessica going to be part of things later on this week?"

"I was surprised she wasn't here Tuesday.

She's usually very supportive. In fact, it might have been because of that scene at the party."

Cam's brain, in full conspiracy mode, wondered if Jessica might have been avoiding the scene of the crime. Having Telly Stevens stalking her sounded like a motive. And having him stalk a bunch of other women, and apparently sleep with them, sounded like a motive for his wife. Cam made a mental note for the time being and left it at that.

The day had a fair bit of structure to it, and Cam had taken care of her tasks, so she decided she would answer some of the emails and put out some fires related to her regular job. She went home so as not to be distracted by other things and ended up on the phone for a couple hours straight.

She felt a sense of accomplishment when she was finished, and she walked back to the Patrick Henry feeling a little lighter.

"That friend of yours, Barry's wife, has called you a half-dozen times in the last half hour. She sounds frantic," Evangeline shouted from her office as soon as Cam entered the suite.

"Oh, thank you. My ringer was off, and I

guess I forgot to turn it on again."

Cam went into one of the other offices and closed the door to return Mindy's call.

"Mindy? What's up?"

Mindy began shrieking and Cam could barely understand her.

"Calm down, Mindy. What happened?"

Mindy couldn't get the words out, but she did manage to convey her room number, so Cam sprinted out. The Travelodge was several blocks away, but Cam was used to walking and could do so quickly. Fifteen minutes later, she knocked on Mindy's door.

The room was a disaster, torn top to bottom. Cam felt sure Mindy had had a break-in, but Mindy explained that she'd done it.

"Why?"

Mindy sniffed and took out a large makeup bag. She unzipped the side pocket and pulled out a Ziploc bag and tossed it to Cam. Inside were a few wilted plants. Cam frowned and held it up, looking at the dejected flowers, petals browning from lack of air.

"Why are you traveling with oleander?"

"I'm not! I think it's a message. I didn't even know what kind of flower it was."

"You didn't bring this?"

Mindy shook her head. "Why would I? And if somebody put *this* in here, somebody could have come in and ruined Lauren's dress!"

"When did you find this?"

"About an hour ago, after I dropped the girls off, I was planning what I'd wear tonight and one of my lipsticks was missing, so I opened that side pocket."

"How often do you normally open it?" Cam asked, though she could tell the flowers weren't months old. If she were guessing, she'd say a day or two, depending on how much oxygen they'd been exposed to.

"Almost never." Mindy said. "It squashes things."

"Mindy, we need to call the police."

"I think someone is just scaring us — they know Lauren is a favorite — someone who stays here, maybe."

Cam swallowed, unsure what to do. The lab thought oleander had been used to poison Telly Stevens, and somebody must want it to look like Mindy did it. Cam didn't think Mindy had put the two together. She might not even know oleander was poisonous.

"Mindy, is there anyone who'd want you to look guilty of murder?"

"What? No."

"No one?"

"Murder?" She paused awhile, frowning.

179

"Barry, maybe. He'd get the girls, but . . . I wouldn't think he'd be that awful . . . or do that to their mother . . ."

"I have to call Jake."

Mindy sank to the ground. She looked frail and helpless and Cam felt bad, but she was sure if Mindy was being framed, someone else was also calling the police to report her.

Cam hit the number already saved on speed dial. "Jake?"

"How do I know I'm going to regret this?" he said.

Cam ignored his jab. "My friend Mindy, you remember Mindy?"

He sighed loudly.

". . . had something put in her hotel room," Cam continued. "She thought it was a fellow contestant being awful — just spooking her — and called me. I recognized it as something more serious, so I'm calling you."

"They aren't there yet?" Jake asked.

"Who's not?"

Pounding on the door answered her.

"I guess they are now. I can count on you to prove we called before they came?"

He made a series of noises, but Cam took them for grudging agreement. She noted the time on her phone and then opened the door.

"You." It was the female deputy who had been there when Telly's body had been found. She looked confused.

"Yes. Mindy called me because she thought another contestant was trying to scare her by putting something in her room. I just called and told Jake, because it looks *to me* like somebody is trying to frame her for murder."

The deputy glared. She was followed in by the greenest rookie Cam had ever seen. He still had acne and she was pretty sure he only needed to shave once a week.

"We had a tip something might be here," the deputy said.

"I'm sure that something is that." Cam pointed at the freezer bag on the bed.

"Did either of you touch that?"

"We both did. Mindy got it from her makeup bag and showed it to me before I had the full story. She didn't know it was evidence, and neither did I, until I saw what it was."

"And what makes you think it's evidence now?"

"Because I know oleander is poisonous and I think Telly Stevens was poisoned."

"It's suspicious that you know so much."

"And don't you think it's suspicious that you got a call about something that was hiding in a pocket of Mindy's makeup bag? Who would know that besides Mindy, unless somebody put it there other than her? My knowledge happens to come from a degree in horticulture. Besides, any plant grower knows oleander is poisonous. It is one of those they warn parents about — to watch their kids."

"Did *you* know oleander was poison?" the deputy asked Mindy.

"By name I'd heard that, but I didn't know this was oleander until Cam told me. I don't . . . well . . . I haven't gardened since I was in high school, other than a few geraniums in a window box. We have . . . had . . . a gardener."

"Had?"

"My husband and I are separated. I can't afford a gardener without him. I had to let him go."

The deputy seemed to be enjoying this a little too much.

"Shouldn't you be searching for break-in clues or something?" Cam said.

"Did they do all this when they supposedly put this here?"

Cam squinted at her name tag: Quinn.

"Officer Quinn," Cam said more patiently

than she felt. "Yesterday somebody sabotaged Mindy's daughter's dress. Today she found evidence someone has been in her room. She freaked a little and looked for any sign of who it was. You can't blame her."

"Maybe *you* can't."

"You can't just ignore that we tried to report this before you got here."

"No. That was clever of you."

"Clever? If this *were* hers and related to the *murder,* don't you think she would have gotten rid of it? *That* would have been clever. Not letting anyone know it was here? Common sense. This reeks of framing."

"Maybe *you* would have gotten rid of it. I hope you don't turn to a life of crime, as you'd be harder to catch."

Cam couldn't believe this.

"Mrs. Blankenship, we need to take you in for questioning," the green rookie said.

"But . . . my girls . . ."

"Their father will have to get them," Officer Quinn huffed.

Cam frowned. Some fathers weren't even in town yet. Some were never coming.

"He doesn't . . . he isn't . . ." Mindy looked up at Cam with a very sad face.

"Do you have a lawyer, Mindy? I can call and have him meet you there about the girls," Cam said. "I won't let them alone

183

until this is sorted out."

Mindy wrote down a name and gave it to Cam. She then left with the police officers.

Cam put together the girls' bags and set them by the door. She found the spare key card and put it in her purse. She didn't want Lauren and Lizzie too traumatized, so whatever happened she would retrieve their things for them once she had a car to do it with.

After the harrowing experience, the walk back to Elmwood Park in the July sun seemed to take a lot of effort. She not only felt overheated but drained when she reached the Arts Commission building. She hoped at least part of the rehearsals were happening. The bright, cut zinnias that had filled buckets at the farmer's market had cheered her, but here, even the hardy shrubs looked tired. They really needed a good long soak and a break from the heat. It was just too hot, for people or plants, to be outside.

Michelle, with the help of two of the teens, was leading the fitness routine. It was easy to spot the girls who'd had years of dance — probably two-thirds of the contestants. What Cam didn't spot, however, was either Lauren or Lizzie. She waited until the group reached a stopping point before she asked

Michelle.

"Nell has the rest of the girls as well as Ashley and the adult volunteers. They are over at the library working on their gardening projects."

"Ah! Thank you!"

Cam hated to leave the air-conditioned building, so she stepped into the hallway and called Evangeline before heading back outside.

"It's Cam," she said when Evangeline picked up. "They just took Mindy to the police station. Evangeline, would Barry frame Mindy for murder?"

"What?"

"She called me because somebody planted oleander in her room. That's not how she put it — she just found it, but that's what it was. Then whoever it was called the police. Fortunately, Mindy had called me first and I called Jake, so we have a credible witness it didn't belong there. But Barry seems the most likely person to want to frame Mindy."

The silence at the other end of the phone seemed too long, then Evangeline said, "I wouldn't think so. He's smart, and that's a wily plan. But he's also selfish."

"Meaning?"

"Well, I can see him wanting custody financially, or to stick it to his wife, but he

185

isn't going to want the kids every hour of every day. It would cramp his womanizing ways. Kids sometimes help — make him look sympathetic. But I can't see him putting his built-in child care in jail. Plus, I'd like to believe the Barry I once knew really loves his kids."

"That's harsh. Other than that last point, I mean."

"I know, honey. I'm just trying to think like I think he would."

"And it's pretty convincing, but who else would want to frame her?"

"Who else looks guilty?"

Cam was annoyed when her mind went to Dylan. He'd been near enough to the argument to have easily overheard. He might know Mindy was an easy scapegoat. Cam didn't want to think about him that way. It would be really lousy to frame another innocent person, just to get out from under the spotlight. She would need to talk to him and see what he thought.

In the meantime, she needed to check on Mindy's girls, and she wanted to brainstorm with someone she trusted. Her experience with friends being blamed for murder suggested if she didn't do some investigating on her own, the wrong person might be blamed. She also felt like she owed Mindy and would like to be free of the debt.

Cam warred with herself about crossing the Elmwood Park lawn. Hurry and sweat but reach the coolness faster, or suffer less extreme torture for a longer period of time? In the end, her shoes decided the matter. The walk to the Travelodge and back had given her a blister, and walking slowly was the only way to not aggravate it.

Thankfully, Lauren and Lizzie, in their respective groups, seemed to be fine. Lauren was reading and taking notes like a much older child. Lizzie was brandishing a thick green marker on poster board. Her idea was already obvious — instead of pesticides, she was recommending toads. For seven, Cam thought the idea had a lot of merit as a green solution. In fact, if cute-factor played in, she had Cam's vote.

Cam talked in vague terms to the group leaders and to Nell about the mom having some trouble and not to release Lauren or Lizzie to anybody but her until they had a definitive answer. They all agreed, but Cam felt her edges unraveling. She called Rob and asked him to come for lunch.

"I'm meeting Jake, Cam. I'm sorry."

Cam sighed and went up to stare out the front library window onto the park. Dylan was watching things, a ridiculous fan contraption hat on his head.

She laughed and, without thinking, went out to give him the morning's news.

He tilted his head as he saw her coming, the umbrella that topped the contraption bobbing.

"You look lovely today, Miss Harris."

Cam rolled her eyes. She wasn't in the mood for sucking up. "Did you see a woman yelling or arguing with Telly Stevens?"

Dylan frowned. " 'bout three of them. I got the impression he was sort of a pig."

That cheered her.

"Somebody was taken in today."

"So I'm off the hook?"

"I doubt it. I think the woman's being framed."

"Who would frame her?"

"Two options. The ex-husband who wants custody, or the person who really did it. But if it isn't personal, then the person had to see the argument to know she was worth framing."

Cam wiped her brow. The heat hadn't been willing to be forgotten for long.

"Here." Dylan pulled her close and she realized between the shade of the little umbrella and the fan, it really was about ten degrees cooler under his laughable hat.

The trouble was, being closer to Dylan made her skin burn for other reasons.

She compromised, stepping back a step but to the side, so she was at least in the umbrella's shade.

"Who else was around when they argued?" She had to describe Mindy before Dylan was sure which argument she was asking about.

"Geez, I don't know. Maybe a half-dozen people. It was when the people were getting there to set up your tents, but the truck with the stuff was late. Lot of loitering while they waited."

"Were there any people from the pageant?"

"Sure, a couple."

Cam pulled a press packet from her shoulder bag. "Would you recognize them?"

"Probably, if their pictures look like them."

That was a fair caveat. A lot of people sent photos that were more glamorous than their everyday appearances.

When they'd gone through the packet to look at pictures, Cam's shoulder was on fire from standing so near to Dylan. He identified Clancy Huggins and Judith Towers-Stevens. He insisted there were still four or five more people who weren't in the promotional materials — probably from the rental company. Apparently Mindy's fight had had quite an audience.

After lunch, the groups of girls swapped stations. Cam positioned herself in the entry of the Arts Commission and pulled out her laptop to get her afternoon tasks accomplished. She wanted to make sure nothing unusual happened and, at least until she got a call from Mindy's lawyer, make sure nobody took the girls.

CHAPTER 10

After talking to Dylan, Cam had a half-dozen tasks to confirm and finalize. It was the second night they would be televised, and it seemed it ought to run more smoothly than the first, but apparently that was only a novice's expectation.

When Annie arrived at three, Cam felt like throwing a party. She'd been nearly ready to throw in the towel, but the mocha fudge cupcake thrust in front of her face washed a lot of that away.

As so often happened with their friendship, Annie's arrival opened a spigot and Cam let the details and worries of the last eighteen hours spill out. Annie, as best friends are reputed to do, nodded, gasped, hugged, and swore at all the expected places.

"So I need you to help me solve this thing!" Cam ended. ". . . Dylan, and now Mindy . . ."

"Are you forgetting the last time I tried

191

this I got accused of murder?"

"Yeah, but that was personal."

"Might have been, but who knew about it at the time? I'd never met the guy."

That was true. Cam couldn't deny the grudge had caught them all by surprise.

"You have no real connection here."

"I didn't there, either," Annie said. "And Mindy resents me at least as much. Probably more."

"Speaking of Mindy . . ."

"Do we have to?"

"Can you dig up some dirt on this husband — strictly internet gossip-column stuff?"

Annie's shoulders fell. Cam knew it meant she'd given in and would help, against her better judgment, or at least her inclinations.

"How long do the munchkins still have in rehearsal?"

"Ninety minutes."

"I'll get some pictures now."

"Get some of Nell at the library, too. I'd like to supply a special-interest piece for her project."

"Got it. Then, while they're showering for tonight, I can look up some stuff, because, as my clean, fresh scent should tell you, I showered after I closed the shop."

Cam raised an eyebrow. Annie didn't look

quite as fresh as she implied.

"Okay, so Jake stopped by and the shower wasn't . . . strictly about getting clean . . ."

That meshed better with Cam's observations, though it also brought up a new question.

"You'd think he had a murder to solve."

"He does! He is! It's just . . . twelve-hour days get long . . ."

"So you were providing a public service?"

Annie punched her in the arm and walked away, though her posture told Cam that Annie was laughing. Cam laughed behind her. There was definitely only one Annie.

Cam headed to the library. The girls were a hive of activity, most of them on a bank of computers. Some seemed thrilled at the project; others were just going through the motions. A few were at tables with press board and markers, having already decided on their direction. Nell had been right about the creativity of children. Cam wondered how she hadn't encountered more gardening projects for kids and made a note that maybe the Roanoke Garden Society should pursue some activities to draw in young gardeners. She was reminded of Lizzie's toad project and thought it was still a winner.

After checking in with Nell and Celeste

that things were going smoothly, she headed back to the Arts Commission.

She was barely in the door when Todd found her.

"Ma'am, it's . . . well . . . I knew you were interested in this guy, so I thought you might want to see . . ."

He led Cam to his tiny little security room and pressed a button. Cam watched the television monitor for several seconds. It was the front door. Finally something interesting appeared — the man — Barry Blankenship. He was tugging a woman by the arm; on closer inspection, Cam recognized her as Deputy Quinn.

"They're seeing each other?" Cam asked.

"I don't know about seeing. But saw?" Todd laughed.

Barry was unbuttoning Deputy Quinn's shirt when Cam looked back.

"In the hall?"

"No. There's a little more in the elevator, but all P.G. Still . . . is this the kind of thing you were looking for?"

"Absolutely! Thank you! Make sure that doesn't get erased. The police might even want to see it."

Cam asked him to email her the footage, then rushed out. As soon as she cleared the outer door of the building, she called Jake.

"Cam?" Jake's voice was dubious when he answered.

"Your Deputy Quinn is cavorting with a suspect. In fact, I think she planted the plant at Mindy's."

"Cavorting? Suspect? That's a pretty serious accusation. What are you basing it on?" he asked.

"She and Barry Blankenship getting it on on-camera at the Arts Commission. Meet me there and I'll show you."

Jake sighed, but Cam thought she had him. He agreed to come, though he said it was because he needed to be there anyway. She sat on the steps to wait.

Unfortunately, sitting was a deed that never went unpunished. Cam's phone buzzed against her leg. She might have skipped answering, but it was Evangeline, so she felt it might be important.

"This is Cam."

"Scene! Restaurant at the Patrick Henry! Hurry!"

The phone clicked off, and Cam removed her shoes and jogged between the Blue Cross building and the Social Security building, the fastest route between the two. She never went this way without wishing the city would give her a free hand to introduce a little more greenery. There were

small trees, but it really could use a little
floral infusion. She debated calling Jake as
she ran, but Evangeline definitely sounded
like the situation was urgent. She just hoped
it wouldn't take long.

When she reached the restaurant, it was
easy to figure out where the commotion
was. Cam rushed toward the shouting and
touched Evangeline's shoulder, causing the
woman to practically jump out of her skin.

"Sorry! What do we do?"

"Thank heavens!" Evangeline said, clutch-
ing Cam's arm. "I think we should divide
and conquer! I'll take Clancy, you take Judith."

They hesitated to catch their breath before
they approached the argument. Cam had
enough spare attention to notice the audience wasn't huge. The restaurant was only a
quarter full. It was the lead-in to happy
hour, but most of the nearby businesses
hadn't closed for the day.

Cam stepped in front of Judith, facing her.
She put a hand on each shoulder. "Judith? I
don't think you want to do this. Certainly
not here."

Judith glared and tried to go around her,
but Cam held firm. Cam suspected she only
maintained control because she was more
sober.

"Judith?" Cam said more firmly. "Come with me."

Cam moved sideways with Judith until her glare at Clancy finally broke. Judith shook her shoulders out of Cam's grasp angrily. "This is none of your business!"

"On the contrary. As public relations manager for this contest, this is exactly my business. You are making us look bad," Cam whispered.

"Me? Clancy's the one who keeps dragging that tramp, Jessica, everywhere!"

"And why would you care who Clancy spends his time with? I would think you'd be glad he was filling her time."

"And what is *that* supposed to mean?"

"That I saw your scene at the party, too. I happen to think you are actually angry with your husband. And while you're at it, keep in mind *you* are why your husband was part of this contest. You insisted. If you hadn't, he wouldn't have been exposed to any of this." She felt cruel for a moment, like she'd blamed Judith for her husband's death, but she quickly changed her mind.

"Hmph!"

Judith stormed away. Cam couldn't deny she was glad to see the woman leave, even if it might make her harder to deal with at the show. She just hoped she wouldn't drive anywhere in her current condition. Cam couldn't hang around to worry about it, though. She worried she'd already missed Jake. She waved to Evangeline, who was still talking to Clancy, and left.

When Cam finally got back to the Arts Commission, she had to run after Jake's retreating form. "Jake!" she shouted, waving her arms. He'd obviously been waiting awhile and had given up.

He finally heard her and turned around; he looked annoyed.

"I'm sorry!" she gasped, trying to catch her breath and talk at the same time. "I had to go break up World War III. Our television producer versus one of our judges."

Jake frowned for a moment, but then turned back and walked with Cam.

She steered him toward the Patrick Henry. They had a water cooler and coffeepot. What she wanted was iced coffee, but cold water in one hand and coffee in the other would have to do at the moment.

They took the elevator to the second floor and he followed her into the office. Evangeline waved as they passed, and Cam took Jake to the office she'd been using earlier and hooked her laptop up.

"Okay, you remember I called you before

the police arrived at Mindy's . . ."

"Cam, I can't talk to you about this."

"Fine. Just listen. Somebody knew the plant was there — before Mindy knew. As soon as she knew, she called me, though probably only because her daughter's dress had been ruined the day before. She thought the two things were related and suggested it might have happened at her hotel instead of at the library, as she'd thought originally. The police were almost on top of me getting there — with a search warrant. Explain to me how they might have gotten that hint unless somebody already knew it was there? She found it. Called me. And I called you. An hour, tops. How long does it take you to get a warrant?"

"Depends."

"And what was the warrant based on?"

"It was an anonymous tip," Jake said.

"From the person who planted it. My money is on your Officer Quinn. Just . . . check with the hotel — did anybody demand access to the room when Mindy and the girls weren't there?"

"I'm the police officer here."

"Then you already thought of that and the proper response is, 'I've already checked, Cam.' Besides, watch this." Cam turned her computer to Jake and ran the clip of Barry and Officer Quinn groping. "This man is married to the accused woman. All over your officer there."

Jake looked up and then at Cam. "Okay. You have a knack for thinking like a cop, but you do *not* act like a cop. One mistake and suddenly evidence is inadmissible."

"And a delay and it looks like an innocent woman is guilty."

"You want to manage me?" Jake asked.

Cam tilted her head. "How long have we been friends? A couple years now? And how was that other murder case? Have you *ever* seen me encounter *anything* I didn't prefer to manage?"

Jake finally laughed. It was good to have the tension broken. Things had grown a little awkward when Jake, Rob's friend, had started dating Annie, Cam's friend. Rob was a cool observer and Annie, a divine distracter, but Cam and Jake both felt the need to control more of situations than they should. Yet they approached control in very different ways. Jake was slow and methodical; Cam, impulsive, intuitive, and if she was honest, a little reckless in her controlling. Their methods clashed when things were too serious to joke about.

"So if my instinct is good, can you look at it a little?"

"Yes and no." Jake stared straight at Cam. She felt uncomfortable. "I will strongly consider the angles you suggest, but you need to understand that, short of a legitimate lead — legitimate meaning fairly overheard, honestly found, or formally investigated — my hands are tied and you're to stay out of it."

Cam doubted she could keep that promise but she promised anyway. She figured when the time came 'round again, she could find a reasonable argument to break the rule and ask for forgiveness later.

Jake sighed and left, but she thought she'd convinced him to at least check with hotel security.

Cam went into the Arts Commission and collected Lauren and Lizzie, explaining that their mom had something big to take care of. It was only then that Cam remembered. It was the woman on the tape questioning Mindy. Jake had been tight-lipped about that, but he must have known. Cam suggested they all go to her house to get cleaned up before the pageant. She called Annie for a ride and ran to pick up the girls' bags on the way.

"Where's Mom?" Lauren asked when Cam got back to the car with the suitcases.

"The police are asking her some questions about something she saw, but I'm sure she'll be here soon," Annie said.

Lauren looked dubious.

When they got to Cam's, Annie led Lizzie in easily. Cam stopped Lauren and looked at her.

"I know this isn't fair. Your mama's having a little trouble. But we could really use your help so Lizzie doesn't get scared. Can you do that?"

Lauren frowned but nodded.

"Can you help her get ready?"

Lauren looked down and stuck her lower lip out, looking her age for a change. When she let out her breath, she stood tall and nodded. "Yeah, I can help the kid."

Cam had to bite her cheek. It was a little self-important and pretentious, especially after her brief display of vulnerability, but it was also cute, and the big sister in her identified with it. Sometimes you had to suck it up for your little sister, even if it stunk.

Cam was glad the pageant had a buffet supper, but these girls would wonder more seriously about their mom very soon. She hoped maybe if Annie were formally standing in, it might help. And she really hoped the questioning would end soon. It would be a shame for Mindy to miss her daughters performing their talents.

Once Cam was dressed, she helped the girls into their outfits. Lauren's replacement dress was very pretty, though Lauren pointed out a number of times while dressing that it wasn't nearly as good as the specially made one had been.

Lizzie wore a mermaid costume, and it was only as Cam examined her miserable face that the question occurred to her.

"How did you two both win if this is all the county winners?"

"Mom entered Lizzie in Campbell County," Lauren said.

"Can you do that?"

"Gram lives there. She used that address."

Cam looked at Lizzie again. The poor girl was examining her tail fin. Cam thought Lizzie would like nothing better than to be disqualified, and Cam now had the grounds to do it, but she only knew because she'd done something that wasn't strictly within the rules herself.

"She's really not supposed to do that," Cam said. She was sure Mindy knew better, but there was no reason to tell the girls that. "She probably didn't know, but I'll tell her, okay?"

"Next year I'll be a junior. I won't be in the kiddie pool, so it won't matter," Lauren said.

Cam frowned. Lauren seemed likely to be as shallow as her mother for the next two or three decades.

Cam knelt and whispered to Lizzie, "After the pageant, would you like it if I disqualified you in the future? No more Little Miss because you were entered in the wrong county?"

"Can you?"

"Only if that's what you want."

"Yes!" Lizzie flung her arms around Cam.

Annie came downstairs in a comfortable-looking sundress. Cam wished she was the photographer instead of the event co-ordinator. Her own pencil skirt, blouse, and heels she'd been so fond of ten minutes earlier seeming achingly cumbersome.

"Looks like you made a friend," Annie said.

"I'll explain later."

Annie helped her load the girls in the Bug and they headed back to the pageant.

CHAPTER 11

When they arrived, Cam sent Annie and the girls to get supper.

"Protect their outfits, will you?"

"It's spaghetti, what could happen?"

Cam's eyes went wide before she realized it was chicken Caesar salad, offered either in a wrap and as a salad. Annie was just scaring her.

"You're evil!"

"No, I'm naughty. I thought I'd explained that difference." Annie took both girls by the hands and headed toward the tent as Cam headed to the amphitheater to check on lighting and sound.

When she went behind the curtain, Scooter was dozing across a large speaker. She poked him and he started, almost falling over.

"Sorry, Miz Harris! Only . . . I'm working long hours!"

"You're done with the setup. Aren't you

just guarding a six-hour shift? Then this is four more — I mean — I know that's a long day, but it's not unreasonable."

"See, for setup, I took a couple vacation days from my other job. But I got back to that yesterday, so it's that, plus the security."

"Oh!" Cam hadn't thought this through. She'd sort of thought these ruffians weren't employed.

"Why are you working so much?"

"My girlfriend is pregnant, so I'm trying to put a little money away."

"For an engagement ring?" Cam blurted.

"I don't think she cares about that, but her job doesn't have insurance. It's my baby, so I need to help her."

"Oh, right. Does your job have insurance?"

"Yeah."

Cam stared at him. She didn't want to say it. It was a stupid reason to get married, except that it really wasn't — the cost of a baby was huge, and if the difference between insurance and no insurance was a ceremony, it seemed stupid not to do it.

That, though, set her thinking about Rob. She was not the kind of woman to trap a man, but how ridiculous was it, with their four years and moving to Roanoke together, to not be talking about it, when it so easily came to mind as a recommendation for someone else? Did she think she was better than Scooter? That marriage for *her* was a bigger deal? She admitted she was a snob about some things, but she hoped not about things like this.

It took her a while to pull herself back to the present. "So you guys have done the sound and light check?"

"We have. We did it at four. Shift change made most sense, as only one extra person needed to show up. Dylan will be back at seven to actually run stuff."

"He ran it Tuesday night, too. Is he the only one who knows how?"

Scooter shrugged. "Not me, anyway."

Cam looked at her watch, thanked Scooter, and went to get some supper. She filled her plate with salad and turned, hoping to spot Annie or Rob milling among the girls. Instead she spotted Barry Blankenship. She stifled a groan when she heard Lauren yell, "Daddy!" and run to him.

Cam steeled herself and walked over, taking Lizzie's hand as she let go of her dad, and trying to grab Lauren's, though Lauren apparently thought she was too old for such nonsense from a non-parent.

"Where's your mother?" Barry asked.

"Girls, can I talk to your dad a minute?"

They both nodded and went back to their suppers as if nothing had happened.

"Mr. Blankenship, you are not on the list. I'm glad you've come to watch your daughters, but the pageant has very strict rules."

"That a stranger watching them is better than their dad?"

"I'm sure that's not true, but I'm not a stranger — Mindy and I have known each other since high school."

"Right. So that's why you're their godmother . . . or where we leave them when we go on a romantic getaway?"

"I'm guessing Mindy's sister, Miranda, or one of her closer friends, is godmother, but they aren't here. And I'm sure there haven't been many romantic getaways since you started sleeping with Officer Quinn."

Barry's mouth did a fish imitation, briefly, and Cam went on.

"In fact, I would doubt Mindy should have gone anywhere with you since your last class reunion and your attempts to date Evangeline a few years ago."

"That was not what I was trying to do."

"Well, then why don't you, Mindy, Evangeline, and I sit down and you can explain what it *was* you were trying to do."

"You seem awfully eager to misconstrue everything."

"No. Actually, I'd prefer you were a nice guy. I like Mindy and I adore your daughters. I'd rather you were worthy. But when your current girlfriend is trying to frame your not-yet-ex-wife for murder, it gets sort of hard to see the good."

"Murder? Mindy's been . . . what?"

Cam was half making stuff up now. There was no proof as to who had done the planting of evidence, but no other story made sense and this particular story seemed likely to make the biggest impact. Cam was only partially confident in her judgment of people, but she thought Barry looked legitimately surprised. She wondered what that meant, but she had too much to do to dwell on it, so she spun and walked away.

She spotted Annie across the crowd taking pictures of the girls and made her way over to her.

"So I just suggested to Barry the creep that his girlfriend had framed Mindy. You mind keeping an eye with me? If he's in on it, nothing. If not, he should confront Officer Quinn at some point."

"You sure have fun friends," Annie said.

Cam rolled her eyes, but she knew Annie would help in spite of her sarcasm. She was a reliable friend and probably as curious as Cam was, even if she tried to hide it.

Cam had to find a quiet spot in the trees to gulp down a few bites of supper. She wasn't known for being a diligent eater, but the night they were having made it highly likely that she and her friends would drink heavily after the pageant as they debriefed from the evening.

Debriefed. That sounded official; but when there was a murder involved, it *was* pretty official. That was when Cam realized she'd been so focused on helping Mindy that she hadn't done a thing to help Dylan. She made a note to think about what she'd do as soon as the night was over. For now, she felt like she just had to survive the next few hours.

The talent presentations were as fraught with bickering as they'd been two nights earlier. Cam even heard a mother scolding a grandmother: "You are not to hex that girl!"

Cam wished she could laugh, but she thought the ill-will was genuine.

Lauren and Lizzie both had their chances to sing. Lauren had real talent, but Lizzie seemed to be mostly getting by on cuteness. She could carry a tune, but her voice was still childish — she reminded Cam a little of Shirley Temple.

And then, as Vonnie LaPear, prima donna supreme, began a pretentious scene from *Othello,* Cam saw trouble in the judges' box. Judith Towers-Stevens had pushed Clancy Huggins in the shoulder; obviously the row from the afternoon hadn't been settled. Judith had the decency not to shout, but as she was not supposed to be there — facing backward in front of the judges — it could hardly go unnoticed.

Cam rushed over, jostling people as she hurried by.

"Judith, can't this wait?"

"*She* didn't wait!" Judith pointed to Jessica Benchly.

"And what did she do?" Cam whispered, trying to transmit the message that Judith ought to speak just as quietly.

Judith looked Cam up and down and then huffed. "Well, I'd hardly tell you."

"You're causing a scene. I thought we agreed you needed some time off."

Judith pulled her shoulder away. "I don't need babysitting."

Cam looked around helplessly. The woman *did* need babysitting, and Cam had a show to manage. She finally found Rob's reliable face and pleaded with a glance.

He came over, pulling out all his charm. He suggested he and Judith take a walk and talk. For all Cam knew, Rob would come out of the night with the scoop of the century, but he'd certainly helped her with a potential bomb, so she thought he deserved it.

Things fell back into routine and Cam tried to relax. The smug expression on Jessica Benchly's face, though, was too much to handle. Cam made her way to her.

"So what set Judith off so badly?"

"Serotonin imbalance?"

"That you caused?"

"How could I cause that?"

"Jessica, don't play dumb. Serotonin imbalance was a good answer — smart — sarcastic. But it destroyed your ability to fool me into thinking you're an innocent idiot."

"Telly left some money in a trust for me. Judith won't have it. I just expressed my willingness to display . . . the true Telly if she refused."

"And what was the true Telly? Brutal? Corrupt?"

"No and yes, but what I was really getting at was pretty."

She held up her phone to Cam and flashed a display. Telly Stevens stood with his hands on his hips. He was wearing a bra of sorts with what Cam would call a Tanga panty —

it was more revealing than she cared to look at, but the phone was snatched away before Cam had time to avert her eyes.

Clancy Huggins looked furious. "This was not for your games."

Jessica pouted and Cam stared back and forth.

"Were you blackmailing Telly Stevens?" Cam asked.

"Of course I wasn't!" Jessica said.

Clancy stalked off with Jessica's phone, even though the next break wasn't for ten more minutes.

"How did he . . ." Cam began, but Jessica sat back.

"I'm apparently in trouble. Never mind," Jessica said. She turned away and wouldn't answer any more questions, though she didn't hide her satisfied smile.

Cam had to do some deep breathing, and *still* her thoughts wouldn't sort. After the show, she went behind the stage curtain. She just wanted to hide.

"Tough day?" Dylan asked.

"You could say that."

"What did step-monster blow up over?"

That was funny to Cam. It was how Annie sometimes referred to her father's wife.

"I think to call her step-monster, your

father would have needed to claim you."

"Hey, if the slime fits . . ."

"Jessica is trying to blackmail her for a piece of the inheritance."

Dylan nodded. "Seems the type. Blackmail-worthy material?"

"If step-monster cares about Telly's reputation." Cam kind of liked the word.

"Which she shouldn't. Guy was an ass."

"What I don't get is why . . . if you had means to blackmail somebody into compliance . . . you'd kill them."

"So you think she was the killer?"

"I don't know who I think the killer was."

"Not me, though, right?" Dylan sat next to her. She could smell he'd been under the hot lights in late July, but it was strangely less unpleasant than baseball stink. Their thighs touched and it occurred to Cam that flight might be a smart idea.

"I don't have a reason to think so, no. And I see some suspicious things in other places. I haven't had time to poke too far, but at the very least, I think I could help a reasonable doubt campaign already."

"That's my girl!" He kissed her forehead, then stood.

It was such an odd, grateful, but non-sexual gesture that Cam felt wrong-footed. She'd always felt he might push the boundaries and she'd have to put on the brakes. Instead, at the moment when she might have been tempted to kiss him, he'd passed it by, offering instead familial gratitude.

She rose and headed back out to Rob. He seemed to have gotten Judith calmed and back to the television booth. He gave her a questioning look.

"Where were you?"

"Just getting out of the public eye a little."

"Behind the stage?"

Cam nodded.

"With that Dylan guy?"

Cam hadn't even realized Rob knew who was back there.

"Well . . . he was *there,* but I wasn't *with* him."

"Annie went to the dressing room for the girls," Rob said.

The girls. How had she forgotten that, for the moment, she was responsible for two little people? "Great. Thanks."

Rob hugged her, nuzzling her neck. It felt strangely wrong after the chaste forehead kiss.

"Let's find them. Can Jake meet us? I think we can give him an earful."

"Oh, and he'll love that," Rob said. Cam stared back. He was usually above sarcasm.

"We didn't go looking for it. It just happened." Cam felt defensive. Her work had solved the spring murders — the police had had wrong suspects across the board. It bothered her that Jake would still see her as interfering. Still, sharing with him was likely to get him to share back, so that was something. And it really was *his* job, not *hers,* to solve the murder.

After Rob talked to Jake, he relayed the message they could all meet at Cam's. The girls would need to be put to bed if Mindy didn't arrive soon. He and Jake would handle snacks. Cam nodded and Rob left. Her forehead burned, making her frown. She was too old for baseless crushes. She went to find Annie.

"Ready, Freddie?" Annie asked as Lizzie came out of the dressing area with her stuff.

Lizzie giggled. "I'm not Freddie."

"Are you Betty?" Annie asked.

Lizzie giggled some more. The two played the game for almost five minutes before Lauren emerged.

"I want to see my mom," she said.

"Hopefully soon. She asked if you could stay with me until she sorted this out. Is that okay?" Cam said.

"Can we watch a movie?" Lizzie asked.

"Only until eleven. You have interviews with the judges tomorrow, so we need to be back here by nine in the morning."

Lizzie scrunched her face, but once Lauren agreed, Lizzie yielded.

"Okay. Let's go!"

"Who's an airplane?" Annie shouted, and rushed off toward the car with her arms out to the side, buzzing loudly. Lizzie followed immediately. Lauren looked at Cam, but finally gave in and ran after them. Cam wondered how it was possible Annie wasn't a parent. That brought feelings of guilt, though. Petunia was about to be a parent, and Cam had been the world's most negligent sister and aunt. She resolved to go online soon and order a fabulous aunt gift, whatever that entailed.

Unfortunately, when she crossed her threshold, it was all she could do just to get Lauren and Lizzie washed up and ready for bed.

"When is our mom coming back?" Lizzie said.

"As soon as she can."

"Why can't we stay with Dad?" Lauren asked.

Cam wondered how much to lie so these girls would blame the rules instead of their mother. They were smart, and she didn't want to get caught in the lie. Then again, who was going to negate what Cam said about pageant rules?

"See, the pageant has rules that only the parent who checks you in can take you anywhere, so without your mom to take you to your dad's, I can't do it."

Lizzie nodded, though Lauren looked a little suspicious.

"Do you girls take baths at night?" Cam asked.

"I do," Lizzie said.

"I usually shower in the morning," Lauren said.

"Can Annie help me when I have to rinse my hair?" Lizzie asked.

"I think so." Cam looked at Annie.

Cam started the bath, then settled the girls into her room. The futon was comfortable enough for one night, and she felt better with the girls in a back room rather than the front. She had a small television in her room and got Lauren watching, stopped the bath, and let Lizzie get in.

"You holler when Lizzie needs Annie's help, would you?" she said to Lauren.

Lauren nodded without looking away from the TV. Cam thought maybe her mom limited TV viewing more than Cam was but wasn't sure how else to entertain them. She turned on a small lamp, turned off the overhead, then joined her friends in the front room.

"I am so not ready to parent!" Cam said as she sank onto the futon between Annie and Rob.

Rob looked startled for a minute, but didn't say anything.

"I mean, how does a person find time to deadhead the roses and camellias between a day job and taking care of children?" Cam asked.

Annie and Rob looked at each other and shook their heads, but at least Cam had calmed the parental panic she worried she'd sparked. The three were nearly zombies until Jake tapped the door and let himself in. It had taken months for Cam and Annie to train him that that was just how they did it — friends just entered.

"Chinese!" Annie jumped to life when she saw the bags he was carrying. "Pot stickers?"

"Always." Jake grinned and kissed her.

He put down his array on the chest Cam used for both a coffee table and a footrest. Cam retrieved plates and a mixed six-pack of beer.

"Annie? Lizzie needs you," Lauren said from the door.

Annie gave each of them an unmistakable leer. "Right. I get two of those six pot stickers or somebody dies."

She rose and left. Jake chuckled. Cam was glad Annie had finally found somebody who "got her," but that made her feel the heat of her earlier contact with Dylan — not the sensation she wanted when her boyfriend was serving her ginger chicken.

She fought it and thought instead about the investigation.

"So did you look at who accessed Mindy's hotel room?" she asked Jake.

"Cam, you know I can't . . ."

"What's this?" Rob asked.

Cam had forgotten that Rob was blissfully clueless on her day's details, and as a reporter, he would dig. So she told him her belief about Officer Quinn and the proof that she was involved with Mindy's soon-to-be-ex.

Rob played off Cam perfectly, posturing about how he'd look into it. Cam wondered why she wasn't always so open, but then, this reveal in front of Jake was a huge part of why her strategy was effective. Jake would have sensed the setup otherwise. He finally seemed ready to talk when the doorbell rang. Cam scowled as she rose to answer it.

Mindy and Barry stood at the door together. Cam felt betrayed that Mindy would show Barry where she lived, but she let

Mindy explain.

"Barry came to the police station with our lawyer; he talked them out of holding me longer. That woman would have questioned me all night."

Cam looked at Jake and was glad to be acknowledged, but Mindy kept talking, so their attention went back to her.

"He didn't know I'd been arrested until you told him, Cam. He thinks that woman, Officer Quinn, thought he might be more of a . . . family guy . . . with daughters and no ex, so she framed me. Barry will testify that's how it happened if it comes to that. He's making a statement tomorrow if I just let the girls stay with him for a few days."

"And you trust him?" Cam whispered, knowing Barry could hear her just fine, but at least the girls wouldn't. "Mindy, once he gets the girls, he can go back on his word. Why didn't you have him sign the statement at the police station?"

"I . . . I didn't know we could . . . do that."

Cam felt someone behind her.

"I tell you what. We can still take care of this tonight. Lizzie's in the bath. I can take . . . him . . . to the station, get it drawn up and signed, and then he can take the girls," Jake said.

Cam smiled at him gratefully.

"That's much too late for the girls," Barry argued.

"Then you won't mind leaving them until tomorrow?"

Barry looked like he'd bitten a lemon, but he finally nodded and went with Jake.

"What would I ever do without you?" Mindy asked as she stepped inside.

"Mama!" Lauren ran out and hugged Mindy, followed just a minute later by a still-damp Lizzie.

"Where'd you go?" Lizzie asked.

"I just had some important stuff to do."

"Annie rinsed my hair!" Lizzie announced.

"Well, that was nice of her. Come here. I want to eat you up!" Mindy said.

The girls tackled their mom and then squealed as she hugged and kissed them. Cam doubted Lauren allowed this very often, as she seemed to see herself as a mature ten-year-old. Cam hoped this chapter was over for Mindy — that enough doubt had been cast that she'd be left alone.

That, though, reminded her of Dylan and the cloud over his head. It seemed her friends were always suspected of murder, but she knew it wasn't that she had the wrong friends.

"Are you three hungry?" Cam asked.

"Pot stickers!" The girls leaped.

Annie had one on her fork, but Cam suspected that was the only one she'd get. Rob served the girls a little beef and snow peas and a pot sticker each and they seemed happy. Mindy refused food but looked fairly content.

Jake and Barry returned nearly an hour later. Barry looked a little sour until he saw the girls. And then he packed them and their things into the car.

Jake's grin was triumphant. When they left, he explained.

"I made it clear that if the statement didn't clearly say he was not doing this in exchange for custody and would not use it to seek custody, that it wouldn't hold up. So right in his statement is a sentence stating that Mindy has had custody for the entire separation and this incident does nothing to change facts related to custody."

"Oh!" Mindy's jaw fell and tears followed. She swooped in and hugged him.

"I never would have thought of any of that," she said.

"Yeah, well . . . one of my sisters is a divorce lawyer, and I've learned that in a town like Roanoke, most ugly legal stuff is domestic, so I just had a hunch."

"You're wonderful. Thank you!"

"You can cite this if, after the contest, he

gives you a hard time about giving the girls back."

Mindy's tears fell full speed now and Cam handed her a napkin.

"I'll be grateful forever. Thank you. But . . . I should probably get back to the hotel."

"Should I call you a cab?" Annie asked.

"I can drive you," Rob said.

It was a good solution. Cam hoped he'd get a good detail or two for the corrupt police woman article.

"You coming back?" she asked.

"If you save me some beef and snow peas," he said.

Cam looked in the boxes and then closed one symbolically and winked.

CHAPTER 12

Cam woke up with her brain in active Dylan-saving mode, and for the first time she realized the easiest way to clear him wasn't to find the killer, but to prove he didn't have means or opportunity. Sure, he had motive, but she believed he didn't know about that until after the fact. She would try to establish where he had been to prove he couldn't have committed the crime.

She looked at Rob, sound asleep, and realized guiltily she'd been out like a light before he'd gotten back the night before. The minute he'd taken Mindy, Jake and Annie had vanished, and Cam had put everything into the fridge. She'd rinsed dishes, but uncharacteristically left them in the sink. She was exhausted. She'd only brushed her teeth and stripped to her underthings before falling into bed and almost immediately to sleep.

She regretted her thoughts about Dylan.

Rob was a good guy. The problem was, Dylan *wasn't* the bad guy he had first seemed. And he was currently being framed by the woman married to the man he hadn't even known was his father.

Cam showered, making mental notes as she did. If she could establish a certain time line, with backup evidence, of course, then Dylan would be exonerated and she could be free of him. Proving him innocent would finally close the door, and she could forget about him.

The pageant day devolved into chaos only moments after she arrived. It became very clear, very fast, that the girls weren't capable of delivering their green presentations in three minutes. Each girl was too proud of her hard work on water-preserving landscape, composting, pest control, or multiuse to give up part of the content. Cam watched for an hour before it occurred to her to just record them, judge in the afternoon, and then have the five finalists deliver five-minute presentations that night.

"You're a genius!" Nell said. "Why I didn't have you plan this with me in the first place, I don't know."

"We can put a paragraph for each girl on your website, too — maybe you'd get their local support to visit and they could all feel like they won something."

"Exactly! It's perfect! In fact . . . could we make each girls' video available?"

"Oh, of course . . . as long as parents approve."

As the green recordings were winding up, Cam spotted Dylan. The planting was now completely done, so she thought he must have had the late guarding shift, which merged into his evening lighting duties.

She rushed out to meet him, admiring how cheerful the begonias made the grounds. "I've been working on your case," she sputtered. "So where were you in the . . . let's call it eighteen hours before Telly Stevens died? I saw him alive that morning, but it probably happened with his first drink of the day. If I can establish where you were the whole time, that solves all your problems."

"Cam, you don't want to do this."

"Why don't I?"

He approached her, close enough that his whisper burned her ear. "You won't like the answer," he said quickly, his lips brushing her earlobe.

Cam's brain promptly emptied. Finally, though, she took a shaky breath and found her voice. "Do you want me to prove you didn't do it or not?"

"I didn't. It shouldn't be that hard. Just find who did."

"It seems a whole lot easier to prove you couldn't have."

"Well, there was some time I maybe could have been all by my lonesome, driving from one place I shouldn't be to another. So why don't you just find the real killer?"

He walked away from Cam then and she stared at his back. Was it possible he was using her to try to prove his innocence when he was actually guilty? But she didn't think so. Why didn't he want her to know where he was, then? Up to something illegal? *With* somebody he shouldn't have been?

Deep down, she didn't believe he was the killer, but it was frustrating to have to start over. She headed back to the Arts Commission building to try to sort her thoughts. She was tempted to leave it to the police after all, even if they didn't seem all that good at finding real killers. But abandoning Dylan and Mindy to the Roanoke PD didn't see very promising after her last experience.

"Oh, honey, your brain's heavy."

"What?" Cam stared back at Nell Norton, not understanding what she meant.

"Sit."

Cam obeyed and Nell brought her a glass of sweet tea from a pitcher she'd requested when they were filming. It wasn't icy anymore, but it was still chilled and Cam drank gratefully. She felt like she hadn't had a break all day.

"My daddy used to say I had a heavy brain when I looked preoccupied. You just look like the world's sitting on your shoulders, and I would have thought the hard part of this contest for you was over."

"It's the murder. Two people I know have been questioned, and I'm sure neither did it, but it looks like it because of the evidence."

"What evidence?"

"One had a bad argument with Telly the morning . . ."

"Oh, honey, everybody had an argument with Telly. The man was a beast. I'm sorry your friend wasn't wise enough to do it privately."

"Did you have an argument with him?"

"Several, but they were small — you may have noticed I'm particular about how things are. Where my business and reputation are concerned, I'm insistent. I mean, the man knew gardening, but you know I do, too, and he kept trying to give me suggestions for my little contest. What that man *didn't* know was kids need some freedom — he kept trying to steer me. I suspect he just liked telling people what to do, and I wouldn't stand for it."

Cam wondered how much to share. "Turns out the other friend is his son . . ."

"Son? Now there's a twist."

"Telly knew about it — mentioned Dylan in his will. The son didn't know anything until the police started questioning him."

"That's a horrible way to learn about your daddy." Nell, though, began to smile. "Who benefits if he's out of the picture?"

Cam smiled. "Sort of what I was thinking." While she'd considered this, she was glad someone else had come to the same conclusion.

"You probably never had a horrible relative try to manipulate money away from another. You're lucky if that's so." Nell smiled and patted Cam's leg. "Now, I need to get to judging these presentations. Only five present tonight, so I have my work cut out for me."

"Good luck," Cam said as she rose, freshly committed to investigating Judith Towers-Stevens, the person who'd already looked most likely to Cam, and who'd just had her motive reinforced. It was the last thing the pageant needed — for the television producer to be accused of murder, but the show only had two more nights, so Cam doubted she could do much harm before it was done.

She went back outside and found Dylan. He was going through the garden and was watering and nipping off the flowers that were done. The once-a-day sprinkler was not adequate for these new plants in the heat wave they were having.

"So have you seen the will?" she asked.

"What?" He stood straight and turned to look at her. He must not have heard her coming.

"Telly Stevens's last will and testament. Have you seen it?"

"I got a copy in my truck. It didn't make much sense to me."

"But you got something? I mean, you're inheriting?"

"Yeah — 'bout a hundred thousand, but it's in some trust — that was where it got confusing. It will pay me ten thousand a year, but there are exceptions for some stuff — a house, education . . . I'm thinking a house sounds good, but I need to establish the rest of the income — you know — work a job that isn't all under the table for a while."

"I imagine if you went to jail for murder, you wouldn't get that?"

"No clue. I didn't murder him."

"I know. I'm looking at why somebody might frame you."

"Oh! You think his wife?"

"That's what I'm thinking."

"I like that thinking. She's nasty, that's for sure."

Cam had seen a little of Judith Towers-Stevens being nasty of late, but all of it had been directed at Clancy Huggins or Jessica Benchly. She wondered how large a chunk of the total pie a hundred thousand *was*? Telly Stevens had been a television figure since before Cam was born. Surely he was worth at least a million or two. Then again, it might be tied up in property or investments. Maybe Judith was loath to give up cash.

The penultimate pageant night finally went into setup mode. Cam ran around throwing scathing looks at mothers who were too demanding. She gave gentle reassurances to girls and checked on props and the volunteers who would be escorting people to their places. Finally, she decided to check on the status in the amphitheater. What she found stunned her.

Dylan was at the lighting controls, and standing behind him, caressing him with some familiarity, was Jessica Benchly. What would Telly Stevens's mistress be doing with his son? All the better to frame him?

Cam watched from the shadows for a minute, but it only made her feel dirty. Finally, she backed up several paces and approached making a lot more noise.

When she reached them, Jessica was back in the shadows — not hiding, but watching from a more appropriate distance.

"Everything set, Dylan?" Cam asked.

"Looks like it."

"Jessica! I didn't know you had stagehand aspirations?"

She laughed pleasantly enough. "Not stagehand. Acting. But the theater groups locally all say if you're willing to pitch in, you have a better shot at being chosen. I was just trying to learn something."

"I bet," Cam said. She didn't think Jessica heard, but Dylan raised an eyebrow. Cam doubted any local theater group would make a former Miss Virginia work lighting before she got an acting role, though, so the story was fishy.

"I need to get to work. Can you find your seat okay, Miss Benchly?" Cam asked.

"Of course I can," she said, and went

through the curtain.

Cam had to fight herself very hard to keep from asking, but she managed. It was none of her business. Dylan and Jessica were both free to see who they liked and she was *not* free to worry about it. It was curious, though, to think that Jessica Benchly, who'd most recently been seen with Clancy Huggins and Telly Stevens, was now chasing the son of one of them, one who'd been left a pretty good-sized chunk of change.

Cam left the amphitheater ready to dive into the night's production, only to be nearly tackled by Hilary Sweeny, Judith Towers-Stevens's assistant.

"Have you seen Judith? She was adamant we not start without her, but she was supposed to be here an hour ago."

"I thought she'd OKed you to do those duties . . ."

"That was for one day only. She called today with new instructions."

"Well I really think she needs some time off," Cam said. "We have to start without her if she isn't here. You know how to do all this, don't you?"

"Of course I do, but . . ."

"Look. The FCC fines groups who don't air what they say — you're saving your network a lot of money by covering for your boss." Cam felt a little guilty playing on the girl's insecurities, though what she said was true.

"Right! But . . . we're behind. Do you know anyone . . ." Hilary looked over Cam's shoulder and said, "No! Never mind! I'm set."

Cam shrugged and decided to take her word for it.

Hilary sped toward Dylan, and Cam hoped there'd be enough time to not have to improvise. That's when Kyle Lance arrived with Jimmy Meares. It was the first time Cam had been glad to see either of them.

"Mr. Lance! Welcome! You're opening tonight?"

Kyle looked at Jimmy, who nodded, then Kyle nodded himself. "When am I on?"

"Talk to Dylan about sound now, but Evangeline Patrick should introduce you in fifteen or twenty minutes."

He looked at his watch. "Got it."

Finally, Judith rushed in, shouting. Cam was too far away to hear what it was about. It looked like poor Hilary was on the receiving end of most of it, though Cam thought Judith owed Hilary a lot for stepping up when she'd been so late. Late, though, triggered another item on her checklist. Cam realized she hadn't seen Evangeline yet, so she went into the library staging area. Evangeline had her own space in what appeared to normally be a book-repair room, but at least it was private.

Mr. Patrick was with her, in a black suit, ready to walk his wife to the stage.

"Cammi! Are they ready for us?"

"Just about. I just wanted to make sure you were set."

"As I'll ever be," Evangeline said from behind a curtain.

Cam wondered how a local celebrity like Evangeline could still get nervous, but then the stalker stuff with Barry and the dead judge *had* made for a rather stressful week.

"Have you seen Nell?" Cam asked.

"She knows she's on after Kyle. She went upstairs to check something. The Wi-Fi connection is better," Evangeline said as she opened the curtain; she looked stunning.

Cam had to smile. A woman in her sixties had chosen her waiting spot based on Wi-Fi reception — the world was changing. Then again, Nell had a lot to keep track of. Running a business across five states was no small feat.

Cam double-checked that she had Nell's number in her phone in case she needed to reach the woman quickly. She'd text her a reminder when Kyle finished his first song. He was doing three at the beginning tonight and then six spread over the following night.

Cam and Neil flanked Evangeline as she finally emerged from the library to start the event.

Out of nowhere, the woman who'd been vandalizing events all week leaped, squirting the three of them from a super-soaker water gun.

"Rob!" Cam shouted.

She hoped he was near enough that his speed could catch this woman, as she took off after splattering the three of them.

"Oh, heavens! Is it . . ." Evangeline said, staring at the front of her dress in horror.

Cam looked, then she touched it and sniffed. "Just paint, but I know it looks bad. Here, I have an idea."

She ran through the crowd to the stage, people staring at her. "Dylan!"

He came over and frowned. "Have you been slaughtering hogs?"

"Never mind me. Evangeline has just been splattered with red paint. It's on royal blue. Any way to choose lighting that makes it look arty? At least not white light . . ."

"Blue will make the red look purple, and it is mostly complementary anyway, though sort of . . . romance lighting . . . but it would work."

"Perfect! That's good!"

She leaned out of the curtain and gave Evangeline a thumbs-up and then ran back to find Rob and the woman. He'd tackled her in the already mourning lilies and the newly planted begonias, though thankfully, they were behind the stage so it wouldn't be visible. Todd, the security guard from the Arts Commission, had seen enough that he'd put her in cuffs and called the police. The woman's super-soaker lay on the ground at her feet.

"Why would you do this?" Cam asked.

"You're exploiting these poor girls!" she said. "Beauty pageants make everyone but the winner feel bad about herself!"

"But they aren't even judged on beauty. It's talent, poise, personality . . ."

"Ha! Those last two . . . you think those aren't about beauty?"

"No. I don't," Cam said. She hoped what she said was true. Rob looked uncomfortable.

They edged away, leaving the woman to the security guard.

Annie approached them with a large grin. "Colorful side piece."

Cam rolled her eyes, wishing she had the

leeway to go home and change.

"No. Seriously! I got pictures of her and she looks insane. And I got Mr. Patrick and Evangeline in the lighting — good idea, by the way. Almost looks planned. I'll get one of her in normal light when she's done — I think it speaks for the brilliance behind the scene — making lemonade of lemons."

Cam had stopped following Annie when she mentioned "good idea," and instead focused on the stage. Kyle was singing and she realized the periphery of the park was packed. They'd sold most of the seats, but there was no way to close everything in, so it appeared all the ten-year-olds in Roanoke had convinced people to bring them downtown for this — a few free Kyle Lance songs.

It wasn't Cam's thing, but she appreciated the tween phenomenon for what it was. After the first song, she texted Nell to let her know it was probably time to make her way to the stage.

"I'm almost there," the reply came, and Cam spotted her. She was stately and had no red paint anywhere. Perhaps she'd been the smart one.

A minute later, Cam spotted Claire, one of the volunteers, leading a group of girls to the front of the stage. She didn't think they knew it meant they were green finalists, but she was pleased to see Lizzie skipping at the back of the group.

Kyle Lance sang one more song, blew a kiss at the little girls, and left the stage, setting off shrieks from the hundreds of girls who had gathered just to see him. He had a limousine behind the shell, and security had held a path. They made their way to the Patrick Henry, where Cam knew he'd be escorted up to a suite of food and entertainment. It was a bit much, but he'd agreed to do this show at a fraction of his regular price because he was from Virginia and it was a warm, fuzzy public relations thing.

Cam was surprised at the presence Nell Norton had on stage once Evangeline had introduced her. She could have been the Queen Mother, at least to the extent Cam had seen royalty on TV. She was proud but pleased, smiling down on the girls and the crowd.

"As a part of my participation in this event, and in exchange for my support as CEO of Nelly's Nurseries, the Little Miss Begonia Pageant has indulged me in a little side competition. You see . . . children are more creative than the rest of us. And so I thought I would offer a separate one-thousand-dollar scholarship for the best presentation of a green gardening idea. All the girls entered, and you are about to meet the five finalists, all of whom have already won a hundred-dollar gift card to their nearest Nelly's."

The audience clapped and a few of the girls shrieked, realizing why they had been led to the stage.

"Girls, do you think you can remember your talks from this afternoon? Two of you had posters, and those are here."

All the girls nodded with varying degrees of confidence.

"Okay, first up is Lily Andrews."

Lily, a timid blonde girl, rose and walked up the stairs. Nell calmed her and then whispered something that made Lily giggle. Lily looked out at the audience and smiled and began her presentation about keeping pigs as pets. She said the pigs could eat the weeds and scraps, and that pig poo could fertilize the garden. There was a lot of appreciative laughter and indulgent smiling.

The next presentation had to do with edible flowers and pretty vegetables: doubling up space to both enjoy the sight, but also then eat what was grown, saving money and improving a house's carbon footprint.

The next two presentations were more about composting-related issues, obviously researched by smart girls and well done, but not as entertaining. And then Lizzie was called on stage. Several audience members made cooing noises — Lizzie wasn't just the youngest contestant, she was by far the smallest.

She began the presentation, "You like toads, right? And bugs eat your garden!" Cam knew she had them right from the start. She couldn't help but grin through the whole presentation, and spotted Mindy and Barry actually sitting together and smiling.

On impulse, she looked around. Officer Quinn was on duty near the fringe of the crowd, presumably to make sure the Kyle Lance groupies didn't get unruly. She was staring at Mindy and Barry, scowling. Being on duty meant she had not been disciplined. Cam wondered what the process was, and if it meant she was innocent or that the proof hadn't been strong enough.

As Lizzie finished, the crowd gave a standing ovation and then Evangeline took over to introduce the next feature — the first group of girls performing their respective fitness routines.

Cam's phone vibrated.

"Hello?" she whispered, not wanting to disturb her neighbors. It was Dylan.

"Miz Harris, I've been trying to get the

step-monster for ten minutes. She's not picking up and I think she wanted each of these fitness groups in different lighting, but I don't know the order."

"I'll find her." Cam didn't look forward to it, but she knew it was an important decision.

She headed to the television control station. The cameramen were off in various directions to get better angles, but Judith Towers-Stevens should have been manning the box with the monitors so she could direct the others. The box was more a tent of sorts, with a window at the front and enclosed on the other sides, to keep the audience and heat out, along with the commotion. Cam reached the window and looked for her. She wasn't there.

She crossed the box to the door and entered to see if there was any clue where the woman had gone and almost tripped over her.

"Crap."

Cam knelt to feel her throat and saw the same foam she'd seen from Telly Stevens. She was sure Judith was dead.

She called 9-1-1, explaining the crowd and her preference not to cause a panic, since the woman appeared already dead. They said they'd send a policeman and an ambulance, but a medic would come in alone initially.

When she hung up, she called Jake. She was far more comfortable with her ability to continue this event if a police officer who would communicate with her was involved.

Finally, she flagged Rob and had him run out to tell Hilary they had a problem. The filming would still need directing and she was the one best able to do it.

Unfortunately, Rob came back ten minutes later and said the head cameraman was on his way. Hilary was nowhere to be found.

CHAPTER 13

The cameramen began a round of what looked like musical cameras. By the time the head man arrived, Jake had, too, so an argument ensued over the cameraman's need to go into the control booth. Jake insisted it was a crime scene and could not be touched, but the cameraman swore he needed access to the equipment to run the show.

"What do you really need?" Jake asked.

"Two of the laptops and the master headset."

Jake nodded, put on gloves and retrieved them, setting the man to the side of the box with the computers. He had them on chairs facing him and the man looked thoroughly annoyed.

"This is hardly ideal," he said.

"Your boss is dead. Probably not a good time to complain about working conditions," Jake said. Cam glared, hoping no one in the crowd had overheard.

The man frowned, nodded, and began checking in with the other camera people. They were into the final fitness routine when Hilary Sweeny returned with a cardboard tray that held two coffees and two pasta boxes from a local takeout place.

"Wh . . . what happened?" she asked.

"Where've you been?" Cam asked.

"Judith asked me to pick up supper — she was in a right rage when she finally got here, so I didn't question her. I went over to 24 Church Avenue for Italian. Will you please let me take Judith her food? It will get cold."

"I don't think Judith will care," Cam said. "Seems she already ate."

"What?"

"You need to wait for Jake."

As Cam said his name, he came out and placed a crime tape strip across the entry.

"Jake, this is Hilary Sweeny. She's Judith Towers-Stevens's executive assistant."

Jake repeated Cam's question about where she'd been, then asked when she'd left.

"When the little girls started that green thing. I was sure I'd be back before they were done, but it's Friday night, so it took longer."

"And Ms. Towers-Stevens was fine when you left?"

"Well . . . fine for a recently widowed woman — a little terse maybe. Isn't she fine now?" She eyed the crime tape nervously.

Cam wondered why she'd tempered "right rage" down to "terse." Maybe the rage had been directed at the assistant and she was worried there would be repercussions if other people knew.

"She's dead," Jake said.

Cam wished she'd thought more carefully how this would go down. Jake's bluntness led to Hilary's shriek and everybody in the audience looking their way just as the medic finally arrived.

Cam pushed Evangeline's speed dial, knowing the crowd would panic with no information. By the time the routine was done, Evangeline stepped calmly to the microphone.

"Just so nobody panics, I've just been informed there's been a medical incident. It's being handled. The show will continue unless we receive word we can't. All we ask of you is to stay seated unless the medical team asks you to move so they can maneuver. This is critical for somebody's safety."

Spin was a beautiful thing. The crowd relaxed immediately. There were still curious eyes, but they gave the two men with the stretcher room to move and didn't seem to have noticed the police officer and medical examiner making their way to the box. Cam closed the flap over the window opening before they began taking pictures. The flash would have been hard to hide or explain.

Things then went smoothly up until the poise routines were over. At that point, Jake called Evangeline and Cam died a little inside. She could hear Evangeline through the phone.

"Are you sure?"

Evangeline finally announced that the police had asked to document everyone there and requested everyone to stay in their seats until someone took names and phone numbers.

"Why? Was there a crime?" somebody yelled. It was a reasonable question.

"They don't know at this point," Evangeline said smoothly, "but if it was, they need to be able to reconstruct details. We really appreciate your cooperation. I wish Kyle Lance was here to sing for you, but in his absence, maybe I can sing you a tune or two."

The crowd clapped enthusiastically, and Evangeline called Mr. Patrick to the piano. It had never occurred to Cam that he played, but a lot of society gentlemen had cultural talents, so it shouldn't have surprised her. Another bond between the glamorous Evangeline and her much older husband.

Evangeline sang Nancy Sinatra's "These Boots Were Made for Walkin'," and then Carole King's "Natural Woman" to an enthusiastic crowd before they judged that about half the crowd had been released and the rest might believe they wouldn't be there all night.

Cam remained preoccupied. She'd been ready to pin Telly Stevens's murder on his wife, but who would want them both dead? Aside from Dylan, anyway . . .

The two arguments Cam had witnessed, first between Telly and Clancy, then Judith and Clancy, kept nagging at Cam. To her knowledge, Clancy was the only person who'd actually argued with both of them. It was hard to picture Clancy as a murderer, but the evidence presented itself as such.

Then again, both arguments had been *about* Jessica Benchly, and Cam thought she was a much easier suspect to consider.

As Cam's mind wandered, she decided to find Dylan and make sure he knew what was going on. When she reached backstage, however, Dylan and Jessica seemed to be rather entwined, so she snuck away, fighting the feeling in her gut that she knew shouldn't be there. She had no business being jealous of who Dylan saw.

Sneaking back off the stage, she found Annie. She was glad to see Annie had put her camera back in her bag.

"Looks like Jake will be tied up all night," Cam said. "Chocolate therapy help?"

"Better than nothing, though preferably someplace with a red wine rack."

Cam frowned. She wasn't a true connoisseur of either chocolate or red wine, preferring a custard or something a bit tart for dessert, and a much lighter wine than Annie would choose. She knew her friend, though, and where Annie was concerned, dark chocolate and red wine had a certain alchemy.

"I'll find Rob." His taste buds were more like her best friend's than her own where wine and chocolate were concerned.

Unfortunately, when she found him, he, too, was engaged. "No way. Murder number two? I can't leave!" He was shadowing Jake. Cam felt annoyed with men in general, and men who had to keep up with criminal events, specifically.

"Come on!" she grumbled. Annie followed her. They headed toward the Patrick

Henry and went into the bar. She was surprised the piano music she always heard in the lobby didn't come from there, as she'd assumed. She asked at the bar before they sat down if they could get dessert as well as drinks.

"Matter of fact," the bartender said, "I got a cheesecake, plain or chocolate, and brownies."

"Perfect. One of each cheesecake. A merlot with the chocolate one and a white zinfandel with the plain. Over there." She pointed to where Annie was sitting.

"Excellent choice!" It was exaggerated, but as the man was about sixty, it was also cute. Cam joined Annie.

"So Mindy probably didn't off Mrs. What's-her-name," Annie began.

"No. Telly Stevens, either. In fact, I think Barry's current girlfriend is trying to get the ex out of the way through framing."

"No!"

"Seriously." Cam explained the Officer Quinn evidence and the scowling she'd seen earlier that evening.

"That's awful! I mean . . . I never liked Mindy, but being framed because somebody else wants your loser ex? That's too low for anybody."

"Not to mention her kids," Cam said.

"Yeah, those girls are great. Did you see Lizzie tonight? The audience was eating out of her hand!"

Cam laughed. Annie's grudge was based on Mindy's history of materialism and snobbery. Annie didn't carry it over to the girls.

"So . . ." Annie changed the subject. "Who's killing people?"

"Heck if I know."

"I know you don't *know,* but you *did* solve the last one. What do you think?"

"Until tonight, I had Judith Towers-Stevens nailed for the murder of her husband. You can see how accurate *that* probably was."

"Unless this was a revenge killing."

Cam frowned at Annie. It was a fresh angle but it seemed implausible.

"Think about Telly. Who would avenge him?"

"Rabid fan?"

"Who would have to be close enough to know who did it, yet delusional enough to respond with murder instead of calling the police with evidence?"

"Okay, unlikely. What about someone who loved him?"

"Like who? He was horrible."

"Right. And horrible men never find saps

to love them." Annie's sarcasm was bitter. She'd loved a horrible man at one point.

"I just can't think who would kill over it."

"I still think you need to ask around about who might have been 'so in love.' " As Annie sighed and fell over in her booth seat as their wine and cheesecake were delivered. She sat back up quickly, looking embarrassed.

"I just wish the most logical answer wasn't somebody I wished it wasn't."

"I'm glad I haven't had any of my wine yet, or I might not have followed that. No, wait. I still didn't follow that. You have a suspect?"

"No! It's not him. But the motivation *looks* like him."

"Who?"

Cam felt ashamed for caring, and Annie figured out it was about her crush.

"Why would Dylan care about Telly Stevens?"

"Dylan is Telly Stevens's son."

Annie gasped. Her jaw dropped, though she had the decency to then cough briefly into her napkin and take a large drink, as if she'd just had a crumb in her throat. When she recovered, she asked, "Okay, so do they think this is daddy issues?"

"They seem to be pursuing inheritance."

"What was he getting before Telly died?"

"No clue. Nothing, I think. He didn't even know who his father was until the police told him. So he had no reason to think he'd get anything from him, dead or alive."

"Ouch. That sucks. I'll have to spank Jake for that. Both telling *him* rudely and *not* telling me. A double spanking."

Cam smirked. Leave it to Annie to provide the necessary comic relief.

"So how did you learn about all this?"

"Benny brought him over the other night because of the questions."

"That and the fact that you want him," Annie said.

"I do not!"

Annie raised an eyebrow.

"Fine! So I want him like I want Sam Winchester from *Supernatural* — bad boy, good heart, *not* a good idea — not *real,* even. I would never cheat on Rob."

"I know you wouldn't, even for Sam Winchester, which is totally *insane* if you want my opinion — and I *like* Rob. I just . . . have noticed a certain mood . . . tendencies . . . attitude . . ."

"Shut up."

"See. That's proof. For you, 'shut up' is profanity." Annie pointed at Cam with her fork.

"Annie, for the sake of our friendship, can we please drop Dylan."

"Fine. Not the wife. Not the son. Who else?"

"Business might have been likely, but not with the wife dead, too. It seems more personal. Has to be about relationships," Cam said.

Annie stared at her like she'd grown a third eye and then downed her last taste of wine.

"Hater? Mistress? Insane fan?"

"All possible." Cam frowned. "There were a few pictures of him in women's underwear. Jessica Benchly had them . . ."

"Oh, now that's an interesting twist. Who could have thought he had that in him? But it doesn't seem smart to kill someone she was trying to blackmail."

"No, but I wonder if there's a story," Cam said.

"There undoubtedly *is* a story. The question is, will anyone tell it?"

Cam nodded. There was no disagreeing there. She was sure *somebody* would talk, but finding who was something that needed careful consideration.

"The people who know about those pictures are Jessica Benchly and Clancy Huggins. Clancy was mad when Jessica tried to

show them to me. And there were arguments between Clancy and both Telly and
Judith."

"So that looks like Clancy's responsible,"
Annie said.

"Do either of those men seem like guys
who'd get into ladies' underwear and take
pictures together?" Cam asked.

"No. That's not what I mean. I mean,
maybe Clancy set him up."

"But if he had the goods on him, he
wouldn't need to kill him — like you said,"
Cam argued.

"No, but then Jessica got ahold of them
and was talking. Heck, maybe it was self-
defense!"

"Self-defense by poison?" Cam sighed.
Poison was a plotter's . . . erm . . . poison.
And Judith appeared to have died by poison,
too.

"Okay, switch modes. Who knows plants
well enough to poison by oleander?" Cam
said.

Annie frowned. "You'd know better than
me, wouldn't you?"

"What do you mean?"

"The Garden Society?" Annie said as if
Cam was dim.

"Well, duh, but no! There's no motive
there!"

"How do we know that?"

"Let's look for somebody else first."

"The nursery lady would know."

"Nell. That's true, but I can't see a motive in any direction . . . but . . ." The suggestion had given Cam an idea.

She pulled out her laptop. Annie rolled her eyes and flagged the waiter for another glass of wine. As it arrived, Cam finally said, "Yes!"

"Enlighten me?" Annie asked.

"The V-SCAMP website has a biography page for past contestants. Almost all the contestants since 2000 are here. Prior to that, it is mostly the top three. But in the bio are interests. I can see who gardens."

"Okay, first . . . V-SCAMP? Nice! Next . . . assuming the killer is a past contestant."

"Well, it's not his wife."

"It could be a lot of people. Even . . . what's his name . . . Benny would know this."

"Benny wouldn't commit murder — certainly not for somebody else."

"He might have had a hypothetical conversation with somebody about plants that kill."

That was true enough. Cam didn't like the idea at all, because it made it possible both Benny and Dylan had had a role in these murders. She'd believed Dylan about

257

not knowing who his father was until after the murder, but how easy was it to lie?

"Look, I don't wanna poop on your party," Annie said, her serious tone cracking Cam into laughter, "but I have another sixteen-hour day tomorrow."

"Why are you open on Saturday?"

"Downtown art festival. I can't *not* be open. I can only be open eleven to three, but there is still the baking that has to get started at eight and then this silly pageant thing in the evening. You need anything that doesn't require time?"

"A hug?"

"Done!" Annie threw herself at Cam. Cam was five inches taller, but the two weighed about the same. This gave Annie an advantage in body slamming, so Cam toppled with Annie over her.

"Um . . . do you two need anything else? A third, maybe?" the waiter asked.

Annie sat up laughing and held a hand up for a high five.

Cam sat up, mortified.

Annie laughed for another five minutes after the waiter had been sent away, Cam leering at her. Finally through, Annie rose.

"We have work tomorrow. Are you coming or not?"

Cam had hoped to hear from Rob, but

hadn't, so she rose and followed Annie out to the car.

It hadn't meant anything to Annie, so Cam hadn't pursued it at the table, but when Cam got home, she pulled up the list of past contestants again. One year in particular sounded alarm bells. Jessica Benchly had edged out Olivia Quinn to win the Miss Roanoke pageant among teens in the late '80s. That same year, Nelly's Nursery had offered a scholarship very like the one they were currently offering, and Jessica Benchly, pageant winner, had won that, too. That meant at least Jessica had some gardening knowledge.

Cam wanted to see what Nell remembered. The woman seemed a standard "early to bed, early to rise" sort, so Cam dropped an email to her that she'd like to take her to breakfast. She expected to have her call in the morning, but the woman surprised her by ringing her cell immediately.

"I heard about how you solved that last murder case," Nell said without preamble. "Do you think I know something about this one?"

"Ms. Norton! You're up!"

"Who could sleep when a second murder happens at a children's pageant?"

That was a fair point, and Cam mumbled something to that effect. "You know, the thing is . . . that last murder . . . I was only able to figure it out because I also collected a lot of information that didn't end up mattering. You don't know what's important until the pattern emerges. So I don't know if you know anything important or not, but I hoped maybe we could have breakfast together so I could just check out a few things."

"I'd rather have a few glasses of wine with you now, if that works. Tomorrow is the only day this week I might sleep in, and it just helps me to think there is no alarm to answer to."

"Of course! Should I meet you in the Hotel Roanoke bar?"

"How about Table 50 — fewer prying eyes. The hotel is hosting so many pageant folks . . ."

Cam understood. It was true; they had a better chance of privacy elsewhere.

"That sounds perfect. Twenty minutes?"

Cam wished it wasn't so humid, though the night-blooming jasmine she passed cheered her — a sure sign of a careful gardener, as it really was too fragile for a zone seven. A midnight walk should have woken and refreshed her, but mostly it just made her feel damp. She was relieved to step into the air-conditioning of Table 50.

Table 50 was a nice restaurant, one of the few favorites she and Annie agreed was cool. Cam loved the artistic presentation and Annie liked that they purchased the majority of ingredients locally, much of it from the farmer's market practically outside the door. Sadly, the men in their lives didn't quite appreciate these points because portions were attractive, rather than generous. So it was usually a girls-only splurge. Cam looked around. It was dark colors and low light, but still looked and sounded cheerful, containing a mix of date couples and happy larger groups. It didn't look like Nell was here yet.

After about ten minutes, Nell walked in with her husband. He headed to the bar to take a stool as Nell joined Cam at her table.

"Are you sure he doesn't want to join us?"

"Quite sure. We've been married forty-three years, and he is prone to unwanted advice, which only creates friction. We've learned when a subject is touchy we should approach it on our own, and then share once a decision is made. It's made thirty-seven of our forty-three years significantly easier. I'm just too hardheaded to want advice, and he is too opinionated not to give it. He does have a fairly peaceful response, though, once a thing is already done."

At first Cam thought this dynamic made them sound poorly matched, but the more she thought about it, the more it seemed they'd done well to figure out such a simple solution.

"That never would have occurred to me."

"No. It's the very desperately arrived at conclusion of two people who love each other but can't manage to live together. It took quite a while to figure it out. Now, what are these questions you wanted to dig into?"

The waiter brought over a bottle of wine, even though nobody had checked on their table. Cam and Nell looked to Mr. Norton, and he smiled and waved at them. It was a cabernet sauvignon, drier than Cam would have chosen, but it was probably best if Cam only sipped, and this would ensure she did.

"How many of these pageants have you done?" Cam asked.

"Oh, dozens over the years, but not very many Young Misses. I know it's the first time in Virginia — the other two were in Georgia."

"Well, I'm actually only interested in

Virginia, but the age of the contestants doesn't matter. Are there people helping with the pageant this year who you remember — either who have helped before or participated in other pageants?"

"Oh, honey, I don't think you've met a postmenopausal memory! I recognize a lot of people, but that may not have anything to do with pageants. Can you ask anything more specific?"

"Okay, let's start at the supper party, and we can go person by person. The judges — Telly, Clancy, and Barbara — had you met any of them before?"

"Well, I'd met all of them, though I only consider Clancy a friend. He and Byron were fraternity brothers many years ago, so I've known him since I was pinned to Byron in college."

Cam definitely wasn't comfortable following that answer with the ladies' underwear line of questioning, so she went the other direction. "And Clancy's date, Jessica Benchly?"

"Oh, I've met Jessica separately on several occasions."

"Since she wasn't formally with the pageant, I wasn't sure where to find out about her."

"Well, to start, she *should* be formally with

263

the pageant. She was Miss Virginia at some point. It was a year I offered my scholarship and she won that, too!"

That last piece was one Cam actually knew, but she felt it was important to let Nell establish herself as the expert.

"And was that . . . stiff competition, or pretty easy to judge?"

"Easier than today — the age range in these younger girls seems so much bigger, and it's hard to tell what is judging on merit, what is merit for age, and what is strictly cuteness of presentation."

"The toad idea?" Cam asked, without revealing she knew Lizzie.

"Wasn't that fantastic?" Nell chuckled and took a drink.

"So the year Jessica was in, this woman was in, too. Do you remember her?" Cam pushed the picture she'd printed from the pageant website of Olivia Quinn at Nell.

Nell frowned and pulled a penlight from her purse to look closer. "I do know her. She threw quite a fit, if I remember right, at losing to Jessica, both rounds. In the green scholarship, she lost for a great idea that was already being implemented — before the internet, see — but she may very well have thought she invented it, composting kitchen debris — something I learned about from West Coast gardeners in the mid-'80s — and I think she was third runner-up in the main contest."

"She's also a police officer who has been investigating this murder case . . ." Cam said.

"Is she? I don't think I've seen her since. I doubt I'd recognize her."

Cam didn't think there was a reason to mention the romance with Barry Blankenship. It didn't really seem relevant at the moment. She was also a little confused. If Jessica were involved, she would have thought Jessica and Olivia were working together because of Olivia's apparent role in framing Mindy, but this made it seem more like they would be rivals.

One thing it meant was that Barry Blankenship had traded his early-thirties wife for an early-forties version, which, based on what Cam had seen of Barry, didn't seem consistent.

Cam thanked Nell for the conversation and Mr. Norton for the wine and headed out. The moon was bright, so she didn't worry about her walk home. She was just glad to finally be getting to bed.

CHAPTER 14

Cam regretted at least one of the glasses of wine from the night before. It wasn't that she was hung over, but she'd woken up with a wild hair related to the investigation — several things she felt she needed to look into. It meant a full day, so it magnified the irritation with the dry mouth that plagued her. She wished Annie was giving her a ride, if only because she would have had an excuse for a fatty breakfast. Instead, she ate oatmeal like a good girl, and it didn't erase any of the pressure in her head.

She had just rinsed her bowl when her doorbell rang. She answered, confused as to who could be there so early.

"Dylan!"

"Quick! I shouldn't have this. It's Jessica's camera. Copy the memory to your computer. I have to get this back."

Cam was totally confused, but too curious to refuse, and so turned on her laptop. As soon as it was going, he stuck a memory card in the side. It uploaded, she copied its contents, and then he pulled the card back out and stood. He almost bolted out but stopped long enough to give her a very lingering kiss on her hand. She took a deep breath and by the time she looked up again, he was gone.

She was way too curious to let this slide, so she sat and opened the file. Clancy Huggins in three different ladies' dresses.

"Okay, then. I see a tit for tat," she said to herself. "No wonder Clancy didn't want the pictures of Telly getting around . . ."

She frowned at the screen. That was all it meant to her — that both men cross-dressed, given the chance. But it potentially gave Clancy Huggins a motive, provided these pictures were older, though they were also a lot milder.

Cam had to stare at them a while longer before it registered where Dylan must have spent the night to be in possession of Jessica's camera. He'd been with Jessica Benchly at the end of the night prior, and this morning he was in a hurry to look like he'd not been gone and he had *her* camera.

It was smart, as it gave someone else at least a hazy motive to murder Telly Stevens, and lent a story to the earlier facts, but Cam also knew it would never hold up — stolen evidence never did. That wasn't her real issue with the matter, though. Sure, it was distasteful to have embarrassing stolen pictures on her computer, but she was fighting very hard not to feel jealous about Dylan and Jessica.

And there was another layer not sitting right with Cam. Clancy Huggins had been nothing but decent, and she didn't feel right bringing something like this into the case without giving him a chance to explain. She looked up his number on her computer and pushed it into her phone.

"Hello?" He sounded confused.

"I hope I didn't wake you, Mr. Huggins. This is Cam Harris and . . ." She wished she'd rehearsed, but there was no way to make this less awkward. "Somebody anonymous," she lied, "sent me some pictures. They thought they might be related to the murder investigation, but I'm not so sure. I wondered if you might talk to me."

"Off the record?"

"Of course." She was hardly likely to go public that one, or rather, two, of the Little Miss Begonia judges liked to wear women's clothing. She'd either keep quiet, or pass the photos to Jake, and Jake alone.

"I was headed down for breakfast. I'm at

the Hotel Roanoke if you'd like to join me."

"Jessica's not with you?" She kicked herself when it came out, but he seemed nonplussed.

"Jessica is a notoriously late sleeper. I doubt anyone will see her until noon." He laughed.

"I'll see you in about twenty minutes, then," Cam said as she hung up.

She hoped she managed to sort what she wanted to say before she got there. She left a message for Evangeline that she'd be late checking in, and then began walking.

She arrived a little more quickly than expected and found Clancy waiting out front, fingering a philodendron that sat in a pot. She wondered if he was worrying about the poisonous properties it had — it was something that had crossed her own mind more than once when she passed the plant. They hardly needed more murder weapons growing nearby. He greeted her, led her inside, and then raised a finger to the girl at the station. She smiled and picked up two menus. Clancy held his elbow out and Cam took it, feeling very bad for the questioning she was about to put him through. Clancy Huggins was clearly a very nice man.

He gave non-verbal clues as he sat that

told Cam to wait on questions. She kept quiet as he ordered, only ordering coffee and a fruit plate herself. She wished she were hungrier, but the oatmeal had stuck, so, even if the bacon smelled good, she had to pass.

"You don't want to eat anything?"

"Oh, I wish I hadn't eaten already, but I did. I had oatmeal before the morning visit that caused me to call you."

"And I wish we could trade. My doctor would be pleased if I were too full of oatmeal to eat an omelet; surely your cholesterol rating is better equipped to handle three eggs with the Santa Fe fixings." He smiled kindly. "So what's all this about?"

Cam bit the inside of her cheek, looking for the right words.

"Mr. Huggins, I don't know how to say this, except just to say it. I saw some incriminating photos of you this morning."

"Oh," he said, his coffee stopping just before his mouth.

"I've also seen sort of similar pictures recently of Telly Stevens."

He sighed. "It's a long story. Jessica thought . . . one-upping him on those photos would stop Telly from using them."

"Using them, how?"

"Well, I suppose this will come out, and

for my part, it's really only shameful that I was so gullible. It's ironic, really. I was contacted by a woman claiming to be putting together a fund-raiser for breast cancer — men in women's shoes. Jessica took some pictures of me in various dresses. We then sent the pictures to the woman. Then a few weeks later, Telly and I were up for the same broadcast journalism award. A man claiming to have a duplicate file threatened to sell the photos of me to Telly so he could use them against me. I thought it would have ruined the fund-raising campaign. Turns out there was no campaign; it was all a trick. Jessica, as my good friend, without my knowledge, managed to get comparable pictures of Telly so that we had the means to keep him quiet. That was it. As far as it went."

"He didn't threaten to go public then?"

"No! He had more to lose than I did! My public is rather more liberal than his — public radio is very different from network television, and my pictures had been taken for the purpose of a campaign, or so I believed. And as a radio personality, people wouldn't necessarily recognize me. Besides, the pictures of me have considerably more clothes."

"What's your relationship with Jessica?"

"I'm terribly fond of her."

"It's not romantic?"

He narrowed his brows, then said, "I didn't say that."

"It *is* romantic?"

"I didn't say that, either. We'd really prefer it was nobody else's business."

"Okay. I'm sorry." He really was sweet and she felt bad for prying. "Are you willing to share anything about the lingering look Telly threw at Jessica at the opening supper party?"

"I don't like to speak ill of the dead, but there is no denying the man was a letch."

"Did you know Judith at all?"

"Of course. She was a producer, and I have done a fair bit of broadcast production myself, though she is . . . was . . . a much more broad programmer, whereas I've just done a few special series. Still . . . well-researched, accurate series, rather than the fluff Telly was known for . . ."

Cam thought that statement actually had to do with the award competition, but she didn't bite. She wanted to pursue Judith. "What did you think of her?"

"We worked together smoothly a handful of times. Until Telly's infatuation with Jessica, she was always very pleasant."

272

"Why would that stop her being pleasant?"

"Jessica and I are very open about our friendship. I think Judith assumed I'd take sides."

"Would you have?"

"I don't see that sides needed to be taken. Telly was awful to both of them, and Jessica never asked for his attention. I think they might have been friends. But I think Judith meant to defend her husband no matter what."

"Would that defense of her husband extend to . . . an illegitimate child?"

"Yes, I imagine it would. Was there one?"

Cam wasn't sure he looked quite as clueless as his words, but she didn't want to accuse him of lying, so she just went on.

"I think so, though as far as I know, it hasn't been tested," Cam said.

"Poor little tyke."

"The little tyke in question is my age, or nearly." This *did* appear to surprise him and she wondered if there were other little tykes. "I think he will land on his feet . . . unless somebody succeeds in framing him for murder, which they seem to be attempting."

"Why are you telling me this?"

"Because I think you're not the kind of man who lets an innocent man be framed.

You seem nice."

"Well, I really hope to not disappoint you on that point, Cam. I try to be nice."

After just a bit more small talk, she left him to his breakfast and decided to brave the day.

She checked in briefly with Evangeline, but things seemed in order, so she decided to double-check on Petunia. It would be the pageant's night for a sit-down supper, and it was quite a large group for Spoons' typical capacity.

Nick answered. "Yeah?"

"Nick! Happy Saturday! How are you?"

"Oh. Hey, sis."

Cam rolled her eyes, glad for the phone between them. She felt very much like she wanted to give a schoolmarm-style manners lesson.

"So are you guys okay for this evening?"

"I guess."

"That's not very convincing."

The phone crackled and Nick whispered. Cam thought maybe he'd stepped outside.

"Okay, so Petunia's not doing so hot. She's got that . . . morning sick . . . but all day long. She'd kill me if she knew I said so, but we could use a little help."

"I'll be there."

Cam was now familiar with the wave of guilt that washed over her. While Petunia was pregnant, Cam would need to be more attentive. She should have thought more about morning sickness, but her only friends who'd had babies lived far away, so she hadn't been through this before.

She arrived at Spoons a little after eleven. She'd taken the time to go home and change into restaurant-worthy clothes — no bare shoulders, no toeless shoes — and then came back toward town to join Nick and Petunia without Petunia being warned.

When Cam arrived, Petunia's face soured briefly, then she sprinted toward the bathroom and Nick came over and hugged Cam.

"She's miserable. I can't get her to go home, but she spends half her time in the bathroom or washing up from being in the bathroom, so we really appreciate the help! Erm . . . even if Petunia says we don't need it."

"I've been Petunia's sister for thirty years, so I know what she'll try to do here. Thanks for letting me help you," Cam said.

"If she asks, you just had a hunch."

"I got it. How can I help most?"

"Chicken?"

"What?"

"That's what keeps sending Petunia out. We're doing stuffed breasts for supper, but it's raw chicken at the moment, and everything about it sets her off — the texture, the smell, the sight."

Cam felt her own stomach turn. She wasn't vegetarian, but almost, for this very reason. Raw meat was repulsive.

"It's half a breast, sliced this way," Nick showed her how to split them into thin, wide half breasts. "Then spread this paste on it, roll them, and stick in a toothpick."

The mixture for inside smelled of prosciutto, rosemary and garlic, and she thought maybe hazelnuts. Nick had put a few spinach leaves under the mix and a sprinkle of crushed roasted red pepper over when he showed her how to prepare them. She was willing to bet the rolled half breasts would be delicious, cooked. At the moment, though, a little gross.

"You have a nut allergy alternative?" Cam asked. She knew hazelnuts were actually a seed, but she didn't think complicated explanations would help the night go any more smoothly.

"Did them already," he said. "That will be the first batch to bake. They're in the walk-in already."

Cam turned to eye the gleaming walk-in

refrigerator. A grant from a foundation heavily supported by Evangeline and Neil Patrick had bought that recently, which ironically caused Nick some grief. Cam knew, though, Nick wouldn't blame the fridge for that. He was just glad for the state-of-the-art business support to keep his fresh things fresh.

"Got any gloves?" Cam asked, eying the chicken breasts suspiciously.

Nick pointed to a box of thin kitchen gloves, and Cam pulled two out. The chicken would still feel gross, but at least she'd be protected from the slime.

"Show me one more so I don't screw it up," Cam said.

Nick did, slicing the breast the long way and setting half aside, layering the stuffing mixture, and then rolling the whole thing.

"Okay! I think I can manage."

Her first effort wasn't as nice as Nick's, nor the second, but by number three, she thought she had it. Cam heard water run around the corner, and Petunia returned from the bathroom.

"That bimbo Jessica!" she shouted. "You know my body was happy with plain old nausea until I saw her puking her guts up! Oh!"

Petunia had walked around the corner.

She seemed to have forgotten Cam was there.

"What are you doing here?"

"I just knew you had a busy day, so I thought I'd offer to help a little."

Petunia narrowed her eyes, suspicious as always.

"Jessica who? Benchly?" Cam asked.

"That prom queen at that party of yours."

"She was sick?"

"Yeah. When we were delivering food, I found her puking behind a gardenia. Got her dumb life story. I haven't been able to walk past a gardenia without puking since — stupid cow! That used to be my favorite smell!"

"And her life story was?" Cam said, hoping to get Petunia back on point.

"Blah, blah, blah, baby daddy, couldn't handle it, something something."

Yes. Petunia had a gift for storytelling, Cam thought, though at least she'd gotten the important detail: Jessica was pregnant. "Did she say who the baby daddy was?"

"Just that he was at the party and something about him was what set off the puking."

Cam pretended to concentrate on the stuffed chicken breasts, though she was remembering Jessica running out after Judith had shrieked. So Jessica Benchly was pregnant by somebody at the party. And it couldn't be Clancy Huggins, or she wouldn't have accompanied him if seeing him would make her sick. Cam had been under the impression Jessica had refused Telly, but he really was the obvious answer when Judith had reacted like she did.

"Did she say how far along she was?"

Petunia frowned. "What do you care?"

Same old irritable Petunia. "Just a hunch about something."

Petunia opened her eyes wide and stared. Cam recognized the expression as meaning, "And?"

"And I think this baby daddy in question was murdered not long after."

"She offed him?"

"I don't know, Petunia. I doubt it. But the secret pregnancy certainly gives a couple people another motive if I'm right that he's the baby daddy."

"Who besides her?"

Cam looked to Nick for help, but he just winked. Petunia could be tenacious and he wasn't willing to cross her.

"Well, anybody who cared about her, if Telly was treating her badly or refusing to acknowledge her. Or Telly's wife, if Telly planned to leave her for Jessica . . ."

"Those rich people are all sick."

That had been the response Cam had been waiting for. Petunia thought the rich were a bunch of undeserving, lazy, pampered wastes of space. This was amplified if the person in question was attractive or famous. At least this judgment ended what Petunia had to say on the matter.

Cam finished helping, and finally all the trays were stacked in the walk-in. They'd need to be baked that evening, but that was a straightforward task that Nick could handle.

"Thanks for helping out," Nick said as she left.

Petunia just rolled her eyes, but Cam knew she was at least a little grateful. Being Petunia, though, Cam was certain her sister was annoyed to feel that way.

CHAPTER 15

As Cam walked home, her cell phone buzzed. She looked at the screen and didn't recognize the number.

"Hello?" she answered.

"Cam, Mindy thought you might be able to help me." Cam scrambled to recognize the caller, but the inexplicable kept coming back up. This was Barry Blankenship.

"Erm . . . no offense, but *why* would I help you? As far as I can tell, you're a creep who's been stalking one of my friends while cheating on another."

"I know I deserve that. I've been lousy to Mindy — I'm a bad husband. But really . . . this is about protecting Mindy. I'm being stalked now, and I'm worried the woman will do something to Mindy because of her obsession with me."

"Something besides framing her for murder, you mean?"

"Yeah. That was what clued me in."

"Look, I don't like you, Barry. And if you have a stalker, I think you deserve it. But I like Mindy and this might be related to the murders, which I'm looking into for other reasons, so I'll talk to you. I want my friend Jake in on it, too, though."

"He's the cop?"

"Yes."

"I don't know if we need the police involved."

"Humor me."

Barry agreed to meet Cam and Jake at Metro!, which was pretty chichi for a working lunch, but Barry had named the location and it sounded like he was buying. Honestly, eating there on Barry's dime was sort of appealing. Heck, eating there on anybody's dime was divine. She'd only been there a few times, and it was very nice. When they hung up, Cam gave Jake a call.

"I'm sorry, Cam. We've got something going down and I can't get involved in this supposed stalker thing. Olivia's already being investigated by internal affairs."

"But it's connected to the murders!"

Jake gave a pained laugh. "No, Cam, it's not. I think we have that one about wrapped up. I'll tell you what: Stop by the station before you meet this guy. I'll leave you a recorder and you and Rob can talk to him — a little investigative journalism. Then, if he says anything important, you have it on tape."

Cam growled and told Jake that Rob had his own recorder and thanks for nothing, then clicked her phone shut.

Rob agreed to go with Cam, so at least something went right. When he got to her house, she told him what she'd learned that morning about Jessica as they drove.

"You really think it's Telly's baby?"

"I sure do."

"You know they're bringing someone in this afternoon. They think it's the guy."

"Who?"

"That Dylan guy."

"No!"

"Why are you defending him?"

"I've talked to him. I know his story. I think they have the wrong guy."

Rob shook his head, his expression disgruntled. Cam knew it was about the inexplicable attraction between her and Dylan more than anything else. She decided to drop it for the moment so they could concentrate on Barry.

Downtown spaces didn't always have plant life, but at least Metro! had a couple large planters out front, which looked well attended. There was some greenery Cam thought was permanent, but it was complemented by annuals. The space inside was open and light and the window front invited in the daylight. There was a modern elegance and clean lines, the space was spare on extra decorations, and Cam wished she could just enjoy it.

"You're not Jake. You're that reporter," Barry said to Rob as they sat.

"And you're not some idiotic jerk, you're a jerk with some observation skills," Rob said. He sat, like he'd never been more bored, and clicked on the recorder.

"Jake's busy, but he asked us to record this in case it sheds any light on anything." Cam knew Barry would not see this as a huge effort in making nice, but then, he was the one asking for a favor.

"So I didn't know Olivia was . . . bad news until you told me about framing Mindy . . ."

"Why don't we ask the questions?" Rob suggested. "That way we aren't stuck with any more of your excuses than we want."

Cam pinched Rob under the table, but he ignored her. She was worried being too harsh would scare Barry off, or worse, make *her* laugh. It hadn't yet, though.

"I know I deserve your scorn. I'm a bad

284

husband," Barry repeated the mantra he'd told Cam earlier, and she felt like she might reach across the table and thunk him in the head. It was a good thing the restaurant was so elegant, or she might have done it.

"When did you meet this . . . Olivia?" Rob asked.

"When I was training for the position here."

"What do you even do?" Cam asked. She knew he sold real estate, but Mindy had said he was successful, which didn't seem to fit with the location change he'd made.

"I'm a regional sales manager — real estate. When I accepted my promotion and transfer, the company put together a training with representatives of several local resources . . ."

"Don't tell me. *She* was public safety," Cam said.

"Well, yes . . ."

"And the most attractive female at the conference?" Rob asked, his voice rippled with disgust.

Barry had the decency not to meet his eyes. "I said, I know I'm a jerk."

"Yeah, well, it would help if there was any evidence that you tried not to be," Rob said. "So how long ago was this . . . training?"

"About fourteen months."

"So she's not the bimbo you left Mindy for?" Cam asked.

Barry clenched his jaw. "I didn't leave Mindy for a bimbo. I never would have left Mindy for any bimbo. Mindy threw me out because I also couldn't seem to *give up* the bimbos."

Cam distinctly remembered Mindy saying Barry left *her,* so she chalked this up as proof he was a liar. She rolled her eyes and Rob scoffed. Rob's feelings on infidelity were at least as strong as Cam's. His mother had cheated, then left, and he and his sister been raised by his dad through high school.

"And you accepted the promotion for a fresh start?" Cam asked.

"I know it sounds bad, but Lynchburg isn't that big . . . everybody was on Mindy's side."

"So how'd your lady friend turn psycho?" Rob asked.

"Because the video from Monday night looked like you were getting along just fine," Cam added.

It was Rob's turn to pinch *her.*

"Video?" Barry asked.

"Undressing each other on the way into the Arts Commission? They have cameras."

"Why would you watch that?"

"We have had some vandalism and have

been watching for suspicious activity." Cam felt like a badass talking that way, though it was probably silly. "And then I recognized you. It's how we were sure you were Evangeline's stalker."

"I wasn't stalking her," he said, but Cam ignored him.

"I suppose that night might have been when things got weird. I mean . . . she was clingy anyway, but since I don't know anybody here, I didn't mind. I said something that night about my daughters coming into town with their mother."

"Okay," Cam interrupted. "Explain this. You leave and don't try to see the girls for nine months, and *then* tried to get custody, right?"

"I didn't want full custody. I guess maybe I wanted Mindy to just make us a family again. I missed my family."

"Brilliant, approaching that by suing for custody," Cam said. "And what did you tell Olivia?"

"That I missed my daughters . . . and being part of a family."

"You idiot. She couldn't have you get your whole family back or she was out of the picture. This framing was to get Mindy out of the way so she could be the wife and you could have the girls together."

"I guess."

"So when did this little fantasy of hers start?"

"I don't know. Maybe as early as her suggestion I try to get custody — months ago . . . I mean, I agreed because it woke up the family feelings, but she planted the idea. She just didn't realize how I saw it."

Rob slapped the table, causing a lot of stares from the high-class clientele. It also brought the waitress rushing over in alarm. They ordered as if nothing had happened. Cam chose the salmon cakes, wishing the prices were higher — she thought Barry really should be stuck with a bigger bill.

"So do you think she'd kill these people to frame Mindy?"

"Kill? No, I don't think so! I think the case fell in her lap, so she thought of framing. I think if she was going to kill someone, it would be a person more obviously tied to Mindy."

Barry clearly didn't know about the agreement with Mindy that Telly had reneged on. Rob started to say something, but Cam pinched him again.

"Does Olivia *know* any of the potential suspects?"

"I don't even know who they are, aside from Mindy."

"Dylan Markham?" Rob said.

"Clancy Huggins? Jessica Benchly?" Cam added.

"Jessica? Jessica and Olivia are friends," Barry said.

"Friends? Not rivals?" Cam asked.

"No. Friends. I've met Jessica a few times. She lives in Lynchburg."

"Did Olivia know Judith Towers-Stevens?"

"Not that I know."

"But you're sure Olivia and Jessica are friends?" Cam said.

Cam was trying to work out what this might mean, but it seemed important in any case.

"I've seen them together — they're friends. I also know that the handful of times I've tried to make plans with Olivia and she wasn't available, it was because she had plans with Jessica."

"So back to Olivia getting strange," Cam said.

Barry shrugged.

"Strange like she feels you don't take her seriously," Rob elaborated, an eyebrow raised.

Cam knew what he was getting at. Barry really was a jerk who probably wouldn't commit. Any woman wanted evidence she was special, but Olivia thought the relationship was serious, or, at least, she had at one point.

"And did she know where to find Mindy and the girls?" Cam added.

"She helped me track them down — traced the GPS on Mindy's car. I had wondered if the girls would have time to see us." Barry paused. ". . . and then I changed my mind. That was when I said it wasn't a good idea — that the girls probably weren't used to the separation yet and I should see them alone. She acted like it was okay . . . suggested Mindy must be seeing someone, too, by now."

"And?" Cam asked.

"I denied it — told her Mindy would put our daughters first and not rush in . . . I might have sounded jealous."

"You basically maximized your mistress's jealousy. Nice move," Rob said.

Barry put his face in his hands.

"Barry?" Cam said. Something had just occurred to her. "The girls have been staying with you. But Olivia hasn't, has she?"

"Of course not."

"I think Mindy might be in danger — if Olivia is trying to make some delusional happy family, she might think getting rid of Mindy is the fastest route."

"That was why I wanted to talk to you —

I'm worried."

At least they agreed on that much. Cam agreed to keep an eye out, then she and Rob left Barry with the bill. Cam deadheaded a sticky petunia in the planter on the way out, though, so she felt like she was ahead, as karma went.

Rob and Cam agreed to let Mindy spend the afternoon at Rob's. Barry had pleaded not to leave her at the hotel. They didn't think it was safe to put her at Cam's or Annie's, as Olivia might think of those, and Cam thought Annie was as likely to wring Mindy's neck as Olivia was.

Cam went to her office and called Mindy to make arrangements for Rob to pick her up. She meant to get a little work done but couldn't concentrate.

Instead she felt she had a list of follow-up questions for Clancy Huggins. Was Jessica's baby his? Did he know Olivia Quinn? And what did he have to say about the friendship?

She dialed his cell but got no answer, so she decided to head to the Hotel Roanoke to see if she could find him in person.

On her way out, she saw Barry Blankenship and Nell Norton sitting in the Patrick Henry bar. Barry seemed to be a busy boy.

He wore his earnest salesman face and Cam wondered what he was up to. She felt she'd only get an honest answer if she asked for it from Nell later, so she headed to the Hotel Roanoke where she thought her chances of finding Clancy were higher.

When Cam finally ran into Clancy, she'd almost forgotten he was the person she'd come to see. He looked a little alarmed to see her, but only briefly. His Southern politeness kicked in and he greeted her warmly.

"Mr. Huggins, how are you? I had an interesting morning and wondered if I could ask you a few more questions?"

"I answered questions already, didn't I? Part of that interesting morning?"

"Of course you did. Can I buy you a tea?" She gestured toward the bar and he looked momentarily panicked, but nodded.

"Jessica will be meeting me shortly," he said.

"Oh, good. I have some questions for her, too."

"And we're on a tight schedule . . ." he reminded her.

"I'm on the same one. I'll be brief."

He finally appeared resigned to having a drink with her, and they went into the bar and sat down.

Cam ordered a sweet tea for both of them, and Clancy ordered a Scotch as backup for himself.

"So who is the father of Jessica's baby?"

Clancy sputtered and stared, but then answered, "Well, I am, of course."

"I thought you weren't romantically involved."

"Well, if I gave you that impression, I'm sure I misspoke."

Cam was sure he was lying, though she knew his earlier answers had been intentionally vague. She wasn't sure, though, how to get him to tell the real story, so she pretended to believe him.

His phone buzzed.

"Jessica, darling! I'm sure you're busy, and I can just meet you later . . . you're sure . . . yes, well . . . I'm in the bar with Cam Harris, then . . ."

It was a nice attempt to protect Jessica, but Cam was glad it hadn't worked. She definitely had some questions for the woman and, thus far, had barely exchanged a greeting with her.

When Clancy closed his phone, he looked at Cam with pleading eyes. "Please don't ask her about the pregnancy."

"Why not?"

"She doesn't want it public."

"But I already know. She told my sister."

"Your sister?"

"She was catering Monday — they threw up together behind the bushes."

He looked pained and patted his forehead with a handkerchief. The waitress delivered drinks and so laid down an extra napkin and looked at him in concern. He waved her away and took a large swallow of Scotch.

"I won't mention it to her, but I think it's relevant for the murder investigation. I'm not going to keep it from the police."

Clancy pursed his mouth and then rushed out. Cam hoped he didn't plan on a heart attack. She'd feel very guilty if she thought she'd caused one.

Jessica found her before Clancy returned.

"Where did Clancy go?"

"I'm not sure. He didn't look well."

"Oh, dear. But in any case, it's nice to have a chance to talk to you more formally, Cam. What business do you have with Clancy?"

Cam swallowed, steeling herself. "With Clancy? He's a judge in the pageant I'm coordinating. But it turns out I might have some business with you."

"Me?"

"How long have you been friends with

Olivia Quinn?"

"Olivia? Years, why?"

"She's trying to frame a friend of mine for murder . . . and she seems to be stalking a man. She just . . . doesn't seem very stable."

"Frame? Stalking? That doesn't sound like Olivia at all."

"Yet the man she's stalking has met you with her."

"Barry? That's mutual. He wouldn't accuse her . . ."

"It seems a relationship that was sort of normal until this week got strange when Barry's wife and children showed up in town. Olivia appears to want something with Barry that she can't have, so she tried to frame his wife, I think because she had that relationship at one point."

"What do you mean, 'sort of normal'?"

"I mean Barry Blankenship is a jerk who has never been faithful, even when he was married with a family. I suggest you let Olivia know what a dog he is and that she's much better off without him. But if Olivia makes another move against his wife, the ax will fall. Tell her that her job is on the line."

"Oh!" Jessica looked surprised. "Well, I only know Olivia casually, but this doesn't sound like her."

"You just said you were friends."

"We've known each other for years, but only recently began spending time together — maybe a year ago."

"And why was that?"

"We ran into each other. I hadn't known she'd moved to the area before that — she used to live in Lexington."

Cam stood and set some money down for her tea; Jessica looked relieved. Clancy returned then, eyes searching. Cam shook her head and left the two of them to each other.

CHAPTER 16

When Cam left, she tracked down Rob so they could pool their information.

"You get Mindy settled?" she asked.

He nodded. "You know Jake still thinks the murderer is Dylan?"

"And as usual, Jake is wrong."

"Why do you have to defend this guy? Do you realize what this looks like?"

Cam rounded on Rob. "Like I'm defending a wrongly accused man?"

"Cam." Rob's tried patience stopped her. "The man has . . . feelings for you." He paused and Cam thought continuing was painful. "And unless I'm deluded, you have feelings for him."

"They aren't feelings!"

"Then what are they?"

"He pushes buttons. Flusters me. That's all."

"So you're attracted to him?"

"No! I mean . . . not rationally. Not if I

step back. But he sort of . . . pushes the right spots."

"And you still want to defend him?"

"Rob, the . . . so-called feelings have nothing to do with his guilt or innocence. He's Telly Stevens's son."

"He's what?" Rob asked.

"Jake didn't tell you that?"

"No. You didn't, either." His glare accused Cam, and she had to look away.

"Oh, geez. It looks to me like he's being framed because he has the most to gain."

"And does he?"

"There's some money in the will. But he didn't know about it until after the death."

"I mean you."

Cam stared at Rob. This was the last thing she expected. Rob wasn't a jealous guy.

"Of course not."

"Are you sure?"

"What are you implying?"

"The two of you are obviously attracted to each other."

"Rob, I'm only interested in *you,* no matter who I happen to encounter and how much they tweak whatever random attraction thing there is."

"So you admit it?"

Cam growled. "There's chemistry, yes. Am I tempted? No! That's a compliment, moron — that I choose you, even when I find another guy hot!"

Finally Rob seemed appeased. "So you're not tempted." It sounded like he just needed to hear it again.

Cam rolled her eyes.

"He is *not* you. Couldn't hold a candle to you. So no. I'm not interested!" she said.

Men and their insecurities could be so ridiculous. She let it go, though. It was not worth fighting over.

"Say, when do you see Jake next?"

"Soon, I hope. Want to come?" Rob asked.

"As a matter of fact, I do."

Rob texted Jake to see when he'd be free. Cam was relieved it was soon, as she only had about ninety minutes until she had to be back on location coordinating the final night of the pageant.

"Let's meet him at Horizon," Rob said.

Cam nodded. Horizon was a bar not too far from Elmwood Park, so it was located conveniently for her. She was still a little offended Rob seemed to blame her for Dylan's attraction, but despite her general disgruntled mood, she was glad to see Jake. She hoped he'd resolve several pertinent questions.

Cam and Rob both tiptoed carefully over conversation as they waited for Jake. They didn't want to fight, but the Dylan topic was like a scab, with edges itching to pick, and if they didn't resist, they might both end up raw and bleeding.

Jake was more than twenty minutes later than he said he'd be. Cam wished they'd invited Annie, as she could always keep things light. Finally, Jake pushed through the door in full uniform.

He turned a chair around and faced them, leaning on it. "Man, I've had a day."

"It's done?" Rob asked.

"Yup. Perp's in questioning now. Just need to break him."

"It isn't solved," Cam said.

Jake pointed a thumb at Cam and looked to Rob for explanation.

"Hey, this is her deal. Though I suppose I recorded supporting evidence at that meeting with Barry you skipped." He set the recorder on the table.

"It's not Dylan. Jessica Benchly is pregnant with Telly Stevens's baby," Cam blurted. "She has the most to gain with both Telly and Judith dead. And since she found out that Dylan is Telly's son, with Dylan framed for the murders, that leaves just her to claim what's left."

"You tried to claim Mindy was framed for it, will you make up your mind?"

"Mindy was framed by Officer Olivia Quinn because she is trying to play family with Barry Blankenship. He wanted to tell you himself earlier. As it turns out, Jessica and Olivia are friends, so maybe she was also covering for her friend. But when Jessica learned about Dylan, Dylan became someone to get out of the way."

"Cam, Dylan's a lifetime con man. He is a much more likely suspect. Besides, his hair — a lot of it — was found at Judith Towers-Stevens's death scene."

"What?"

"All over the periphery."

"Okay, does that make sense to you? One hair, two, maybe. But how would a lot of hair ever happen by delivering poisoned coffee?"

"Doesn't matter — it's proof he was there."

Cam narrowed her eyes. "He is event staff — doing the lighting — so there is every possibility he was there helping one of the television people with something while they were setting up. But there is also this: He spent the night with the most likely real murderer the night before and may have left hair on the pillow, so she decided to use it to frame him."

"What are you talking about?" Rob asked.

He was loud enough that the couple at the next table looked over in alarm.

"This morning, Dylan brought me pictures of Clancy Huggins in women's clothing — he'd spent the night with Jessica and saw them on her camera."

"Clancy Huggins?" Jake said.

"It was some charity thing, or so Clancy thought," Cam said.

"Dylan came to your house early this morning?" Rob said.

"Someone threatened to sell the photos to Telly. Jessica panicked and arranged for pictures of Telly that were even worse," Cam said, ignoring Rob's question. "And you're saying none of this matters?"

"Doesn't appear to."

"Unbelievable! Can't you just look at this?"

"Of course we'll *look*. I just don't see it going anywhere."

"I know . . . and Annie's a murderer and so is my brother-in-law, Nick." The pair of them had each been police favorites in the last murder investigation Cam and Jake had locked horns in.

Jake looked to Rob for help, but Rob just shrugged. Cam could see he was annoyed at the new evidence, but was also swayed by it. She suspected it was because she'd been right the last time and he'd also been ignored regarding Annie — the police had not dug deep enough and both Jake and Rob had stubbornly stuck to wrong candidates for much of the investigation.

Cam looked at her watch.

"Look, I have to be at Elmwood Park to start the double-check for tonight. Just promise not to drop this."

Jake wouldn't meet her eye, but his expression was resigned. Rob left with her, claiming Cam needed a ride, though he knew she didn't.

"Guess you showed him," Rob said as they walked to his Jeep.

Cam sighed. Now that they were away from Jake, his attitude about Dylan resurfaced.

"Can we not do this now? I have a thousand things to keep straight over the next five hours."

He raised an eyebrow, but gave a nod.

"Shoot!"

"What?"

"We'll need a lighting person if Dylan is being questioned."

Rob grimaced as Cam called Evangeline to give her a heads-up.

"Are you sure? I just saw him," Evangeline said when Cam explained.

"What?"

"I watched him walk across the park with Jessica not ten minutes ago."

Cam wasn't sure what to make of that — Dylan being there, *or* his being there with Jessica. "I guess that's good, then," she said, and clicked her phone shut.

"Emergency resolved?" Rob asked.

"Apparently. Either Dylan wasn't formally arrested or he's out on bail already."

Cam thought Rob's frown was less confusion and more irritation than hers had been.

Cam checked in with Evangeline again when she reached the park, looking around quickly with satisfaction at how nice they'd made things look — at least the setting was right. Then she made a beeline for the shell to find Dylan. Her curiosity had gotten the best of her.

"How are you here? I thought . . . Jake said you were stuck at the police station, but then Evangeline saw you here. Were you . . ."

"Questioned for murder, yes . . . but my reason for my hair in that booth was verified by that Sweeny woman. Not enough evidence otherwise. Besides, they could tell I don't have the resources to leave town," Dylan said.

"Why were you in the booth?"

"Ms. Sweeny needed help with all the wiring. Remember?"

She did, now that she thought about it.

"You don't seem that upset." It was true. He was fiddling with a trio of lights and hadn't even looked at her.

"I thought there were other suspects anyway," a voice said.

Cam started and realized Jessica Benchly was sitting on a chair at the edge of the shell. She was in shadow.

Cam jumped. "What are you doing here?"

Dylan let out a stream of air to show irritation but Jessica answered.

"If you must know, I overheard a hissy fit from Judith on Tuesday that Dylan was Telly's love child. I happen to be carrying Telly's baby, who is therefore Dylan's brother or sister. Family . . . And frankly, Dylan has been a lot nicer about this family thing than Telly was, though I guess the fact that Telly rejected them both might be a bonding point, too. Dylan and I have become friends."

Cam looked to Dylan, who nodded. Cam wasn't sure why Jessica had just confessed this love child to her — maybe she knew the news would soon be public? She doubted Dylan had confessed to stealing pictures. Though he also hadn't confessed to Cam that Jessica was pregnant, so maybe he was just a secretive guy. Whatever the case, Cam wasn't sure how to assimilate it at the moment, and she had way too much to do to try.

"Well, I'm glad — for both of you. Dylan, you set for tonight?"

"Aren't I always?"

Cam rolled her eyes and left him to it.

The pageant began with an announcement of finalists, which promptly led to minor chaos.

Lizzie Blankenship was announced as the first finalist and took her place as expected, accepting her bouquet of daylilies, as begonias were far too short for a pageant bouquet. But when, by the end, Lauren had not been announced, Lizzie began to cry and kept trying to explain something. Evangeline gave a pleading look, and Cam came forward and took Lizzie to the side.

"What is it, Lizzie?"

"It should have been Lauren. Not me!" She sniffed.

"But honey, that's not what the judges thought."

"But it was my fault! I ruined her dress!"

"What?"

"I just wanted to go home. I didn't want to be here. I thought maybe if Lauren's dress was ruined, she'd want to go home, too."

"Oh, Lizzie, does that sound like your sister?"

Lizzie looked down and sniffed again. "No."

The poor thing was devastated.

"Lizzie, the judges wouldn't count Lauren's dress against her. She got a new pretty dress. And she was only judged on the talent anyway, and Lauren did really well on the talent part. You need to tell your mom, though. Can I have your mom come talk to you?"

Lizzie wouldn't look up, but she gave a sad, dejected nod. Cam took her to sit with the other contestants and then went to find Mindy.

Mindy was sitting with Barry, who had a hand on Mindy's leg.

Cam grimaced. She couldn't imagine a scenario where this was good news. Barry pressuring Mindy was bad. Mindy forgiving Barry was bad. Barry was bad.

She tried to ignore it and snuck in behind Mindy. "Can I talk to you for a minute?"

Mindy jumped at the touch, but when she saw Cam, she nodded. Barry started to rise, too, but Cam said, "It's a mom thing."

Barry nodded and sat again.

"What happened?" Mindy asked as they worked their way to the finalists.

"I think Lizzie should tell you," Cam said. She was heartbroken for Lizzie, but felt some glimmer of hope that Mindy might finally understand this wasn't Lizzie's thing.

Cam left Mindy and Lizzie to talk everything through and made a round to check the other places where things might go wrong. The television crew seemed fine and on target. Her volunteers knew the agenda and where they had to have girls and when. And Kyle Lance was waiting in the wings to be introduced by Evangeline. Everything was set.

Cam could see Annie near the stage, shooting pictures of everything from the activity on it to the people in the audience picking their noses, if Cam knew Annie.

Kyle made his way on stage and sang two songs, accompanied by masses of little-girl swoons. For the second song, all the contestants went on stage, an inner half circle of the finalists, Lizzie finally back with them, and a much larger half circle around them.

Kyle hoisted Lizzie onto his shoulders, which finally brought her out of her funk, and when he finished the song, he kissed her hand when he put her down.

As the last girl came off the stage in one direction and Kyle Lance in the other, there was a huge commotion.

A familiar voice screamed, "Look out!"

It was followed by a loud crash and several explosions and flashes. One of the lighting tracks had fallen, and the bulbs exploded as they hit the stage.

Cam dashed up the stairs and saw Dylan lying on the floor, breathing heavily. The warning had come in time to save him, but the falling structure had caught his ankle as he dove to the side.

Dylan's face, even in the dim lighting, shone slightly green and sweat beaded on his forehead. His eyes were terrified. Jessica was nowhere to be seen.

"What happened?" Cam asked.

Dylan swallowed. "I guess Evangeline just saved my life."

Cam turned to see Evangeline, also apparently in shock. She stood to the side, positioned to take the podium again as the girls left, but was too stunned to move.

"Did you see who did this?"

Evangeline shook her head, and finally approached the podium.

"We've had a small accident back here. If

everyone could just stay calm until we get this cleared up — it should only be about ten minutes."

The audience calmed considerably.

Jessica rushed up and ran at Dylan. "Heavens! Are you okay?"

"Like you care," Cam muttered.

"What?"

Cam regretted saying it and hoped the "what?" meant Jessica hadn't heard.

"I said we need to get him out of here. He needs medical attention."

Jessica frowned.

"What about lighting?" Evangeline asked.

"He can't do it. Maybe Benny?"

"Oh, I don't think . . ."

"Benny can do it," Dylan said. "He's helped me at a few band shows. Nothing fancy, but he can point and change which lights — gives you maybe three shades and all the locations."

Cam dialed Benny before Dylan finished.

"But do you think . . ." Evangeline protested.

Cam knew what her argument was. Cam had learned a few months earlier that Benny and his father had gone to great pains to make the Garden Society believe Benny was dim because of a minor crime he'd committed as a teen. Evangeline, Cam thought, needed to believe it because of some of the things he'd done more recently. If Evangeline believed Benny had full mental faculties, it might destroy their friendship. On the other hand, the show needed him, so she took on a confident expression and nodded.

"If you're sure," Evangeline said.

A few of the "muscle" helpers arrived to clean up the glass and metal, and an EMT who'd been on site arrived to look at Dylan's ankle.

"You'll need stitches and maybe to have this casted, sir. I'm not sure if it's broken or just a very serious sprain, but you need to go to the hospital. If another person can help, I can get you to the ambulance."

Cam didn't want to do it, but the only person she could think of was Rob. She went on stage and shouted for him, certain that Dylan and Rob spending ten minutes together was the worst idea imaginable. She couldn't justify not giving Dylan the help he needed, though. Rob was the only person she knew present she could ask who was strong enough, aside from Jake, and Jake was on duty.

She watched as the EMT and Rob helped Dylan off the stage. The crowd considerately parted for them as they made their way to the ambulance, which was only a short distance away.

Cam turned to Jessica. "You really don't know who did this?" she asked.

"Why would I?"

"Because it seems to me, if your baby is the only heir left, you stand to inherit an awful lot."

"For your information, I'm wealthy in my own right. I don't need Telly's stupid money. Even if I did, half is plenty and family is worth more. I have a mother with Alzheimer's and no one else. I really want Dylan as family."

Jessica was quite the actress. In fact, Cam really wanted to believe her. At the moment, though, the show had to go on and she didn't have time to second-guess herself.

CHAPTER 17

Benny arrived a short while later. Evangeline introduced the next segment under the bluish lights that had been up for Kyle Lance's second number, less the row that had fallen. Benny was able to get them adjusted as the finalists lined up for the poise routine.

Cam finally left the stage, relieved things seemed to be on track to at least finish the night.

"Psst!"

Cam looked around, unsure at first that the call was meant for her, but it was Annie.

"What?"

"This is it."

"This is what?"

"Where the lighting unit was jerry-rigged." Annie was standing at one of the spots where the lighting gadgets were anchored, but there was no rope.

"So you think it *was* on purpose?"

"Look at those other knots. You think they untied themselves?"

"Crap! Wait, what are you doing?"

Annie was fumbling in her camera case for something.

"Calling Jake. He needs to get over here."

Cam started to argue but knew she'd only offend Annie, and it *was* Jake's job. Maybe he could get fingerprints or something. She also felt a little satisfied that the most logical suspect for this was the person she'd spent so much time arguing for as a murder suspect.

"I knew that Jessica was evil," Cam said.

"Why?"

Cam spun to find Evangeline behind her.

"Look." Cam pointed to the empty anchor. "Someone set the lighting thing up to fall on Dylan on purpose."

"It couldn't have been Jessica," Evangeline said.

"Why not?"

"She's been helping me all night. She's hardly left my side."

That couldn't be right. Even if it were true, it wouldn't be the first time Jessica had had an accomplice. They both looked around for clues as to who the culprit was when Evangeline's eyes lit on Annie.

"You!" Evangeline shrieked and Annie

314

yelped, looking betrayed. She'd been accused of something she didn't do before. Cam started to protest, but then heard the rest.

"Were you shooting the crowd when Kyle Lance was playing?" Evangeline asked.

"Of course I was. You didn't think I'd shoot *him,* did you?"

Cam bit her lip at Annie's sarcasm, glad Evangeline caught it for the humor it was.

"Silly me. But that's perfect. We can see who left their seats!"

"Oh, yeah! Reliable Annie," Annie said.

"Funny. That phrase has never occurred to me," Cam said.

"Really? That's where you want to go right now?" Annie said.

"No! You're right. Steadfast, never-failing Annie!"

"That's better." Annie began to scan her pictures. "Crowd shots are way too small. We'll need to do it on the computer."

Cam sighed. She'd figured as much.

A big screen dropped after the last routine and the finalists were called up one at a time to give a brief statement as to what being Little Miss Begonia would mean to her. After the girl's very brief rehearsed answer, her talent and a clip of her interview were shown. Then the next girl was brought onto the stage.

Cam barely paid attention. She was alternating coordination of the show with scanning the audience for suspicious details. She didn't spot anything that stood out.

Only when Lizzie, the last finalist, got up did Cam listen.

"I wish my sister was picked," she began. "She really wants to be Little Miss Begonia, and I'm only here because I want to be like my sister."

She looked down then and gave a sniff. There were a lot of "Awws" from the crowd, but Cam knew the reality: Lizzie had basically stepped out of the race without knowing it. The other girls — or more notably, their mothers — would be outraged if somebody won who didn't want it, and, frankly, the criteria mentioned having a passion for the program and being a good representative. How good was a representative who didn't want to be one?

When the finalists were done, the audience was given a ten-minute intermission while the judges met to make their decision. Cam was ready to spend the time problem solving, but Evangeline caught her.

"Come with me, will you? I need to change, but I want to ask you something."

"Of course."

Cam followed Evangeline around the crowd and into the library.

"Do you have a plan," Evangeline asked quietly, "for keeping the murders disentangled from this?"

"Stalling," Cam answered honestly. "The people interested in this pageant will be frenzied through Monday, and then all interest will drop off except for the individual girls. If we can keep the deaths ambiguous until then, we should be okay. Then, when the information on the murders begins to be more public, it will only be tied in passing to the pageant."

Evangeline sighed. "Okay. Not ideal, but I can't see a better plan. Will it work?"

"Unless a motive related to the pageant is uncovered, and I can't see that happening."

"Good girl."

When the audience was called back to their places, the judges went on stage. Each gave a brief speech regarding the qualities they were meant to judge on, the high caliber of the participants, and the spirit and benefits of the competition.

Toni Howe then called up the second runner-up, Andromeda Barrows. Barbara Mackay called up the first runner-up, Venus

DiAngelo. And finally Clancy Huggins called up the winner, Daisy Rae Hawthorne.

Cam was a little annoyed to see Andromeda in the finals, as she'd proven herself a poor sport, but the judges had not been informed of that. Cam made a mental note that perhaps they should hear such things if she ever did this again. Venus was a bit of a know-it-all, but really was very talented and charming when she tried. Daisy Rae, on the other hand, was kind, pleasant, talented, and most of all, she seemed genuine, so Cam could be content with the results.

Once the girls were assembled, Kyle Lance came out for a last ballad and then walked to the front of the stage, formally escorting Daisy Rae.

When the pageant wound up, Mindy approached Cam, Barry clinging to her hand.

"Thank you so much for everything! You've been so great."

Cam had to bite her tongue. A reunion with Barry wasn't the outcome she'd hoped for now that she'd met the man, or even before, based on Mindy's description. He just wasn't a good guy. Instead, Cam addressed the girls.

"Your daughters are really fabulous. I had a great time getting to know them. And it's wonderful Lizzie got Nell's runner-up award — I know $250 isn't a thousand dollars, but it's a lot more scholarship than most people have at seven!"

Mindy laughed. "It sure is, and I hope our money troubles are over anyway. Barry and I are going to try to work it out."

Drat! Cam hated it when an avoided topic became unavoidable. "Well, if that's what you want, I hope it works. I'd just like to see you and the girls happy."

Barry had the decency to look sheepish; she had to give him credit for that.

It took a long time to get everybody on their way. All the girls needed to collect their props, receive congratulations from friends and family — no matter how they had done — and of course, have their picture taken with Kyle Lance. He was a great sport about hanging out, especially given the annoyed expression of Jimmy Meares.

Rob interviewed the top three girls, promising that in addition to the Roanoke newspaper piece, he'd send a more extensive interview to each of their local papers. Cam thought he'd be up all night typing up the interviews. It would no longer be news in a few days, so it was best to shoot for the Sunday and Monday papers. She wasn't sure about the other towns, but the *Roanoke*

Tribune deadline was two A.M. to get the results into their bulky Sunday paper and midnight the next night for the Monday living section, where the in-depth interviews would go. The only exceptions the papers made on deadlines were the unavoidable, huge-news events that preempted page one — natural disasters, violent crime, or political scandal. Little Miss Begonia, when they'd known the date for weeks, would not qualify.

"Hey," she said to Rob. "I know you have a heck of a deadline, and I'm here awhile. I can catch a ride from Annie."

"Why does Annie have to stay?"

"Erm, or Evangeline. Go! I'll get a ride from someone or walk twelve blocks."

"Not at night, you won't. No walking." He pointed a finger at her and she rolled her eyes.

"Fine. I promise. Ride. Annie or Evangeline."

He finally nodded, kissed her, and left. Cam was tired anyway. The only thing she'd miss about the walk was the jasmine.

As Cam wound her way to Annie, she ran across Nell and Byron Norton. She stopped to thank them profusely, then pulled Nell aside.

"I saw you earlier in an odd conversation with Barry Blankenship. Do you mind my asking?"

"The man was trying to sell snake oil — rural property on the outskirts of Roanoke — as if I don't *have* rural property." She sighed and walked away.

The audience finally dispersed as Kyle Lance drove off in his limousine, so only the contestants and their families continued to mill, alternately retrieving their things from the library and thanking the contest staff and judges. Cam had to work hard to be gracious when she was so distracted.

"What did you find on Barry Blankenship?" Cam asked Annie when she managed to find her. She looked thoroughly done with photography for the evening.

"What?"

"Did you look?"

"Yeah, two days ago. I thought you didn't need the information once Mindy was cleared."

"I don't think we do on the murder, but he seems to have wormed himself back into Mindy's life."

"Sick. Why?"

"I don't know, but I'd rather give her a heads-up if there is anything there."

"Well, yeah — there was stuff — real

estate stuff. There was something about a sexual harassment suit, but I didn't end up reading it all in depth because we ran out of time and then Mindy showed up."

"You saw it?"

"Of course."

"You ready for a long night?"

"Not so much. Can't you stick with one crime at a time? I got pictures for Dylan, philandering for Mindy, and neither looks like murder."

"I'll give you twenty free hours next week-end."

"Huh?"

"Roanoke Garden Society is still on hiatus. I'll work for you in exchange for helping."

Annie sighed. "I hate you, you know."

"I know you don't. I also know you're the best friend anybody could ever have."

"And you're a giant, demanding suck-up, which is almost as bad as being the ordinary favor vampire you always are. But I suppose if you must suck the life out of me, the butt kissing is appreciated."

"I love you," Cam offered.

"Shut up. When can you leave?"

"Not for another hour, at least. Evangeline can give me a ride if you want to head out and get started."

"You're too kind." Annie's unenthusiastic

tone oozed sarcasm.

Cam made a kissy face. "I'll see you in an hour."

Cam did her part then, seeing families off, thanking staff and judges, and making sure the clean-up crew had things under control. Finally she found Evangeline.

"Would you mind giving me a ride home?"

"I'd be happy to, Cam, but I have several things still to do. Could you check with Benny?"

He hadn't occurred to her, but there was no reason why not. Cam found him on the stage, stowing the last of the rented equipment.

"Hey, Benny. How's it going?"

"Almost done."

"Can I ask you a favor?"

"Probably," he said.

"Would you mind giving me a ride home?"

"Well, sure. You mind if we stop at the urgent care and check on Dylan first? It's just the clinic right over there." He pointed — it couldn't be seen through the shell, but Cam knew what he was talking about — there was an outpatient clinic that was part of Carilion Hospital. It sat just kitty-corner from the far end of the park.

Checking on Dylan wouldn't have been

her first choice, mostly because she had a full night ahead, but she did want to see how he was, so she agreed. A half hour later, she and Benny finished up at about the same time, so it worked well.

They walked across the park and intersection together after Benny had stowed the things that needed to be picked up by the rental company.

Dylan was waiting outside an ER-style waiting room. They'd put his ankle in a splint while they waited for the X-rays to come back, but as Cam and Benny arrived, the doctor was explaining that he had a break and his leg needed to be casted.

"How long will that take?" Benny asked.

"He should be back in a half hour," the woman said.

"Does it hurt?" Cam asked.

"Why, Miss Harris, I didn't know you cared," Dylan said.

Benny snorted and Cam blushed.

"You didn't see who did this, did you?"

"No, but I saw something."

What?"

"Man acting real fishy — whispering and telling some woman off, then kissing her, but making her go — it was that guy in the video with the lady cop."

"That toad!"

"Sounds right."

"But you didn't see anything else?"

"Maybe. Ask when the drugs wear off. My memory is a little fuzzy."

Cam rolled her eyes.

"I'll come back for you, okay?" Benny said. "You probably aren't supposed to drive."

"Especially not with the pain meds, and I'm definitely going to demand more of those." Dylan grinned.

"I'm really sorry it's broken," Cam said.

"I know what you can do to make it feel better."

"I'll send a card right away," Cam said, blushing even brighter.

"See you," Benny said, and Cam led him back out, hoping her face wouldn't burst into flames.

Cam was glad Benny didn't feel compelled to ask about it. She wasn't sure what she would have said, aside from her protest that she was happy with her boyfriend. She was deeply relieved to be dropped off at home.

"About time!" Annie shouted when Cam finally got home. It was almost one in the morning.

"Yeah. Sorry about that. I had some trouble finding a ride." She didn't confess

325

to stopping by the clinic with Benny. She wasn't sure if Annie would tease her or scold her, but she wasn't in the mood for either.

"So pictures or trash about Barry first?"

"Pictures. I've already got a little trash to work with, so let's work with what we don't know."

Annie gave her a strange look. She knew something was up but didn't press Cam about it, for which Cam thought she had the time rather than Annie's sense of decency to thank. Annie pulled up a file of pictures on her computer and then clicked on one. She must have been searching and found the spot they needed before Cam got home.

"See, this is where Kyle Lance started his last song of that first set. I have a few of him, and that blue lighting is reflected on the audience."

"Okay."

"And back here — the song before, the audience is in white light — remember that obnoxious starlight thing?"

Cam did. The song was sappy, and there'd been white-on-white disco lighting, which had threatened to give her a headache. "Yeah."

"So what we're looking for is audience differences between the white pics and the blue ones, right?"

"Sounds right to me, when you put it like that. I guess that's why we pay you the big bucks."

"Yeah, still waiting for *that* check."

Cam sat next to Annie as her best friend tried to identify audience shots of the same places, one white and one blue, so the pictures could be compared, one spot at a time.

It was tedious, but finally Cam spotted it.

"There! Can we get closer? Someone's leaving; looks like a man."

Annie selected the area and enlarged it.

"It looks like *the* man, you mean. Headed in the right direction, even."

"And Dylan said the man had been arguing with Olivia Quinn but then he kissed her."

"Man, what a jerk! Wait. When did Dylan say that?"

Cam ignored Annie. "We need to warn Mindy."

"Oh, that'll go over well. But I wouldn't wish that whack-job on anyone. Even Mindy," Annie said.

"You're too generous," Cam said. "So what did you *find* on him?"

"Restraining order — situation sounds a

little like what happened to Evangeline, and then this . . ."

Annie hit a tab and a blog popped up.

"What is this?"

"Not proof positive, but I cross-referenced Barry, real estate, cheating, and various swear words on the blog search engine. This one looked good, so I checked out the author profile. She's in Lynchburg. She claims to have been drawn in and duped, first sexually, then for an investment, by a real estate bigwig named Barry who has since been transferred to Roanoke."

"Yeah, awfully high on coincidence, but a blog . . . people can say almost anything, can't they?"

"Well . . . they can . . . but maybe we could contact her."

"Some stranger? Online?"

"Oh, come on, Cam. Where's your sense of adventure? Don't tell me you've never emailed a stranger before."

Cam frowned. She had. Quite often, but always in a professional context. This just seemed sleazy.

"What do we say?"

"The truth! That the sleaze is trying to get back with his wife, and we are friends . . . *you're* friends with her anyway, and are concerned. You're looking for information to convince her not to get back together."

"Okay?" Cam agreed in theory, but the whole thing still felt sordid.

Annie tutted and pushed the computer at Cam. "You're the P.R. person. Think of it like convincing someone to contribute to a cause."

Cam narrowed her eyes. Annie fetched her a glass of wine, made her take a drink, and then repeated herself. Cam finally managed to get the words out.

Burned by a Real,
I stumbled across your blog and think I know the identity of this horrible man. He is technically married to a friend of mine, and has recently made inroads toward reconciliation. As her friend, I'd like to warn her about the kind of man he really is. I know you can't say publicly, but hoped you might give me a few more details so I can prove to her she should stay away.

The Barry in question is 40, dark-haired, about 6'2", and has two daughters, seven and ten, who would be heart-broken if there was a reconciliation and then more bad behavior.

Could you please let me know if it sounds like the same man, and if it does, share some details to dissuade his wife? I'd be very grateful.

Cam Harris

"Daughters are a nice touch," Annie said when she read it. "I would have left them out, but thinking about it, you probably tripled her chance of responding."

"Now who's sucking up?" Cam asked.

"I *do not* suck up. I'm a truth-teller, my friend. So take your compliment like a man."

Cam snorted and pressed Send. "Now what?"

"I was thinking bed, but if you have a line of Chippendale dancers in your closet, you might convince me to stay awhile."

"No dancers."

"Then I say we call it a night. Maybe this woman will respond by morning."

Cam had to admit the idea of sleep appealed to her. She'd had far too little for a week. She hoped she might even sleep in.

CHAPTER 18

Unfortunately, Cam had trouble sleeping. She thought with the pageant over, it should have been easy — her stress was finally gone. But the blogger troubled her, and she had strange dreams. When the sun peeked under her curtains, she gave up and got out of bed. Since she was up anyway, she decided to check her email.

Nothing. She put on a pair of Crocs with her pajama shorts and tank top and went out to do a little early-morning weeding to clear her head. It occurred to her she did this too often, as the task took less than an hour, but then she came in and showered and checked her email again.

It felt early, but it was actually almost nine. If the woman got up early, she might have responded.

Cam logged on and was pleased to see there was in fact an email from 'Burned.'

Dear Cam,

I can't be specific. I happen to be a public figure of sorts and need to keep my identity private — the foolishness I displayed would ruin my reputation.

It does sound like the same Barry. In fact, recently I had to endure watching him trying to win his wife, so I know what you say is true.

As for details to help you convince your friend, I spent a weekend with him two years ago when he was meant to be at a real estate conference in Arlington. He also took me on a hot-air balloon ride once at Virginia Beach. Accommodations at the time were comped — he was trying to get me to buy a beach house . . . he called it our love nest.

I got the impression, after the fact, of course, that he frequently used sex to sell real estate. I guess I wouldn't have objected, had he been more honest about it.

Burned

Cam put on coffee and tried to digest the information.

Mindy was probably still in town, if the signs of reconciliation could be trusted. Cam thought that she and the girls were probably staying at Barry's, since they'd checked out of the Travelodge when the risk of Olivia had first come up. That made it very hard to contact Mindy without alerting Barry.

She pressed speed dial for Annie so she could share the news.

"Are you freaking serious? I have one day to sleep in and you call me at . . ." She paused, probably looking at a clock or her phone. "Nine-fifteen?"

"That woman responded."

"Big whoop."

"And I need help figuring out what to do."

"You are so helpless. Is coffee made?"

"Just about."

"Cream?"

"What do you think?" The two debated cream versus skim milk frequently.

Annie gave an exaggerated sigh. "Fine. I'll bring the cream."

It was only five minutes before she heard Annie stomping down the stairs rather too heavily. She wore slippers, boxer shorts, and a T-shirt that Cam thought belonged to Jake. She set a carton of half-and-half on the table as she sat. Annie's expectant look demanded coffee, so Cam obliged.

"Nice outfit," Cam said.

"Yeah, I went for maximum embarrassment. I put on Jake's clothes, then when he wakes up, he'll have to put on mine."

"Oh, geez. Jake's there?"

"Where else would Jake be? Rob's place?"

"Oh, stop it. We just were so late. I didn't think . . ."

"That I had a cuddle-muffin up there waiting for me? Cam, open-door policy. I got up there last night and there he was."

"Okay, then I don't feel quite so guilty. At least you got lucky."

"Not so much. He was asleep already. But had it been winter, I suppose the body heat might have been a bonus."

Cam laughed, then she turned her computer to Annie, who doctored her coffee first, then read. Cam waited, sipping her own coffee.

" 'Had to watch him wooing his wife'? You don't suppose she was *here,* do you?"

That hadn't occurred to Cam, but if Mindy was to be believed, it had to be the case. "Either here, or he tried to reconcile before. But that's not what Mindy said. Do you think we should ask her?"

"No. I don't think we go to Mindy until our arsenal is full. I think we talk to *him.*"

"About?"

"What Dylan saw. What I saw. Jake's not scheduled to work today. Maybe I can get him to go."

"Oh, yeah. That will fly," Cam said.

Annie squinted for a minute. "You're right. Jake won't work. Just remember the rules: public place — don't give too much away . . . record it."

"You're coming, too, aren't you?"

"Probably, but I'm not changing until you have something set up. You might not be able to get him to meet with you, and I might get to go back to bed. Do you have his cell?"

"As a matter of fact, I do. He called me, remember?"

"So call him."

Cam had to psych herself up. She wasn't a big fan of confrontation. She stepped out her back door and breathed in the rose fragrance. It reminded her of her mom, which always helped. Finally, she pressed the numbers into the phone.

"Yeah?" Barry whispered, giving away that he wasn't alone.

"I take it you have Mindy and the girls there. I need to talk to you — I think you'll want to hear me out."

"Why would I?"

"We have photographic evidence that it may have been you who rigged the lights to fall on Dylan Markham."

"Who? Why would I hurt a guy I don't know?"

"That's what we want to know. Will you meet me or not?"

"No."

"Then my next step is to call Mindy and share some information from a blogger called 'Burned by a Real' . . . She gives pretty good detail of a brief affair." Cam went on to describe some of those details.

"Fine! I'll come!" He stopped Cam before she could finish, in her mind confirming the connection. He named a downtown diner and said he'd meet Cam there.

"Okay . . . Aesy's," Cam said. "I'll be there."

"Hey, I know their morning cook," Annie said after Cam hung up. "He comes in for muffins before they open — early. I'll go in the back way and back you up . . . take pictures."

"I don't think that's necessary."

"Yes it is. I know what kind of trouble you get up to. Rob ever leave a wire here?"

"Wire?"

Annie rolled her eyes. "So someone else can listen? Jake has one. I'll be right back."

Instead of going upstairs, Annie looked either way, then pulled keys from somewhere and went out to Jake's police car. She rummaged for a minute, then came back with a handful of gadgets.

"Get there first. Sit near the kitchen. If you are within twenty feet, I can hear with no wiring."

"Then we need to hurry."

"Pants me!"

"What?"

"Shorts, sweats — give me something to put on."

Cam grabbed a lightweight pair of capris and tossed them at Annie, pulling a sundress over her own tank top and shorts. The two took off.

Cam was glad for how close to downtown they lived and how negligent Annie was about the speed limit. They parked behind the diner, Annie's downtown entrepreneur pass allowing them to park in a spot not open to the public. They actually entered through the back.

In the kitchen Annie did the talking. Ronny, the head chef, called over one of the waitresses, who nodded a lot and then seated Cam at a table near the kitchen. As Cam followed the waitress, she saw Annie tuck a chair against a wall, out of the way of activity, and out of sight from the main restaurant.

Barry was already seated, but the waitress went over and explained to him that his party was waiting at another table. He looked confused but followed her back to Cam's table.

"You seem to be the bane of my existence, Miss Harris."

"And you, mine. Maybe you could clear some things up and then we can leave each other alone . . . if you're not rotting in jail, I mean."

"I don't know what delusions you have, but I know there is no reason I'd rot in jail."

"Then explain this." Cam pulled out a cheap camera that nevertheless managed to play the memory card from Annie's pictures. It was a duplicate. Cam was glad Annie was used to such things and was paranoid about backing up her files.

"I don't know what I'm looking at."

"You, leaving your seat toward the side of the stage, just as somebody was booby-trapping the lighting to fall on Dylan Markham."

"I have no idea who Dylan is."

He'd said that once before, but she still didn't believe him.

"Lighting guy? He saw you argue with, and then kiss, Officer Olivia Quinn."

"I was letting her down easy," Barry said.

"That's why I went back — to say good-bye."

"Nice, prolonged good-bye kiss?"

"She asked for a kiss good-bye! I was leaving her! I felt bad."

"I'll be sure and explain that to Mindy."

"No! She couldn't understand."

"She's not alone there. Kissing the woman who framed your wife can't possibly be popular."

"But she didn't do it."

"You aren't the first idiot to believe your mistress, but I thought you'd switched teams."

"No. I'm serious. I believe her — I talked to the maid who had falsely accused her — and I let Olivia talk to her!" Barry said.

"You can't get real answers when you let a cop intimidate a witness!"

"Then get that cop friend of yours to check. Olivia didn't do it. She's being set up, too."

"Give me a break."

"I'm serious. Have that cop friend talk to the hotel worker."

"And she's innocent like you're innocent. Man, you two deserve each other."

"Cam, I know I'm a cad. And I'll be the luckiest man on the planet if Mindy forgives me. But I didn't hurt what's-his-name. And

I *was* saying good-bye to Olivia."

"Okay, so tell me about the sexual harassment suit in Lynchburg — the one you left town for."

"Geez. You *are* a snoop."

"A snoop with Mindy on speed dial."

Barry gave a small shiver, which Cam took to mean he was squirming, so she went on.

"And the blogger? She's under the impression that your real estate sales appeal includes a Barry boink as standard."

"Another woman jealous I wouldn't leave my wife for her. I *told* you I had trouble resisting bimbos."

"Then why on Earth would *anyone* think you might change?"

The waitress brought coffee and asked for their orders. Cam laid a five on the table and left. She didn't care if Barry ordered or not. She knew she wouldn't get any more out of him, at least not with his neck still intact.

When Cam and Annie got back to their split house, Jake was sitting on the front steps with a cup of coffee. There was a small stack of weeds on the sidewalk and Cam wondered just how bored he'd been.

"Dare I ask?" he said.

"Cam had some questions. I was just

providing backup," Annie said, kissing Jake.

"With police equipment?" He raised an eyebrow.

"Hey, you were gardening. It was trade-jobs day," Cam said. Jake ignored her.

"You know what trouble she gets herself into." Annie blinked.

"And *my* underwear?" Jake added.

Cam smirked as Jake pulled Annie into a hug.

"You're incorrigible," he said.

"You wouldn't have it any other way," Annie said.

"I suppose that's true," Jake admitted. "So what did you learn?"

"Well, Barry left his seat just before the lights fell last night. But he swears he was telling Olivia Quinn good-bye. Dylan witnessed a kiss — a good-bye kiss, Barry says. And Barry insists Officer Quinn is being framed in the framing," Cam said.

"He does, does he?"

"We don't believe him," Cam said. "But he thinks some third party is framing Quinn."

"Who would do that?" Jake said.

"It seems like the only person who knows for sure is that maid."

Jake narrowed his eyes. "I can certainly bring her in for more questioning."

Cam thought Jake looked strangely at peace with this development. Annie sat by him and looped an arm through his. "You did hear we're not saying we believe Barry — just that it's worth asking?"

Jake removed her arm. "And you're saying the two of you feel up to police work without a police officer?"

"Oh, don't be like that." Annie stuck her lip out. It was such an obvious pout that Cam knew Annie was joking, but Jake either missed the teasing or enjoyed it.

"Then don't run off questioning witnesses with my equipment . . . and my underwear . . . without at least letting me know first."

Annie looked guilty, but Cam wasn't feeling it. Jake had failed to follow through too many times for her to feel bad for getting an answer or two. Still, she was relieved when Annie convinced Jake to let them watch the questioning of the maid.

It didn't take long for Jake to round her up. Her address was on file as a witness, and she apparently had Sundays off. They asked her to come to the station and she did, in her Sunday best, annoyed to be disturbed on her free day.

Jake began with the idea of an alternate

witness with a different story, the fact that the woman could lose her job over the testimony — but only if the alternative was true, not it if was false — then slipped in the accessory to murder charge if the original testimony was proven untrue and had helped the killer get away.

"Killer? I thought it was just about love! Love and money," she admitted. "The woman paid me a great deal."

"Which woman?"

"I don't know her. I only saw her once."

"This woman?" Jake held up a picture of Officer Quinn.

"No — she was the one I was to blame."

"What did the other woman look like?"

"Tall. Dark. Very curvy . . . the good kind of curvy."

Jake opened the folder to another page. "This woman?"

"Yes! That's her!"

"And she paid you to blame this other one?" He turned the page back to the picture of Olivia Quinn.

The woman nodded happily, apparently relieved they'd figured it out. Unfortunately, Cam just felt more confused.

"Jessica Benchly is our briber. I'm not convinced she's our murderer, though," Jake said when the woman had left.

"Well, of course not," Annie said. "She's got huge . . . tracts of land . . ."

Cam snorted in spite of the situation. Jake didn't seem to grasp the reference, or at least didn't have their same appreciation of Monty Python or innuendo.

"You know we're on our own," Annie said when she and Cam were on their way out of the station.

"Yeah. Men don't think straight when huge 'tracts of land' are involved. We're looking for a connection between Jessica and Barry?"

"I'd say so. Jessica snowing men doesn't seem very searchable."

"Wait a minute. Maybe huge tracts of land really is the answer," Cam said.

"Erm."

"Barry's a realtor. Maybe he met Jessica . . . buying or selling . . ."

"Barry's the one who told us Jessica was a friend of Officer Quinn. Why would he make a connection for us like that if he's part of it?" Annie asked.

"Maybe he planned to turn on her the whole time?"

"That double-crossing . . . I like it! So *he's* the killer?" Annie said.

"Or maybe he was just scamming Jessica

and she got into something."

"Oh, make up your mind."

"That's just it. This isn't a nice, neat story. But I bet if we search public records for sales and purchases, we can connect them, and maybe it is the hint we need." Cam felt triumphant as Annie pulled into the driveway and then followed her inside.

"Or maybe we go talk to Mindy, then you distract her and ask for something, and I look in drawers for proof her husband is rotten while she shows you."

"Are you nuts?"

"I thought we'd established that already. Yes. I'm nuts. I'm *your* best friend, aren't I?"

Cam stuck out her tongue.

"Guess it wouldn't hurt to talk to Mindy. She doesn't know what we know, and maybe she should . . ." Cam started.

Annie nodded. "Call her."

Cam sighed but obliged her friend. She wondered if Mindy knew Cam had met her husband for breakfast. A little voice in her head that sounded like Annie followed up with, "and got nowhere." She pulled up Mindy's number on her phone.

"Cam! I'm glad you called!" Mindy answered.

Cam prayed Barry wasn't in the room. "I

hoped maybe I could say good-bye to you and the girls. Are you back at the Travelodge?" She knew they weren't — Barry had obviously had someone there when she called earlier and her money was on Mindy. But she felt it was in her best interest to play dumb.

"Well, no. We stayed at Barry's last night — and before you warn me — I know what he's been, but he seems to sincerely want to try!"

"Well, I hope that's true — that he really wants to put you and the girls first. Are you at his place at the Patrick Henry, then?"

"Yes. Should we meet you in the park?"

"It's already ninety degrees out. Is Barry home? Maybe I could just come up?"

"He's not, as a matter of fact. I can call the doorman and he can let you up."

Fortunately, Mindy had interpreted Cam's question as permission for access and not the avoidance it was. "Do you mind if Annie comes?"

"Annie?"

"She got really attached to Lizzie. She'd like to say good-bye."

"Oh. Well, of course."

Cam was glad Mindy found rudeness mortifying, or surely Annie would have been excluded.

"We'll be there soon."

Cam and Annie both changed to more appropriate day-time clothes — a sundress for Annie and capris and a tank top for Cam — before they left. They easily found street parking for the Bug, and the two told the doorman they were expected by Mrs. Blankenship.

"Yes. She called. Here." He led them to the elevator and when it opened, used a key to signal the right floor, then stepped out and let Cam and Annie rise.

"He must be rich," Annie said, referring to Barry, not the elevator attendant.

"I think that's a safe bet." Cam knew most of the building was more affordable, but this special treatment did indeed seem rich.

"Do you get rich in real estate?" Annie asked.

"You can, I guess. It depends on the kind you sell and how good you are at it."

"Yes, I suspect Barry Blankenship relies heavily on being good," Annie said.

Cam gave an annoyed nod at the innuendo but didn't comment.

The elevator opened to a wide hallway with only two doors, one at each end. It wasn't the penthouse, which had the whole top floor, but it was certainly up there.

They turned to the left and knocked. Mindy opened the door a little ways, only to be mowed aside as Lizzie rushed out into the hallway and hugged Annie.

"Heya, Squirt! How's it going?"

"I have a cool room at my dad's. Want to see?"

"Sure. If it's okay with your mom," Annie said.

Mindy didn't look thrilled but nodded. When they'd gone, she frowned at Cam.

"I would have thought you'd think better of Annie by now. Your girls love her," Cam said.

Mindy pursed her lips then sighed. "Maybe that's the problem. They don't think much of me. Lauren prefers her dad and Lizzie prefers this stranger."

"I suppose Annie is a stranger, but I think, for Lizzie, that takes the pressure off. She doesn't have to try and figure out who she needs to be to make Annie happy. She can just be herself."

Mindy stared at this foreign concept. Cam thought the idea of some *other* "normal" terrified Mindy.

Cam explained Lizzie's wish to be disqualified from further pageants to a gaping Mindy, then changed subjects. "So you want to show me this fancy place?"

That set Mindy right. She smiled and took Cam's wrist. "It's amazing!"

"Does Barry own it?"

"Only leasing — the building isn't selling . . . ever. He's leasing a number of apartments below and keeps dangling this one, but he's priced it way too high for now because he'd rather stay here until the units below go."

Cam got the grand tour: four bedrooms, large entertainment space, formal dining room, modern kitchen, study . . .

"Someone put in a lot of money," Cam said.

"The developers were really looking for high-end clients for these top few floors. The rest is . . . you know . . . to revitalize downtown Roanoke."

"How many super rich can there be in Roanoke who want an apartment downtown? Does he have a who's-who — Barry's fancy list?"

"Oh, he does, but he tries to be discreet. Some people prefer not to be in the public eye for things like real estate."

"But it's all public record — people can just go to the county and see — why would he be secretive?"

"It's not as public on leases — they're more private."

"Are they clients he doesn't want *you* to know about?"

"Why would you say such a thing?"

"Mindy, I don't want to hurt you, but . . . can you log us onto the internet?"

Mindy frowned but turned on the computer. She glanced at Cam irritably several times as it turned on and the internet loaded. Cam pulled up *Burned by a Real . . .* and pointed out the Barry clues.

"Well, I don't believe *that.*"

Cam took a deep breath, aiming for understanding. "If you can't believe, you can't. But I couldn't know and not tell you. Answer a question, though. Does your husband know Jessica Benchly?"

"Jessica? The former Miss Virginia?"

"The same."

"Not that I know of. Why would he?" Cam thought perhaps her responses sounded rehearsed.

"We thought maybe she purchased some real estate from him."

"*We?* This has Annie all over it. She is always judging me."

"Actually, I'm just as paranoid as Annie on this. We both just wanted you to have your eyes open. That's all."

Mindy was more terse through the rest of the tour, but Lizzie found them again, insisting Annie had said Cam would like the flower boxes on the balcony. Cam and Mindy followed her out. The flower boxes were nice, but Cam stalled for other reasons. She thought Annie had spotted something that needed investigating.

On the way out, Cam saw Benny cleaning the stage and park. They wandered over and said hello.

"How's Dylan's ankle?"

"Two weeks in a cast, six weeks splint and crutches. Could be a lot worse. You nailing whoever did it?"

"Now there's a concept," Annie said. Cam punched her. It was just like Annie to turn everything into innuendo.

"Trying. We have a couple of leads."

"Well, you shout when you know."

"I'll tell Jake when we know. We want the person arrested, not beat up by thugs."

"Thugs? Miz Harris, I'm crushed."

Cam rolled her eyes. "And you call me if anything weird happens."

"Of course. You're my queen of weird."

Annie snorted and gave Benny a thumbs-up as they left. Cam punched her again.

"What? He got that right."

"This is *you* calling *me* weird?"

"Hey, I'm eccentric across the board. You're weird here and there, which is weird."

Cam shook her head as they headed for home. Annie dropped her off and promised to be back after she handled some Sweet Surprise business.

CHAPTER 19

Cam spent the afternoon trying to get her press releases in order. Ideally, they'd be sent before six so the pageant could be included in Monday's Living Section along with Rob's interviews, but it was tricky business, with the chaos the event had seen. The side piece about the gardening competition had been far easier — what with Nell coming through with not only the extra scholarship, but donating so many flowers to make the grounds gorgeous. But that wouldn't be featured until Tuesday, regardless, when the paper ran its gardening feature.

Still, she knew what the pageant committee wanted for the main press release. She decided to keep it sweet and light, and offer her name if anyone had any questions. She was sure they would, but she could stall those until the next afternoon, and so by the time the extended story came out, those with a personal interest in the pageant would have gone on to other things.

Just as she was attaching the last accompanying documents to an email that would be sent to dozens of papers, her phone buzzed.

"Benny?" she answered.

"Remember that 'if you see something strange' thing?"

"Yes?"

"Well, I've been sort of eying that new girlfriend of Dylan's all week."

"Girlfriend?" Cam hated that the idea turned her stomach.

"I don't know. I mean they've been spending a lot of time together . . ."

"Jessica Benchly?"

"Busty brunette? Hotter 'n a firecracker?"

"That's her." Cam sighed.

"Anyway. I sorta noticed who she was friends with and who she wasn't. But today she meets this other chick — the one you been hanging out with."

"Mindy? Are you sure?"

"I'm sure. They're both pretty. Guy like me notices a couple pretty dames."

"That doesn't make any sense."

"Why not?"

"No, I mean it makes sense that you notice. It doesn't make sense that they are hanging out together."

"You said call if I see something strange. If it wasn't strange, I wouldn't have called."

Cam scratched her head. "What did they look like together? I mean . . . were they just talking, or maybe arguing, or . . . ?"

"Their heads were close. I thought maybe they were sharing secrets. Not arguing, anyway."

Cam managed to say something incoherent and hung up. She couldn't see any way this fit. At the moment, Jessica was the most logical suspect and Mindy had been framed. What would they have to say to each other?

Then she remembered the Jessica-Barry connection and decided Barry might be using Jessica to set Mindy up once and for all. Or would he be using Mindy to set Jessica up? Either way, these two women with their heads together, in Cam's opinion, pointed to a Barry Blankenship who was surely evil.

Annie didn't return until almost four, but she'd brought Frappuccinos as a peace offering, and Cam hadn't noticed Annie was late until she hung up with Benny at 3:40.

"Coconut mouthgasm," Annie announced as she set the drinks down.

"It is not called that," Cam said.

"Well, not to the public, no, but I know people."

Cam took a sip. It was indeed fabulous. When she sat back, Annie opened her laptop and plugged in the cable from her tiny little camera. Cam hadn't even realized she had it with her when they were at Barry's earlier.

"Well, duh! I'm not the speed-reader you are. Besides, better to be able to check later."

"Not admissible in court," Cam said.

"Court schmort. What are we? Police? And look at" — she clicked a few folders until a document popped up — "this."

It was an agreement with a woman named Jessica, but Cam thought Annie was mistaken until she pulled up a credit form that had other names on it. It was Jessica Benchly, and she'd bought a house through Barry Blankenship. It wouldn't have seemed strange, except Barry said he only knew her through Olivia.

Cam jotted the address and frowned. "This looks fairly normal to me."

Annie shrugged. "I only had five minutes. It proves Barry and Jessica knew each other before Olivia — if he is telling the truth about when he met Olivia, anyway."

"I guess so."

"And then I copied both their email folders, but I need to figure out passwords to open them." She set a thumb drive on the table.

Cam didn't think the pieces made sense. It looked like Jessica knew Barry, Mindy, *and* Olivia, and she seemed to be the lynchpin in the puzzle, but Cam couldn't figure out how. She decided maybe Evangeline was the best person to help her sort at least part of it, so she called her.

"Oh, hon. Come on out. What's a week with murder but no mojitos?"

"Do you mind if Annie comes? She's my ride."

"Of course she can. Three heads are better than two."

So Cam and Annie got in the Bug and drove out Blue Ridge Parkway to La Fontaine, the Patricks' house. Cam admired a field of sunflowers as they went, though mostly they passed immaculately manicured large yards in front of impressive houses, not least of which was La Fontaine. Giselle, the housekeeper, led them to the covered patio, where a fan blew a virtual monsoon to keep the air at a comfortable temperature. The hibiscuses danced happily in the breeze.

The patio was covered by the deck above, but Evangeline sat with her long legs out in the sun, a book perched in one hand, and a cocktail on the table next to her.

Cam admired several pots of ripening tomatoes she thought must have been returned to their normal spot after the meeting here several weeks earlier. The plump fruit gave off an aroma that made her mouth water.

"Oh, hello, girls. Sun or shade?"

Cam said shade as Annie said sun, and so Evangeline pointed to a chair sitting in each.

"Mojitos okay with both of you?"

Cam's memories of her last gin experience weren't that great, but she didn't want to be argumentative, and Annie said, "Perfect," so fast that Cam just nodded.

"Ooh! Nummy!" Annie said once Giselle had brought their drinks. "How do you make them?"

"Well, Giselle does it, but the trick is to soak the mint and sugar in the rum overnight first, I think."

Rum. So much for Cam's cocktail knowledge. Hopefully rum was better, but Cam was still planning on pacing herself. She took a small sip.

"So what's on y'all's mind? You sounded like you had a bee in your bonnet, Cam."

"It's all these former Misses who seem to know each other. You told me about Jessica and Olivia being rivals, but here they pop up as friends. This morning, Benny saw Jessica and Mindy with their heads together."

"Well, I think Jessica's their neighbor."

"Whose neighbor?"

"The Blankenships . . . well, before the separation. I don't know exactly, but they're on the same street in Lynchburg."

"This street?" Cam pulled out the address she had for the property Jessica had bought with Barry Blankenship's help.

Evangeline looked at it. "That looks right. I didn't notice until I started to pull thank-you letters together, but — wait a minute . . ."

Evangeline went inside and returned with a list and reading glasses, scanning the list over the rims. Evangeline looked unfairly beautiful, considering she was several years older than Cam. But Cam was relieved to see the small sign of aging, even if the glasses looked great on her.

"Yes — only twenty apart in address — either neighbors, or almost."

"And if Barry sold her the house?"

"Probably hand-picked as a neighbor — you don't try to sell next door to people you don't want to see a lot."

"So Mindy really does know her?" Cam asked.

"This says 2006 is when she bought it."

Annie held out her laptop and spun it. "But that doesn't eliminate an affair and a framing."

"That's true," Cam said.

"What about this Jessica-Olivia rivalry?" Annie asked, looking at Evangeline.

"Ongoing since they met. They hated each other. Finally, maybe two years ago, Jessica went out of her way to make peace and they've been friends since then."

Cam doubted the motive after so long. It seemed likely Jessica had put a plan in motion. If only Cam could figure out what it was.

As they drove from Evangeline's, Cam called Rob.

"Could you and Jake maybe meet Annie and me?" she asked.

"I've got another two hours to try to make the most of this feature. You can ask Jake, but you really can't count on me for a few hours."

Cam didn't like it, but she passed on the message to Annie, who called Jake as soon as they pulled in their driveway.

When Annie hung up, she looked at Cam. "Half hour, Macado's."

"Sounds good. Showers, then we leave?" Cam said. She was feeling overstressed and overheated and a shower seemed a good way to resolve both.

"Perfect. When did you get so smart?" Annie asked.

"I've been smart. It's you recognizing it as smart that's been slow in coming."

"That could be. Your intelligence is very subtle. Most people wouldn't notice it at all."

Cam reached for Annie to flick her, but Annie escaped for her shower.

Cam felt considerably cooler as she and Annie headed to Macado's in the Bug. The air had lost a little of its humidity to a warm wind, so though it was still uncomfortably warm, there was a breeze and less moisture to cope with.

They arrived about ten minutes after they'd told Jake they'd be there, but Cam was sure Jake was familiar with Annie-time. Annie could keep a schedule professionally, but socially, she had internalized the idea that "On time looks desperate," a belief Cam had never shared.

As expected, Jake was waiting at a dimly lit side table, a pitcher of beer in front of him. Macado's was laid out like an old-fashioned pub, so most of the activity centered around the U-shaped bar that came out into the center of the room. They would have at least a fair amount of privacy where they sat.

"Not on duty?" Cam asked.

Annie poured herself a beer as Jake answered.

"Today was my ninth day in a row, so I think they're okay with a six-hour shift."

"Ouch. But what happens if we break your case?" Annie said.

"I can share information after a beer. I just can't go chasing bad guys. Beer and guns are a bad combo."

"Yeah, I can see how that would be." Cam flagged over a waitress to order her own, more see-through variety of beer.

"Oy! You shame me!" Annie pretended to faint against Jake. Cam thought maybe in the dimmer light, he copped a feel. She couldn't be sure but Annie sat back up, grinning, which supported the theory.

"So how are you breaking my already solved case?" Jake asked.

"We learned today that Jessica Benchly is a neighbor of Barry and Mindy Blankenship."

"And?"

"And she had a long-term rivalry with Olivia Quinn, which she only ended two years ago."

"So grudges die hard," Jake said.

"What if it never died? What if she decided on revenge instead?" Annie asked.

"Revenge?" Jake rolled his eyes. "That is what you wanted to share?"

"There's more," Cam said defensively.

When he sat back, he looked a little more content. Cam thought Annie's hand was on his thigh.

"So she made nice in order to *wait* for the chance for revenge?" Jake said.

"It sounds so far-fetched when you say it that way." Annie pouted. Cam knew she was goofing around, but Jake looked a little confused.

"She saw her opportunity this year when . . . erm . . . well . . . we're not sure . . . either Barry wanted to frame his wife or to play hero to his wife — either way, Mindy needed to be accused of murder."

"Why kill Telly Stevens?"

"All those witnesses to Mindy arguing with him."

"But then his wife turned up dead."

Cam frowned. It was true that piece was a lot harder to fit into this puzzle. She began a half-dozen different scenarios, but could shut down each of her own ideas before any of them made it all the way out.

"Decoy?" Annie finally offered.

"Yeah, like last time," Cam said. The second murder in the spring had been to throw off the investigation. The victim had been killed largely to throw off investigators and frame Annie.

"Do you know the odds of that?" Jake asked, an eyebrow raised.

"Okay, so we have some puzzle solving to do."

"Cam, this matter is going just fine in police hands."

"Right. And you still think Dylan is your guy?" Cam asked.

"I'm not doing this," Jake said.

"Right. You want our plausible details, but it doesn't go the other way," Cam said.

"Cam, he *is* the cop."

"*Et tu,* Annie? I never would have thought it." Cam sat back and stared.

"Oh, geez. You know I'd never put authority over you. I'd never hold back. But you have to see why Jake does."

Cam did, but she didn't want to, so she took a large sip of beer and walked out on both Jake and Annie. She hoped maybe Annie would be guilted into probing Jake after she left.

She hadn't planned ahead, of course, which

was a problem for a girl with no car. She didn't know what she wanted to do, but letting herself be strung up on technicalities wasn't on the list.

She would have liked to go talk to Dylan. She wasn't sure why she felt this would help, except that she thought the new information about Jessica Benchly suggested Dylan might be in danger, or that he was at least being used. He seemed to have let Jessica into his life, so he needed to be warned.

She wandered toward Elmwood Park, hoping to trigger her memory. As she got close, she could see the trees that still had the tissue dogwoods in them. She would need to coordinate getting those removed. Benny would help, which pushed the nagging feeling about Dylan toward the front of her mind again. Before she knew it, she called him.

"Cam?"

"Hi, Dylan. I just wanted to check and see how you were."

"I'll be okay eventually, though . . . erm . . . did the pageant have any liability insurance? I won't be able to work for a month, probably."

"We do, and if it doesn't cover this, I'm sure the Patricks won't leave you hanging. They're good people."

"Well, then, I'm pretty good — that was my main worry."

"Listen. I think you have another one."

"What's that?" She thought she heard amusement in his voice.

"Jessica Benchly. She's neighbors with Barry and Mindy, and I think Barry and Jessica framed Mindy and you both — I think she's after Telly's money."

"Cam, that's ridiculous. I've gotten to know her. She has her own money. Look, I'll tell you what. Just because you're so concerned about my safety, I'll poke around a little and find proof."

"You do that. Poke around. I really hope you're right . . . And be careful."

"Always am . . ."

CHAPTER 20

Cam stood up from the short wall she'd been sitting on and debated heading home. She couldn't think of another angle to approach this from. Her cell phone buzzed, and she looked at the display. Mindy. She'd really hoped to have concrete evidence as to what was going on before she talked to Mindy again. She answered anyway.

"Cam, you and I really need to talk."

"Okay?"

"I thought maybe we'd go to supper. The girls are with my mom for the night before we drive back tomorrow, and Barry has an obligation, so just us?"

"Sure. I'd like that."

"Let's meet at Table 50 in a half hour."

"I'll be there."

It was only a short walk, and she didn't have time to go home, but she could drop into the office and check her email for questions about the press releases. It seemed strange that normal things like newspapers were continuing forward when everything else was so out of whack.

She was glad she'd taken the time when she checked. The Virginia Beach reporter had a half-dozen questions. Their representative was first runner-up, but apparently she was also a childhood cancer survivor, something Cam wished she'd known sooner, though it sounded like the girl had kept it quiet in order to avoid favoritism. *Portfolio Weekly* was doing a large feature on her now that it was over, and the reporter wanted many more contest details.

By the time Cam left again, she was running late. She called Mindy on the elevator to let her know, but lost track of her thoughts when she walked through the lobby and saw Barry in the bar talking to a rather unsavory pair of men. She stood behind a plant and snapped a picture with her phone and then sent it to herself via email. She had no clue who they were, but she couldn't imagine them doing anything good.

She walked the four blocks to Table 50 and found Mindy waiting. She wasn't sure what Mindy would have to say, but she clicked the record button on her phone as she walked to meet the woman. If anything important happened, she would be able to refer to it later. Mindy let Cam order a drink before diving in.

"Cam, I don't know why you want to go stirring up trouble for Barry and me. He wants to reconcile, and I really don't see why you'd try to block my happiness."

"I'm not trying to block your happiness, but I'm worried about you. Just two days ago, he was carrying on with a woman who tried to frame you for murder!" As she said it, she remembered it hadn't actually been Olivia but Jessica who'd done the framing. She tried to double back, but got uncharacteristically tongue-tied, only managing to blurt she was sure Barry was involved.

"Well, which is it?" Mindy finally asked, annoyed that Cam kept skirting the point.

"Jessica Benchly is your neighbor," Cam said.

Mindy twisted her face in a way Cam didn't understand. "So?"

"You and Barry both claimed not to know her. It looks to me like maybe Barry and Jessica are working together, setting you up, setting Dylan up. I'm worried they both want you out of the way."

"That's the most ridiculous thing I ever heard. I've been miserable since Barry left. Can't you just be happy we're working it out? And . . ." Mindy looked flustered, then seemed to come to a decision. She looked either way and leaned in. "Look, you may be right about Jessica . . . In fact . . . honestly . . . I think you are. Did you know this is Telly's baby she's carrying?"

Cam nodded.

"Well, I think she thinks she deserves that fortune, if you want the truth. But I'm positive she's working alone — she wants his money for her baby. Can't you just leave Barry and me out of it?"

"I can try if you will promise to be careful and watch your back."

"Well, thank you for worrying about me. You're a good friend."

Cam sipped her wine and the two ordered supper.

"So where is Rob tonight?"

"Newspaper deadline. He had to get all his pageant stuff in."

They continued their small talk as the food came and Cam began to eat, but on about her third bite, her phone buzzed. It was Benny again.

"I'm sorry, I have to get this," she said to Mindy and got up from the table.

"Benny?" she said as she walked away. "I was going to call you earlier."

"Where are you guys?"

"Us guys? I'm having supper with my friend, Mindy. Who am I supposed to be with?"

"Dylan. He's gone and he left his phone here — looks like he left in a hurry — it's a mess. You were his last call, so I thought he was with you."

"I talked to him maybe an hour ago, just to check on how he was doing. We talked about the pageant covering his disability time."

"Yeah, very legitimate stuff, I'm sure. I'm just . . . this doesn't look so good, Cam. He's not a neat freak, but there's a half sandwich . . . and he wouldn't leave without his phone."

"Are you suggesting someone took him? Benny, Dylan is about six-foot-two and injured. Do you know what size people those would have to be to take him?" A picture of the men at the bar with Barry crossed her mind; she tried to squash it back.

"Will you help me?"

She sighed. "Yes. Pick me up at Table 50."

"Be there in about fifteen minutes."

Cam clicked her phone shut and came back to the table, distracted.

"What was that?"

"It looks like something happened to a

friend of ours — one of the grounds staff from the pageant."

"Friend? Are you friends with those . . . workers?"

Cam raised an eyebrow. This was the Mindy whom Annie hated so badly. "Most people have to work, Mindy."

"Oh! Of course they do. I just mean . . . well . . . laborers."

"How is their job a bigger deal to you than the fact that something might have happened to one of them?"

"Oh, you're right. You probably think I'm terrible."

Cam didn't agree out loud, but she couldn't bring herself to deny it. She took a few more bites of food, then called their waiter over.

"I've just gotten a call and have to go. Could I get a to-go box?"

"Of course."

He rushed off, then returned with a box and the check. Cam slid her rotini in and Mindy grabbed the check.

"You don't have to . . ."

"Oh, no. It's my pleasure. You fed my girls and took care of them, so it's on me."

"Well, thank you. I should probably run now."

"Of course. Go! Save your friend!"

Benny took another five minutes getting there, and Cam opened the to-go box and picked at her pasta while she waited. She was glad to have escaped the snobby version of Mindy that had emerged apparently because of this reconciliation. Barry was obviously bad for her friend.

"Miz Harris! Hop in." Benny stopped in a no-parking spot, but Cam was right there. He took off before she could secure her seat belt.

"Do you know where we're going?" Cam asked, unsure why he seemed in such a hurry.

"No clue."

"Did you try Jessica?"

"Wouldn't know how to reach her."

Cam frowned. She didn't either, without calling to ask someone. "Then where are we going?"

Benny frowned and pulled into the parking lot of a law firm. Nobody else was there. He hit his steering wheel with both hands.

"I just can't think of anywhere!"

"Okay, breathe, Benny. Does Dylan have any enemies?"

"Everybody does, don't they? But I can't

think of anyone who'd . . . take him. His enemies are more like . . . try-to-sleep-with-his-girlfriend-type enemies."

Cam frowned. What would her enemies do? Talk behind her back? Maybe spread a rumor? Funny how different walks of life did things differently.

"Has anything happened with those enemies lately? Has Dylan done anything to make them mad?"

"Not that he said. I don't think that's it."

"So you think it has something to do with the murders and the inheritance?"

"Don't you?"

Cam sighed. "Yes. I just hoped otherwise. Listen, before I met Mindy for supper, I saw her husband, Barry, in the Patrick Henry bar with two guys who looked like mob enforcers."

"Mob?"

"I don't mean that literally. I just don't see large, menacing men in a nice place like that very often."

Benny whistled and leaned back. "Where would people like that take Dylan and why?"

"I think the 'why' has to do with Jessica Benchly. And I think a call to the hospital isn't a bad idea — in case they just beat him up and dumped him somewhere."

"Sucks to have that be what you hope for

as best case," he said.

"It does. But I think our next best bet is one of the properties Barry is representing — he has houses and buildings he has access to where people could hide out."

"Would he do that?"

"In the short run, it seems the smartest thing to do if he has him. I can't imagine someone like him has places he regularly does this. So one of his properties would be private — he controls access. He knows the places. He could have just scanned his brain for the best one."

"How many places would he have?"

"I wish I knew — a bunch — but I think we can narrow it down. He won't want neighbors who could spot what's happening, so it's either rural or has a huge fence."

"Or a warehouse or something he could drive into."

"I'm hoping you just watch too many movies, but yeah, that would fit, too. We need to think like criminals."

"That shouldn't be too hard for me," Benny said.

"Oh, stop it. You're not bad."

"You've never asked me why the Patricks and them think I'm an idiot."

"They don't think . . ."

"Okay, dim . . . not very bright."

"I did wonder. I mean, it wasn't hard for me to figure out otherwise."

"That's because you followed me into my lair. And I appreciate you not saying anything. My dad would probably get canned. When I was fourteen — the first day my dad ever took me to work — it was at Samantha Hollister's, actually. Anyway, I spotted this fancy little boom box with removable speakers and great sound, considering it was maybe five pounds. At the time I'd never seen such a thing — Dad is pretty low-tech — and I wanted it so bad. So when my dad was off down in the garden and I was tending one of those fussy trumpet vines, I snatched it and hid it away in our truck. I got caught, of course, by my dad that night. And the story was born. He said we had to not only return it and apologize, but explain that in spite of me being fourteen, I didn't know any better because I wasn't really capable. I've had to act it out since. See, all his clients are these rich people, and he couldn't have a thief for a son, especially not when I work for him."

"That's harsh. A lot of kids that age make a stupid mistake. Why do you still work for your dad if you have to keep that up?"

Benny shrugged. "It's a pretty good job. I get to be outside a lot. And I guess as Dad gets older, I worry a little. He had a minor heart attack a year ago, so I like to be there to help him with the big stuff — to do the heavier jobs."

"Noble" had not been a word Cam had ever expected to apply to Benny, but that was her first thought when she heard his explanation. He nudged her out of those thoughts, though.

"So how do we figure it out?"

"Go to my place — Annie's, actually. She's good at this kind of thing — both the computer search piece and thinking like a criminal."

Benny laughed. "I like Annie."

Cam grinned back. "Yeah, me, too."

Cam called Annie as they drove.

"You cooled off now?" Annie asked. She didn't sound thrilled but agreed to let them come over.

"You guys are pulling me into that trouble-making web again, aren't you?" Annie asked as they arrived.

"You don't have to come with us. You just need to help us find where we need to look."

"Ah, yes. Find the lair. Send Cam in. Sit at home and do nothing. Because I have no conscience."

Cam rolled her eyes. "Fine. Come with

us. But we have to figure out where it is first."

"And what are these screening qualifications?" Annie asked as she led them to her kitchen.

"We figure it is one of the properties Barry Blankenship is selling or leasing — that it is either out of town a ways or has a high fence — you know, so two thugs dragging a body from a van isn't observed by neighbors."

"Couldn't that just be an attached garage?"

"I hate you!"

"What?"

"No. You're right. Although it still seems like they wouldn't want to chance neighbors getting too close — in case he screamed or something."

"Well, let's see what our options are. That will give us an idea how carefully we need to pre-screen," Annie said.

"Good idea."

Annie's laptop was on her kitchen table, which was immediately over Cam's kitchen table, as their apartments were almost identical in layout.

"There!" Annie said.

"That was fast. What did you do?" Cam said, walking around behind Annie.

"I went to his agency website and picked Barry."

Cam leaned in. It was a long list, but not as bad as she'd feared — just under forty properties, she thought.

"It won't be anything with near neighbors or current occupants," Cam said. "Wait a . . ." It couldn't be that Barry was actively trying to unload a property he was using, could it? As a salesman it would be more normal just to represent them, but if he knew one was sitting empty . . . She wished Nell had been more interested. As it was, she doubted Nell had gotten an address.

Annie looked at her funny, but when Cam stopped, she just copied the list and then opened a program Cam hadn't seen before. She pasted the addresses, then took the time to add commas between them. Then she pressed Submit and an arrow started to spiral. It took almost a minute, but then a map appeared with a lot of little markers.

"Couldn't match these two," Annie said, pointing at a box in the corner. They're probably in developments newer than the background map. The rest are on here, though."

"Wicked," Benny whispered.

Cam opened her bag and pulled out her own computer. "We can eliminate faster if we tag team, but Annie, you're amazing."

"I know. Either that or a map geek. But I'll take amazing."

Cam sat across from Annie.

"You know what?" Annie said. "If we sort by price, I bet we can eliminate any of these in-town options that couldn't work. Cheap and in town means near neighbors and little privacy."

"Do it," Cam said as she set up her computer.

"Leaves eight in town, a dozen out, but it eliminated half the list."

"Are we just going place by place, then?" Cam asked.

"You have a better idea?"

"I hoped maybe *you* did."

Annie frowned in concentration. "Where did Dylan get taken from?"

Benny stepped closer and pointed at Annie's screen. "About there." Cam walked around to look at where the location was against the dots. It was a west-side neighborhood Cam wasn't familiar with.

"Okay, so these four are pretty darned inconvenient — heavy traffic to reach them. I think those go at the bottom," Annie said.

"That helps."

"But honestly, think like someone who doesn't do this regularly. Would you want to worry about every detail? I think it's most likely one of these remote ones."

"See," Cam said, "that's why we pay you the big bucks."

Annie rolled her eyes. "Again with the promises."

They split up the eight properties on the same side of town, but focused first on ones outside the city limits. Three were eliminated right away, as they were in new developments with a dozen or more houses each.

"That's it," Benny said. He was watching over Annie's shoulder.

Cam walked around the table to look. "Why do you think so?"

"Look at all the trees." Annie had pulled the address up under satellite view. "Even if there were neighbors out, they wouldn't see. And then it's got that shop in back — seems like that might have handy stuff to keep him imprisoned."

"You may be right. I'll write it down, but I don't want to stop checking just because we found one that fits," Cam said.

Benny shrugged. Cam went back to her computer. The real estate listings all had the standard square feet, bedrooms, bathrooms, but Cam was keeping a special eye out for bonus features — details like "secluded" or "fully fenced yard." It seemed the most likely way to spot whatever it was they were looking for. In the end, they had three properties that looked possible.

"What now?" Benny asked.

"I guess we go house shopping," Annie said.

CHAPTER 21

The first place they checked was off Electric Road. It hadn't been a favorite, as trees for blocking the view were quite a ways from the house itself, so it seemed more open than they thought they were looking for. But it was on the way, so there was no harm checking.

When they got near, Cam shook her head. "We're not far from Brambleton. I don't think he'd want to be near two main thoroughfares, even if they are both clear out here."

"Let's just drive up and look," Benny said. "We're here anyway."

They did, Cam noting that the trees were not only distant from the house, but ornamental, rather than privacy oriented. Their answer was confirmed in the driveway: a pair of cars, one with a car seat, the other with FOR SALE signs in the back. The house was being shown — unlikely to be hiding any secrets. Cam thought perhaps one of the family members had been to an open house that afternoon and made an appointment to come back as a family.

Benny pulled back out. "Okay, where now, hot stuff?"

Annie snorted. "You know, nicknames like that make Cam blush."

Benny grinned. "I know."

"We head south on Jae Valley Road," Cam said, trying to ignore them. She was annoyed with herself that she was, in fact, blushing.

The sky was yielding to darkness, purple coloring the east, as they made their turn onto Jae Valley Road. Cam didn't like the idea of doing this in the dark. They definitely looked a lot less legitimate as home buyers — who went shopping for a house when they couldn't see it?

A wrong turn and two correct ones later, they found the long driveway with the FOR SALE sign hung from a tree. Benny edged the pickup onto the narrow drive.

"Turn the lights off!" Annie said, reaching over like she'd do it herself if Benny didn't comply.

"I won't be able to see," Benny complained.

"We'll go slow. If this is it and somebody's

there . . ." Cam began.

"Then a car in the driveway can't hide very well. We should act like we turned in by mistake, pull back out, and then walk in," Annie said, changing her assessment.

Benny looked at Annie and complied without waiting for Cam, though Cam agreed. "Yeah. Does seem smarter, though last time I crept around somebody's property at night was a little more adventure than I bargained for," Cam said.

"Yeah, but you saved me — that's what we're doing, right?" Annie asked.

"Yeah . . . with no backup."

"So call backup. See if it works any better this time."

"Point taken." It really hadn't worked very well the last time.

"And it isn't possible you trust Rob as backup more than me," Annie continued.

"He's faster," Cam said.

"Define fast," Annie joked. "Besides, think about overall style."

Cam laughed. It definitely broke the tension. Benny looked relieved, and they parked up the road by a barn, then returned on foot and started up the driveway, single file, Annie in the lead.

"What if someone comes up the driveway behind us?" Benny asked from the rear.

"We dive into the trees," Annie said.

"They will have seen us already."

"That's true," Cam said. "We'll need to listen. If someone approaches on the outer road, we hit the trees. It may give us some false starts, but at least we don't get caught. And watch for the holly," she added as she looked around. There was some growing in the undergrowth, and holly in the shade tended to be fairly dense, so the sharp leaves would be hard to avoid if they got stuck in it.

"Yeah. Good idea," Benny said.

The problem wasn't the idea itself, but the hyper-arousal of listening for cars while half watching for the safe spots to dive. It was stressful. Twice, as they approached the house, they had to jump back into the trees. Cam reassessed how she felt about it getting dark — the dim lighting meant they didn't have to get back too far to be out of sight, which was definitely a redeeming feature, though the potential for tripping on something had increased.

Finally the road opened up to a wide driveway, large enough for at least three cars.

"I think we should still skirt it," Annie said, but as she said it a car actually turned up the driveway.

They dived for the trees . . . in separate directions.

Cam was alone on her side of the driveway. She wished she'd had time to think, as she'd far rather be near enough to talk to Annie and Benny, but her instinct had been opposite of theirs.

An SUV drove into the driveway and triggered the garage door. Cam tried to get a look — there was only one person in the car; all she could tell was that it was a large man. That was enough to suggest this was the right place. The garage door closed again, and Cam darted across the road to where Benny and Annie were.

"I'm pretty sure that was one of the guys who talked to Barry earlier. I mean, all I have is size, but that's something. That means the other is probably inside — two big, dangerous people. What should we do? Call Jake?"

"Jake can't do anything unless we have something more solid. I'm not even sure he has jurisdiction out here. It's county, not city. He could come, but all he could do would be knock on the door and ask questions," Annie said.

"That won't work! Dylan's in there. I'm sure of it," Benny complained.

Cam had figured that would be how it

worked. She decided having Rob on the way was better than nothing, so she called him.

"Hey, Cam."

"How close are you on deadline?"

"Basic story's in; I'm working on another. Why?"

"Dylan was grabbed by two thugs who are working for Barry Blankenship. We've found the house."

"*We?* Please don't tell me you and Annie are on some insane rescue mission."

"Okay. I won't. But if anything happens, we need someone to know. And besides, Benny is with us."

"Benny? That's supposed to make me feel better?"

"I hoped it would." She relayed the address.

"Look. I'm on my way. Don't do anything."

Cam sighed. "Thank you." She knew they wouldn't wait for him, but she was glad he was on the way.

They crept around the side of the house, darting between weigela, which was easy to hide behind, and the smaller bluebeard. A couple of windows were lit, but they definitely weren't using the whole house. Paper covered the basement windows. The house was quiet, other than the hum of an air conditioner, which was loud enough to drown out any other noise. Thankfully, it would also cover any noise they made.

They went along one side then the back of the house, pushing on windows, testing to see if any would yield.

On the third side they checked, as she ducked behind yet another weigela, this one with white flowers, Cam spotted a window that was open a crack. It wasn't to the basement, though that was just as well. She didn't think any of them could fit through one of those, certainly not without a lot of commotion.

She ducked under it, then flagged Benny, who joined her.

He wasn't so cautious. He slid a pocketknife along the screen and pushed his fingers through, edging the window up a little higher and peeking.

"It's a bathroom," he whispered.

He eased the window up and listened.

"No one near that I can tell."

"You going in?" Cam asked.

"I would, but I think it will be a lot quieter for you; I can lift you in. You okay with that?"

"I guess." She really wasn't, but she had to try. She didn't think, even together, that she and Annie could lift Benny quietly.

"You get in there. Annie will go back for the pickup. She will drive up and honk, create a huge racket. While they are distracted, you let me in the back door, then we'll go get Dylan."

Cam looked at the house and it suddenly seemed huge. "Where? He could be anywhere."

"You're the one who said they probably don't do this often. I bet he's somewhere that seems least visible and where he won't ruin anything in this house — it's for sale, so they won't want him putting a foot through a wall. He's probably in the basement. Try to find something to use as a weapon."

While that was impressive logic, especially given it was Benny, it didn't seem like much of a plan. But Rob was on his way, and they didn't have a better one. She let Benny hoist her through the window and managed to silently slide the window back down and climb into the shower, catching her breath behind the dark curtain. She'd listen and try to get her bearings from there.

It took a minute or two before she finally felt like her own heartbeat in her ears wasn't drowning out all other sound. She could hear a television — the air-conditioner buzz was quieter than outside, but still present. She couldn't hear any voices or movement, though, which somehow seemed worse. If she could hear them, she would know where they were. Without hearing them, they could be anywhere. Her knees shook at the thought.

Swearing filtered up from below her and a commotion that involved a few crashes, a slam, and some muffled shouting. Someone stomped up some stairs, she thought, and stormed into the bathroom.

Cam pressed herself against the shower wall and involuntarily held her breath. It had been hard not to gasp audibly.

"Sucker bit me!" the man shouted as he ran water from the sink.

"I'm sure you showed him who was boss." She heard a man laugh from out in the hallway.

"Could have used your help getting that gag back on him."

That was confirmation someone was there; Cam doubted there were multiple cases of abduction in Roanoke on a given day. She realized, though, she'd really have to do something about that soon.

"You managed," the man in the hallway said.

"How long is this for, anyway? I didn't

sign on to babysit."

"You signed on for what you signed on for, moron. It's not like this is the hard part."

"I don't like it. Grabbing someone, teaching them a lesson, that's one thing. But I feel like sitting ducks here, holding on to him."

At that, there was a crash outside followed by the regular horn of a car alarm. Both men rushed that way, and Cam scrambled out of the tub. She found the back door easily and unlocked it, but Benny wasn't waiting. It took a few doors to find the basement stairs, and she quietly slipped down, cursing Benny's stupid plan.

Cam hoped Annie hadn't just gotten herself in a heap of trouble. It sounded like Annie had crashed Benny's truck into the men's car, though she knew their car had been in the closed garage.

Cam ran through the basement, which didn't take much time. It was mostly one room, but off the laundry room was a door with a padlock. She tugged but it didn't give. These guys didn't seem organized enough to share a key, though, so she felt along a high shelf that held a couple paint cans.

"Pay dirt," she said to herself.

She wiggled the key into the lock and it clicked open. Dylan was lying on the floor in a heap. He tried to open an eye, but it looked like it had swollen shut.

"Oh, geez! This is bad. Dylan, are you okay?"

He made a muffled noise, and she managed to pull a cloth from his mouth, though the bandana that had held it in place was knotted too tightly.

She climbed into the closet behind him to work at the duct tape on his arms, and for a minute she lost herself in concentration. She wished she'd brought Benny's knife.

"What do we have here?"

Cam sucked in a breath and looked up to see a huge form silhouetted in the doorway.

"I knew you weren't just into that Jessica chick. You won't mind if I just lock you back in with this tasty number?"

Cam sensed Benny before she saw him. Behind the thug came a black metallic . . . something . . . Cam remembered she'd been meant to grab a weapon, but things had gone too fast when the time arrived.

The thug fell and Cam saw it was a heavy-duty flashlight.

Benny reached in and handed Cam his pocketknife. She went to work on Dylan's tape.

"What took you so long?" Cam asked as she cut the tape and tried to peel it off Dylan's skin.

"That nut friend of yours. Bozo one was pretty mad, yelling and screaming. But I thought if I took the other out of circulation it would be easier. I broke a plate over his head and he went down. But the noise called this one back inside, so I had to hide. I followed him down the stairs."

"So the other one might wake up?" Cam asked.

"Probably."

"Tie that one, would you?" Cam said. "Dylan, can I help you sit?"

He sat with difficulty, and Cam began to cut the tape from his ankles as Dylan massaged his wrists. The uncasted leg was clamped pretty tightly to the cast. Meanwhile, Benny proved he was skilled with duct tape. He bound the thug well.

"Thanks for coming, guys. How'd you find this place?" Dylan said.

"A little genius and a lot of luck," Cam said.

They left the man in the main room — they wanted him eventually found. The stairs were too narrow for three across, so Cam went up first and Benny helped Dylan. She was glad to find Annie was as resourceful as ever. The second thug was tied with cooking twine and Annie was talking to Jake on speaker phone as she worked.

"No, I swear. We just stumbled across it, but when we did, we could hardly leave Dylan here."

Benny laughed loudly, almost like the dim guy who didn't realize Jake could hear him. Cam glared. The guy on the kitchen floor groaned, so Benny redeemed himself by reinforcing the man's binds with duct tape while they waited for the police.

Jake wanted all of them to go to the station together to sort out what had happened.

"So who were those men?" he asked.

"They were trying to warn me off Jessica Benchly, or so they said. But they also talked about how they'd make me disappear," Dylan said.

"They work for Barry Blankenship," Cam added.

"Cam, that's an extremely serious accusation."

"It starts with this." Cam held up her cell phone and showed Jake the picture. "They looked like they were up to no good then — about four hours ago — so much so that I snapped a picture."

"So he met with them."

395

"And we found them by searching the properties Barry is currently leasing or selling."

Cam pretended not to see the irritation on Jake's face. They hadn't just run across all this at all. Thankfully, he didn't say anything.

"You ever see this man, Dylan?" Jake pointed to Barry on the picture.

Dylan shook his head. "Not since he was kissing that cop last night. Tonight I only saw the lovely gorillas who took me and beat me up. That's them, though."

"And you're pressing charges?"

"You bet I am!"

Cam was shocked Jake had no more questions about the murders. She felt like she had a million. Annie stayed behind to talk to Jake, and Benny ran ahead to fetch his pickup so Dylan didn't have to walk as far. As Cam and Dylan walked out of the police building, Dylan with a borrowed set of crutches, Cam edged closer.

"So did you learn anything from all that?"

"Look through the peephole before opening the door?" Dylan said.

Cam rolled her eyes. "I mean about the murderer?"

"Well, when I was there, it was a bunch of insane talk about how I was helping Jessica frame Mindy, but that isn't true. I mean, I like Jessica, but I don't know her that well. I'd certainly never help her frame somebody innocent. But besides that, Jessica didn't frame anybody. She was with Clancy Huggins until he dropped her off at a telethon the day the body was found. She was there another twelve hours and then went home to collapse."

"There's a maid who says she *did* frame Mindy, and . . ."

"No. It was part of a plan!"

"Do you know how stupid that sounds?"

"Cam, work with me. It was a plan *with* Mindy."

Cam just nodded. She didn't believe it for a minute.

"And look." He shoved a piece of paper at her. It held a handwritten plan to frame Mindy to win back Barry.

"Dylan? This is longhand."

"So?"

"So it could have been made this morning, after the fact."

"I found it yesterday between the mattress and springs."

Cam ignored that this meant he'd been alone in Jessica's bedroom.

"Fine — made yesterday. Is still easily could have been made after the fact. It was probably meant for you to find."

Dylan looked frustrated. "What constitutes proof, then?"

"Well, computer stuff at least has a time stamp, as does phone, text — anything like that."

"Hell! I can't use any of that."

Cam felt sorry for him. "Look. If she were to get arrested, they will look at all that. If it clears her, they'll use it."

"But I don't want her arrested."

Cam sighed. "Well, I'm glad you're okay."

She was contemplating such a tight alibi. She was sure, though, she could figure out a way Jessica had gotten away for the time necessary to spike and deliver the bourbon.

"Thanks to you." He grabbed her shoulder and spun her, an awkward motion with his crutches, and one of them fell, so he sort of toppled toward her. In that motion, he planted a kiss on her lips that sent a fire down her spine, but she pulled away and ducked to fetch his crutch.

"Dylan, I . . ."

"I know. We're both taken. But I just took a pain pill and was pretty sure it was the only time I'd brave that, so I had to do it just once."

"I find it hard to believe you're shy about stealing kisses."

"Maybe you bring out my inner gentleman. You have a lovely night, Miss Harris," he said and hobbled toward the corner where Benny would pick him up.

"There you are!"

Rob ran at her as she climbed out of Annie's car and he pulled her into a tight hug. "One step too late all night! It was the most frustrating thing. Griggs caught me on the way out to give me the bad news about the trial, and I never did seem to catch up. I got to the house after the police and they wouldn't let me near — all of you hauled in! I couldn't believe that! I waited awhile but they said it might be a long time."

Griggs was Rob's boss, so she could understand that holding Rob up, especially in relation to the murder case Rob had scooped a few months earlier.

"Yeah. Thankfully it wasn't. It was nice of Jake to get Annie's car from home while they sorted the questioning. So you said bad news about the trial?" Cam did her best to change subjects.

"District attorney dropped the case! He says 'the other confession in the matter stands,' so he claims the case won't hold water. Griggs thinks somebody flexed some political muscle and practically dared me to figure out who and out them, but as of now, no trial."

"Yeah, I probably shouldn't be surprised. She's connected."

Cam felt sure she should be outraged about the injustice of it, but that wasn't her biggest fear. It had been her investigation and suggestions that had prompted the police to make this particular arrest, and the woman was central to the Roanoke Garden Society. Cam hoped that this dropping of charges didn't also mean a firing from her job. She was so close to her Mustang, too.

"Yeah. That's bad." Then it occurred to her why it was bad for Rob — she somehow had forgotten that his covering the pageant had been a trade for getting to cover the trial. "Maybe if you solve this other murder it will all balance. Would that make it up to you?"

Rob grinned. "It might."

Cam and Rob talked late into the night about the things they knew, suspected, and doubted. Rob thought a confrontation with Jessica was definitely in order, as Cam had tried both Barry and Mindy and gotten nowhere. Mindy had blinders on. Jessica had to know the answers and seemed the person most likely to tell them, unless of course they implicated her in a murder.

It was too late to call, but they decided they'd track her down first thing the next day, no matter what it took.

CHAPTER 22

Jessica had left town the day before. Cam was glad Evangeline knew that and had had Jessica's phone number besides, as she would have hated to go to Dylan as a source. Lynchburg, though, wasn't so far from Roanoke. Cam loaded a small cooler with icy-cold water, grapes, and a couple sandwiches.

Rob rolled his eyes. "It's forty minutes from here. We'll be back by lunch."

"Not if we have trouble finding her."

He sighed, but humored her.

The day promised to be a scorcher, hotter than even the worst of the pageant days, though in the last week of July, that was hardly surprising.

"Now what are we saying, exactly?" Cam asked. "Aside from 'We know you're a murdering psychopath.' "

"We're presenting the evidence as we understand it and are going to give her a chance to give her side. We're on a mission as *reporters,* Cam. Not rogue law enforcement."

"Well, what good is that?"

"We get the truth. She really may *have* a story worth hearing."

"She won't admit what she did."

"Not if she's guilty, probably, but I've been trained to spot inconsistencies. And if we act like cops, she won't talk one way or the other. As a reporter, she may see me as willing to weigh the angles — the facts — fairly, so she might be more likely to talk."

Cam didn't think Jessica really deserved that, but she couldn't deny, at least short a squad of cops, that Rob's approach had a better chance of getting results.

"She'll see that you're impressed with her huge . . . tracts of land," Cam muttered.

"Oh, don't go Python on me. You know I prefer my tracts of land by the handful."

They reached Lynchburg at about ten, and Rob suggested a Starbucks stop, always a good idea. They parked on the street and went inside to order.

"You call," Rob urged. "I don't know her, but this is just an interview. Push the reporter angle."

He left Cam at a table and went up to get them drinks, Cam eying the picture of what

403

was surely Annie's coconut mouthgasm. She knew Rob would bring her a skinny latte. It was what she always ordered for herself. Rob dutifully did what she requested, where Annie pushed her to try things out of her comfort zone. She was glad she had one of each.

Cam stared at her phone as Rob walked to the counter. She doubted Jessica was going to buy her cover story, even if — for Rob — it was the real story. Jessica was a smart woman. To Cam's surprise, Jessica sounded as if she'd expected the call. She invited Cam and Rob to lunch at noon. Cam had barely had a chance to respond in the affirmative before Jessica hung up.

Rob brought Cam's skinny iced latte and his own iced caramel macchiato and sat.

"She's feeding us lunch," Cam said.

"You ought to be a reporter. I never have sources agree so easily."

"She may not really know what we're there for — she knows you were covering the pageant and that I'm doing the P.R."

"What did you say?" Rob frowned.

"That we wanted to talk to her — that was pretty much it."

"Then she can hardly claim you misled her. And honestly, what is the biggest story of the week? She can't be shocked we want to talk about that."

"I guess you're right there."

Killing two hours in Lynchburg when eating and spending time outside were both off the list was a little bit challenging. Rob was relieved to hear that the Anne Spenser House and Garden Museum was unlikely to get them out of the heat. Cam loved the old place with its lush garden and fountain and all the flowering shrubs. She had been there before, though, so they didn't have to go. Instead they found the Legacy Museum and ducked in there for a while to look at a collection on African-American art and culture.

At ten minutes before noon, they headed to Jessica's house. Cam was hyperaware that it was also Mindy's neighborhood.

The houses were large and ostentatious, all boasting columns to their second- and third-story roofs. The yards, in Cam's opinion, were overly meticulous — shaped shrubs and perfectly edged lawns. It was a newer neighborhood; this was where new money and rich young families lived, not the local nobility. Cam thought they'd find a lot of engineers, bankers, and real estate folks, but nobody whose money had been inherited — unless it had been inherited elsewhere and people had relocated to

Lynchburg.

Jessica's yard had a round garden in the center, highlighted by a cherub bird bath and, of all non-surprises, a hearty section of oleander.

They parked in the driveway. Cam didn't think Rob had spotted what she had. His eyes usually glazed over when she discussed plants, and though he'd probably looked up pictures recently, they gave no clues about the height, color variation, or ambiance of the evil that was oleander. She couldn't take her own eyes off the plant as Rob led her up the walk and rang the doorbell.

Jessica opened the door formally and led them through to the back of the house where French doors looked out on what Cam would have called a Chinese garden. Hors d'oeuvres were on a table, as was sweet tea in tall glasses. Lack of condensation suggested Jessica had actually poured them as Cam and Rob were coming up the street. Acutely attentive. It was very detailed hostessing.

"Sit, please. The oven will buzz when I need to fetch the rest."

Cam was impressed this wasn't being done by a servant yet was attended with such care.

"So what was it y'all wanted to talk to me

about?" She eagerly leaned forward, resting her chin on her fingers, looking for all the world like they were the best guests she could have hoped for.

Rob took a breath to begin, but Cam blurted, "How long have you been friends with the Blankenships?"

"What?" Jessica sat back again, her brow wrinkled. "Well, that's not a question I expected." She paused to think. "Mindy and I worked on a pageant together a long time ago. In fact, it might have been the one she was in."

It was Cam's turn to be surprised. It made sense, of course, that that had been the origin of this relationship, but all week they'd acted like they hadn't known each other.

"So when you looked for a house . . ."

"Mindy introduced me to Barry, and I looked for one in their neighborhood. She spoke highly of it."

"So why did you act like you didn't know Barry when we asked? Why the charade and framing Mindy?"

"I *didn't* try to frame her for murder. I helped her look like a victim to win Barry back. It was a scheme of hers, but don't you dare tell him. And my act was because it was awkward, seeing Barry away from

Mindy. But I thought if I played it cool, I could take information back to Mindy. Barry obviously also didn't want to admit knowing me, with a girlfriend about."

"You tampered with evidence?" Rob asked.

"Oh, I told the policeman — he knows. I have some silly fine for their trouble, but they didn't pursue it. I told them as soon as I knew they were involved . . . Well, as soon as Barry fetched Mindy from the police station, anyway. That was the payoff."

"Doesn't that seem a little extreme?"

"It worked, didn't it? I just love love." At that, the buzzer went off. Jessica rose and went to the kitchen, returning with a homemade pizza topped with a garlic sauce, salmon, and capers. Cam's mouth watered. It was elegant in spite of being a pizza. Jessica then retrieved a large salad of garden greens topped with walnuts, cherries, and goat cheese, along with a vinaigrette.

"This looks amazing," Cam said.

They took a brief break from talking as Jessica served them, but Cam felt she had to dive back in.

"But Barry's probably a murderer. Do you want her with a murderer?"

"Why would Barry murder either of those two?"

"Well, who do you think did it?"

"I have no idea, but not Barry — not when he just got his family back."

Cam didn't want to argue, but at the beginning he hadn't had his family back. She decided not to focus there. "The next most logical suspects are you and Dylan."

"And I know how that looks, but it isn't either of us, either."

"Why would Mindy tell us you'd been after a sugar daddy and saw Telly as the perfect opportunity?"

"Mindy said that?" Jessica's hand fell to the table and she stared at Cam.

Rob and Cam both nodded.

Several expressions crossed Jessica's face before she could bring herself to speak. Cam recognized hurt, anger, and fear. "I can't believe that. I think you're just saying that to get me to say something incriminating, but I don't know anything incriminating to say."

Rob pulled out a recorder. Cam was surprised he had it, as it was her own recording made by her cell phone when she'd talked to Mindy. She'd emailed it to Rob, but she hadn't expected him to have it with him. He pushed Play and let it run through Mindy's accusation.

Jessica sat with her mouth agape. "I

can't . . . She didn't . . . why, that . . ."

Her turbulent emotions finally landed on anger. She stood and looked like she might storm over to the Blankenships' house right then.

"I'm sure she's not home yet. Her girls were staying with her mom last night," Cam said.

"Well, that . . ."

"I think maybe we should go," Rob said.

"Yes. I'm sorry we disturbed you so badly and put you to all this trouble. It was lovely," Cam said.

Jessica didn't try to stop them. She clearly wasn't interested in hosting a lunch anymore. Jessica followed them as they walked toward the front door.

As Cam and Rob made their way along the sidewalk, Cam heard her name shouted by a small voice. She turned to look and saw Lizzie running toward them.

"Well, hi there."

Timing couldn't have been worse.

"What are you doing here?" Lizzie shrieked as she threw her arms around Cam's waist.

"Er, Cam?" Rob said. "I think maybe we have a situation."

Cam looked up from the top of Lizzie's head to see Jessica marching furiously toward Mindy.

"Get back in your car!" Jessica roared. "Cam and Rob will watch the girls. You and I need to talk!"

Mindy's eyes were wide. "Lauren, go over by your sister."

Lauren dropped her suitcase and ran to Cam. "She has a gun!" Lauren cried as Mindy and Jessica tore out of the driveway.

"Uh-oh. This can't end well," Rob muttered. Cam hoped she was the only one who heard.

She dialed 9-1-1. Rob called Jake.

Rob hung up a few minutes later. "They're on it. Mindy's car has a GPS. They will find them."

"Did you believe Jessica?" Cam whispered. "She was so convincing as innocent. I mean, other than helping Mindy win Barry. It fit so well."

"Yeah, though weren't you the one who told me she wanted to act?"

"That's true." Cam tried to cling to the idea, but didn't think anyone could spontaneously be that good of an actress.

The two of them pulled it together to help the girls. Lauren had a house key, so they went to the Blankenships to settle in until things were resolved. Rob retrieved the pizza from Jessica's unlocked house, and they tried to get the girls to eat.

"Miss Jessica won't hurt Mama, will she?" Lizzie asked, climbing onto Cam's lap.

"I don't think so, honey. I think they just had some important things to talk about."

Lauren had hauled her suitcase upstairs, and Cam thought she was putting things away. She came down a short while later, though, and announced their dad was on his way.

Cam and Rob glanced at each other, knowing this only complicated things. Cam thought they should have anticipated it and headed it off, but it was done now.

"Don't question him when he gets here," Rob whispered. "If this is what it looks like, he may be volatile."

Cam thought they needed some answers but conceded. She didn't want him to get defensive with the girls there.

Rob had one call from Jake while they waited. He gave them an update before Barry arrived.

"They're at a cave in the valley. It's on somebody's property, Jake gave me an address." As he said it, they heard a car door slam.

Cam was surprised Barry had arrived so quickly; he must have been in town already.

He had a thousand questions, but Cam pretended she'd just been having a pageant-related lunch with Jessica and had no idea what had set her off. Barry reluctantly let them leave. Cam would have hesitated, but she was sure the man wouldn't hurt his daughters. They would cause more trouble by staying than going.

As Rob climbed into the Jeep, he looked at Cam and said, "Are you thinking what I'm thinking?"

"We need to go to the cave?"

Rob grinned. "Here goes, then."

They headed east and then north, following the directions from his GPS. Luckily, the property had a road back to the area with the caves. They drove back toward the rocky protrusion.

Mindy's car sat abandoned, three police cars surrounding it. Jessica had apparently forced Mindy into one of the caves.

They knew they shouldn't go in, but neither Cam nor Rob was inclined to sit and wait when there was a story unfolding.

They skirted the two officers who had stayed with the cars, walking in the sparse scrub. They heard, "Hey, you can't . . ." as they ducked into the opening of the cave, but they kept going.

"Could use a flashlight," Rob said.

Cam pulled out her keychain, which held a tiny penlight. "Better than nothing."

"Barely," Rob said.

Rob held Cam's waist as she led the way. They didn't have far to walk before they found the police and the two women. They stayed back in the shadows.

Jessica was being arrested.

"But I got her to admit it," she argued. "Just listen to my phone!"

"Somebody's a fast learner," Cam whispered to Rob.

"You can't take somebody at gunpoint, ma'am," the officer said.

"I'm not saying don't arrest me for that. I'm saying you have to arrest *her* for murder! She admitted it!"

Cam and Rob looked at each other as the pieces began to fall into place. An officer took the phone and put it on speaker. Everyone moved closer to listen.

"This is ridiculous!" Mindy said. "She had a gun pointed at me. She said to confess or she'd shoot me!"

Cam doubted that was how it had gone down, but it would probably make an effective legal argument.

"Let us listen, ma'am." The policeman clicked Play.

"I can't believe after I helped you win Barry back that you'd implicate me in those murders," Jessica's voice came from the gadget.

"I did no such thing," Mindy said.

"I heard a recording — you said I'd done it, that I was trying to get Telly's money."

"And you *will* get Telly's money," Mindy's voice said.

"No more than if he was alive. He made a trust for the baby when the baby gets to college — it's generous, but it's all I get, then or now."

"Jessica, they were suggesting Barry did it."

"Why didn't you trust the justice system to just catch who really did it?"

"Oh, I couldn't let that happen."

"Why not?"

There was a space of silence.

"Mindy, did you do it?"

"Don't be ridiculous."

"You did, didn't you?"

And then Mindy exploded. "I slept with him once to earn my daughter finalist standing, and what does he do? Doesn't follow through. Ignores me. Won't return my calls. Not even when I told him I was pregnant!"

"You were pregnant?"

"No, but that's not the point."

"Maybe it is. Maybe he knew you were lying. He was horrible but not stupid."

"He had to be stopped! He was a monster! And then I saw . . . how I could use the situation to win Barry back . . . how you could help me . . ."

"But why kill Judith?"

There was a pause where Mindy seemed to remember herself.

"I didn't kill anyone!" she declared.

Too late.

"I think that's enough. Mindy Blankenship, you have the right to remain silent . . ."

"I never would have believed that," Cam whispered.

"I guess you never really know somebody," Rob said.

"Oh, Annie could have called this."

In the days that followed, Rob got a promotion and pay raise for his reporting on the twisted murder investigation, but Cam just felt concern for Lizzie and Lauren. Barry Blankenship was not the selfless person

416

needed to raise two very different daughters by himself.

She hoped maybe Mindy's sister could stay involved, but she was halfway across the state.

Jessica, on the third day after Mindy's arrest, sent Cam an email letting her know she planned to keep an eye on the girls. Barry felt bad enough for Jessica's treatment that he was letting her spend some time with them. She promised to let Cam know how they were.

Cam had been waiting for Annie when the email arrived, and they decided a little celebration was in order. She pulled out her blender and began throwing in mango, lime, tequila, triple sec, and ice.

Annie walked in as the first batch was done.

"Woohoo! You get a star for clairvoyance. How'd you know?" Annie said.

"Know what?"

Annie took her computer out of her bag and pointed at the blender, indicating Cam should pour while Annie loaded.

As Cam handed Annie the mango margarita, Annie pointed at the treasure on her computer screen and tapped the thumb drive Cam knew Annie had brought from Barry's apartment.

"Motive for murder number two." At Cam's strange look, she explained. "Password for Mindy's email was LCBEJB — the girls' initials! So Judith saw the emails Mindy sent trying to blackmail Telly — threatening to expose him, and Judith sent back a counterthreat. Judith said she was sending Telly's emails to the police and Mindy would be charged with murder."

"But what if the murder hadn't been over this?"

"I suspect Judith sent something similar to everyone who'd threatened Telly — I mean, heck, there must have been a bunch or the police would have followed this lead. Judith might have been trying to smoke out the killer, but it worked too well."

"They can't use this."

"Not this copy, but they can subpoena her email records, and even if she deleted, there are recovery methods if they have this to know what they're looking for. Or heck, get it from Telly's computer."

"I feel a little bad," Cam admitted.

"For her girls, maybe. Sucks to have a mom so set on social standing and contests that she'd throw her life away like this," Annie said.

Cam frowned. Annie was right — that was the main point. But still, Cam felt a little sorry for Mindy. As she was thinking it, her phone buzzed. Dylan Markham.

"Hello?"

"Miss Harris, how are you?"

"Fine, you?" She felt strange talking to Dylan after a few days' break — like he was a part of some other life.

"I owed you some information. Is now a good time?"

"Sure."

"I'm out front."

"Oh. Your driving leg is better then?"

"No. I'm with Benny. Can we come in?"

"Of course you can."

When she hung up, she pointed at the blender and supplies and looked at Annie. "You get a couple more ready?"

"We having a party or something?"

"Or something," Cam said as she headed to the front door.

When Cam got back to her kitchen with Benny and Dylan in tow, she caught Annie's expression, but Annie distributed margaritas and the men sat at the table.

Cam picked up her margarita and stared at Dylan.

"So I have a success and a failure on that proof about Jessica."

"We have the killer anyway, but let's hear it."

Dylan frowned. "No further proof when Telly might have been poisoned — just the telethon records, but the night Judith was killed, Jessica was with me all afternoon and evening. And the poison was in her coffee, which means it had to be put in very close to when Judith drank it."

Cam rolled her hands, indicating he should go on. There was nothing new that she hadn't heard.

"And Jessica has been talking to Barry."

"So this is what? Thirdhand?"

"Pretty much. But what he said was all the evidence pointing at Mindy, she told him *I planted* — so he thought I was threatening his wife. He really did the lights and beating-up stuff, but because she'd misled him so he was trying to protect her."

"Still, he can't do that." Cam wasn't sure how Dylan thought that made it fine.

"Look. I just want it done. I dropped the charges."

She wondered if maybe he was getting a nice, big payoff for it. She hated it, but she hated the idea of Lizzie and Lauren in foster care more, so she didn't press the issue.

She was just glad to have the killer caught. It would make her public relations tasks significantly easier. She hoped the media flurry over the matter would die down soon.

With that in mind, she'd put the money from the pageanting project in the bank, hoping in a few months' time — well before winter — she would be able to put it toward the car she'd been saving for. She knew just the one.